The Waterside Secret

A Luca Thriller

A Luca Mystery
Book 17

Dan Petrosini

Print ISBN: 978-1-960286-96-3
Naples, FL
Library of Congress Control Number: 2026906622

"The past is never dead. It's not even past."

— William Faulkner

Part One

Twenty Years Ago

Chapter One

Conrad Bolt strode purposefully toward East Naples Community Park. David Flan, a childhood friend, was waiting for him just inside the entrance.

Conrad said, "We were supposed to meet at the soccer field, not here."

The pair walked into the park.

David whispered, "Are you sure this thing is going to work out?"

"Follow the plan, David, and everything is going to be fine."

"But what happens if we see somebody we know?"

Conrad, a head taller than his friend, sighed. "We went over this. If we're recognized, we'll postpone it to the alternate date next week."

"And what if something happens that day?"

"Tomorrow and May twelfth are the last two days we have classes, and public schools are closed. If we can't do it on either of those days, we're not doing it at all."

"Do you think any of the girls are going be too nervous to do it?"

"No."

"I don't know, Elena is cold as ice, but I'm worried about Cindy."

"She's going to be fine."

"Are you sure? She can be flaky."

"She needs this more than anybody." Elbowing David, he said, "Dummy."

Elena Borelli and Cindy Clermont were sitting on a park bench. A gust of wind lifted their blonde hair.

Elena checked her watch when she saw their friends approaching.

Cindy stood. "Hey."

After the friends embraced, Conrad took a seat in the middle of the bench. David sat on one side of Conrad, and Elena on the other. Cindy sat next to David.

Conrad surveyed the surrounding area, it was deserted. "Is everybody ready?"

Everyone nodded.

"Good. If we follow my plan, exactly, everything will go smoothly. Remember, we must work as a unit. We can't have anybody going off script. We adhere to the plan, avoid improvising, and especially cowboying, and we'll laugh our way to the bank."

David said, "What happens if something goes wrong?"

"Nothing is going to go wrong, but if something unexpected happens, don't do anything stupid. Wait for my lead. If we need to, I'll call an audible."

Elena said, "We've covered every possible thing that could happen. This is going to go perfectly."

Conrad said, "She's right. And remember, as long as

nobody gets hurt, people will forget about it within a month or two."

David said, "Except the owners of the store."

Elena scoffed, "They have insurance, they're not going to lose a penny."

Cindy whispered, "What about the burners and Tasers? When are we going to get them?"

"I have them and I'll bring them tomorrow."

Elena said, "We can't leave anything behind. We don't want anything to trace back to us, especially the Tasers."

Conrad said, "The Tasers came from a gun show near Tampa. I used an alias, even though the recordkeeping they use is a joke. I'll activate the phones right before we do it. When we're done, everyone has to give the burners and Tasers to me, and I'll get rid of them. Nobody is going to find anything."

The group went quiet for a moment and Conrad asked, "Any questions?"

Everyone shook their heads.

Conrad said, "Okay. Just to go over things. Elena speaks Spanish, so she'll get one of the landscape guys to drop a backpack by Seagate School's entrance. Elena, you have the hundred-dollar bill ready?"

"Yep. I wiped it clean. No worries."

"Okay. If for some reason she can't get one of the land-scapers to do it or Tropical Greenery isn't there as they usually are, we'll blow that part off but still proceed with the rest of the plan."

"Sounds good."

"Then we'll make our calls and drive over to Waterside. Elena and David will be dropped off by Saks Fifth Avenue, and Cindy and I will park in the garage. We should get a spot on the ground floor, but if not, I'll back into a spot as close to the exit as possible."

Elena said, "Remember to hold hands."

Conrad said, "Exactly. We need to be believable as couples."

Elena looked at David and said, "Don't get any ideas."

The teenagers laughed as David puckered his lips.

"The store needs to be empty. Another customer is a complication we don't need. Wait for Cindy and me. As soon as we head for the door, Elena and David must be right behind us."

David said, "I'll lock the door behind me."

"Wait until I signal you."

"I will, don't worry."

Conrad said, "We make like we want to shop for engagement rings, and depending on where the lady owner and security guard are, I'll say something close to, 'That ring is perfect.' And then Cindy and Elena will hit them with Tasers. Just one shot each and in the midsection."

The girls nodded.

Conrad said, "Make sure it's the midsection. You understand that?"

Both girls said yes.

"Good. The security guard has to be the first to get zapped since he's the biggest threat. As soon as they're down, David and I will start stuffing whatever we can into the bags we're bringing."

Cindy said, "We've got to go for the big stuff—rings with big rocks and necklaces."

Conrad held up a hand. "She's right, but we can't get greedy. No more than three minutes, maximum. Then we leave. We walk. Not run. Stay calm and we'll be in the car before you know it. Don't panic when you hear sirens. They're going to be headed for the schools."

Cindy said, "When are we gonna get some money out of this?"

Conrad glared at her. "As I said from the beginning, six months, at the earliest. If this goes as it should, it'll disappear from the news, and the cops will move on to other things. It'll be safe to fence the diamonds in Orlando and sell the gold to a buyer in Miami."

Cindy groaned, "Six months is too long. Can't we sell a little bit, like a couple of weeks later?"

"No. If you can't live with that, then this isn't for you."

She pouted.

Conrad said, "Are you good with waiting or not?"

"Yeah, I'm cool with it."

"Are you sure?"

"Yes, I'll wait."

Conrad said, "Good. Look, I realize all of this is nerve-wracking. But it's important everyone stays as relaxed as possible and acts normal. Not only today, but from this day on. I mean like forever. We can't invite questions."

David asked, "Does anyone want to go over anything?"

Elena said, "No. We covered everything."

"Me either."

"I'm good with it all."

Elena said, "This was my idea, but thanks to Conrad, it came alive."

Conrad stood. "All right, everyone, try to get a good sleep tonight."

Chapter Two

Elena hopped in the back of the car. She and Cindy wore straw hats over their black wigs. The boys wore blond wigs. Conrad had a fake goatee and David wore a dummy full beard they'd bought in Miami.

Everyone had lifts in their shoes and wore jeans and mirrored sunglasses.

Conrad drove out of St. William Church's parking lot.

He looked over his shoulder. "How'd it go?"

Elena said, "Perfect. The guy didn't speak English. I told him in Spanish, and he took the hundred and the backpack."

David said, "Are you sure he's going to put it by the school?"

"For sure. I told him two hundred more next week if he did it."

Conrad said, "All right. Let's make our calls. Use the burners and keep them short."

David dialed 911. "There's a bomb in a backpack outside of Seagate School. This is not a joke. We're giving you fair warning to get the kids out."

David hung up and Elena made her call.

"There's a man carrying a rifle by the high school. Barron Collier High School. Hurry, we need help!"

Elena disconnected. Cindy, first, then Conrad made calls to 911, alerting the police to possible bombings at two other Naples schools.

Conrad collected the phones, put them in the glove box and entered the lot for Waterside Shops, pulling over just past the entrance to Saks.

David and Elena got out. Conrad circled around, backing the car into a ground-level spot in the garage, and got out.

Cindy and Conrad held hands and made small talk as they walked past one of the high-end shopping center's water features. Conrad leaned against the glass fence. Cindy put her arms around his waist while Conrad had his eyes on the Van Dores Diamond Showroom.

Conrad faked a cough and scanned for their friends. They were in place. He nudged Cindy and they sauntered toward the jewelry store.

He looked through the windows of the luxury jeweler and picked up the faint sound of police sirens. The store was empty of customers.

Conrad signaled David and Elena. It was game time.

As he opened the door, he kissed Cindy on the cheek. "Let's get you an engagement ring."

Before the door closed behind them, David and Elena came into the store.

The female owner approached. "Did I hear engagement ring?"

Conrad said, "Yes, ma'am."

David said, "Hey, that's crazy, we're shopping for one too."

The security guard smiled. "You're going to remember this day forever."

David chuckled, "I'm sure we will."

Conrad pointed to a display cabinet. "That ring is perfect."

The four friends drew their Tasers. Conrad pointed his at the owner. David did as well. Cindy and Elena pointed their Tasers at the security guard, who said, "You don't want to do this. Leave before it goes any further."

Cindy took a step forward, pointing at the guard's head. "Shut your mouth and show me where the surveillance tape is."

Conrad said, "Tase her."

The owner screamed.

David said, "You'll be okay."

He pulled the trigger, and the woman jerked as she crumpled to the floor.

David and Conrad grabbed the display keys from the floor where the owner dropped them and began scooping jewelry into the small velvet bags they brought with them.

Cindy poked the security guard. "Show me the recorder, or you're next."

The watchman pointed to a door. "It's in the office."

"Well, get it open!"

They went into the windowless office. Cindy eyed the screen and video unit and said, "Get on the ground."

The guard didn't move.

"Get down, now!"

"Don't tase me, man. Please."

Cindy pointed at his head. "On the floor!"

The man hesitated and Cindy fired her Taser, holding the trigger down as the guard hit the floor. He began to convulse. Cindy released the trigger. She went to the recording unit, ejected the disc, and pocketed it.

Conrad poked his head inside the office. He looked at the foam coming out of the watchman's mouth and said to Cindy. "Hurry. We're out of here."

He led the thieves to the door. Before unlocking it, he said, "Take a deep breath and relax. Walk normally and act like couples."

They paired up and kept their heads facing each other. They forced laughs and chatter as they made their way to the parking lot, then jumped into the car.

Conrad yanked his goatee off. "Take your disguises off and keep your heads down until I say it's okay."

Conrad eased out of the parking spot toward the exit.

Police activity a couple of blocks away had backed up the traffic at the Seagate Drive exit.

"We're going to go through Pelican Bay."

Conrad snaked his way through the massive neighborhood and spilled onto Vanderbilt Beach Road. He drove west, crossed Route 41 and turned onto Airport Pulling Road.

"Okay, everybody, you can get up now."

Cindy said, "Holy shit, man. That was crazy."

Elena said, "Yeah, but we did it! We freaking did it!"

David said, "Are they going to be all right? The lady didn't look so good."

Conrad said, "Neither did the guard. Cindy, did you hit him in the chest area?"

"I don't know. He was coming at me, I, I just fired the thing."

"Did you release the trigger quickly?"

She shrugged. "I think so, I held it only for a couple of seconds."

"I was specific, all you needed to do was give a quick zap. On and off the trigger. A long charge raises the health risks."

"He'll be okay."

"You better hope so."

Conrad turned onto Immokalee Road. "I'm going to drop you guys off. I think it's better to wait until tomorrow to put everything in the storage unit."

Elena said, "I'm okay with that."

Cindy said, "So, you're going to keep all the loot yourself?"

"Yes. Is that a problem?"

"It's not fair. You shouldn't have it all."

"You don't trust me?"

She shrugged.

Conrad said, "Fine. Each one of us will hold some of the merchandise."

David said, "No. I don't want to."

Elena chimed in, "I don't either."

Cindy said, "I'll hold some of it."

Conrad said, "Where are you going to keep it?"

"In my bedroom. In the closet."

"Is it safe there?"

"It's better than your parent's self-storage place."

"I doubt it, it's only used to store Christmas decorations."

"Well, keeping it in two separate places is a good idea."

"If it makes you comfortable and nobody is against it, I'm fine with it as long as you're extremely careful with it."

"I will be. I'm staying home tomorrow, all day, to be sure."

"No. Didn't you listen to anything I said? Everybody has to go to school. We have to act as if nothing is different. If we miss school the day after, it'll be a big red flag. Does everybody understand?"

All three of them said yes.

Conrad said, "Don't be texting each other about what we did today. Don't call each other tonight either. We'll see each other tomorrow, at school, like always."

Chapter Three

Conrad Bolt's father was sitting at the dinner table. "That smells good."

Conrad's mother set a platter of string beans on the table. "I'm going to take the pork chops out of the oven."

"I'm starving."

She said to her husband, "Did you hear what happened at Waterside Shops today?"

Conrad's father said, "No. But one of the other lawyers said something about there being bomb scares at several schools. What went on at Waterside?"

"Four kids robbed the Van Dores jewelry store."

"In the middle of the day?"

"Yes, and they killed the owner and the security guard."

"Oh my God. They shot the poor people dead?"

The mother turned the oven off and said, "The news report said they used Tasers."

"Really? They're not supposed to be lethal."

"The lady owner had a heart condition, and the news

said they believed the security guard got a long dose of electricity."

"How do they know that?"

"The newscaster said the poor man had burns, or whatever happens when you get tased."

Conrad's dad said, "They'll catch these kids, and when they do, they should get the death penalty."

"They can get the death penalty, even though a real gun wasn't used?"

"Yes, we have a felony murder rule that holds individuals responsible for any death occurring during the commission of a robbery, regardless of whether they intended to kill the victim or not."

"What's going on with our town?"

"I bet they came over from the East Coast."

"You think so?"

"It's probable. Different jurisdictions. They've got their hands full over there, so this won't get much attention."

"But two people are dead."

"I realize that, but that's reality."

Conrad came into the kitchen. "What are you talking about?"

"The robbery at Waterside."

"I heard something went on, but what happened?"

His mother explained it.

Conrad said, "Dad thinks they came from the East Coast?"

"I do."

Conrad said, "You're probably right, Dad. We need to keep those troublemakers out of Naples."

"That's easier said than done."

"What are the police going to do to catch the people who did this?"

"This is a high-profile crime. They're going to have to respond accordingly."

"You think so?"

The doorbell rang. Conrad's dad checked his watch. "Who is that? We're about to eat dinner."

Conrad stood. "I'll get it."

He peeked out the window expecting to see the police. It was David Flan.

Conrad slipped out the door and closed it behind him.

He whispered, "What are you doing here? I told you—"

"The lady and the guard, they died. This is bad, really bad."

Conrad hissed, "Get a hold of yourself."

"Nobody was supposed to die."

"I know, but they did, and now we have to deal with it."

"How are we doing to deal with it?"

"Nothing changed in the plan."

"How can you call people dying nothing?"

"We stick to the plan. I don't like this anymore than you do, but we can't bring them back to life. We have to concentrate on protecting ourselves."

"We're going to get caught, I know it."

Conrad got in David's face. "You keep acting like this and we will. Follow the plan, stick to your normal routine, and stop doing things like showing up like you just did."

"I'm sorry, but I didn't know what to do."

"You do nothing but follow your regular schedule. I'll tell you when and if we need to deviate from the plan. Do you understand?"

"Yeah, I'm sorry."

"Go home."

THE LUNCHROOM at the Community School of Naples was buzzing with teenagers being teenagers.

Conrad picked up a tray and got in line. Elena slipped in behind him.

She grabbed a turkey wrap and said, "Hey, did you do the biology project yet?"

Conrad slipped a paper plate with a slice of pizza onto his tray. "Yes. I handed it in a couple of days ago."

"Really? I'm struggling."

"If you need help, I've got some free time before soccer practice tomorrow."

"Thanks. I'll let you know."

They finished picking out things to eat and headed to a table in the section where the seniors ate. David and Cindy were huddled together whispering into each other's ears.

Elena said, "Hey, guys."

Conrad glared at the two of them and slid onto the bench. He looked around and hissed, "What's with all the whispering?"

David said, "Sorry."

Conrad leaned across the table and lowered his voice. "Sorry isn't going to cut it. You're not acting normal, and that's going to attract attention."

Cindy said, "Calm down, man."

"I will when the two of you stop acting like you're guilty of something."

Elena said, "Connie is right. If we maintain our cool, we have nothing to worry about."

Cindy speared some of David's pasta salad with a plastic fork. "We were just—"

Conrad said, "Change the subject, you're boring me."

Elena pointed at Cindy's lunch. "Mac and cheese, what are you, ten years old?"

Part Two

Present Day

Chapter Four

In the well of the courtroom, a uniformed bailiff stepped forward. "All rise."

The people seated at the prosecution and defense tables stood along with the spectators as the Honorable Conrad Bolt entered.

The bounce in his step contradicted his prematurely gray hair. Settling his lanky frame into his chair, the judge signaled the bailiff, who called out, "Please be seated."

The jury filed into the room and the bailiff swore them in.

"Have you reached a sentencing recommendation?"

The foreman stood, offering an envelope. "Yes, Your Honor."

The bailiff took the document and handed it to Judge Bolt. The packed courtroom fell silent as Bolt unfolded a single sheet of paper.

He pursed his lips as he read it. Bolt took his reading glasses off and scanned the sea of faces who had waited three months for this moment.

Bolt drew a breath and said with authority, "The jury has previously found the defendant guilty on the counts of murder in the first degree and conspiracy to commit armed robbery."

A collective murmur rippled through the gallery.

Bolt pounded his gavel. "Silence please."

The victim's husband, seated in the first-row behind the prosecution table, dabbed his eyes with a tissue.

The defendant, a career criminal who had terrorized the community for years, stared straight ahead. His attorney patted his client's forearm.

Judge Bolt said, "This court has heard three weeks of detailed testimony in this case. The evidence presented leaves no doubt that you, Mr. Cortez, showed a brazen disregard for human life in your pursuit of criminal gain."

Prosecutor O'Leary nodded approvingly from the prosecution table. In his fifteen years as a prosecutor, he had never seen a judge command a courtroom with such presence. Bolt's reputation for being tough but fair had quickly made him the most desirable judge for Collier County's most serious cases.

"We've heard several victim impact statements as well as a statement from the defendant."

Bolt shifted his gaze to Cortez. "But before this court imposes its sentence," Bolt said, "I want to comment on the impact of your actions. Mr. Martin lost not just his wife but the mother of his two young children. The Martin family will never feel safe in their store again. You didn't just steal their possessions—you robbed them of their peace of mind."

Cortez's attorney jumped up. "Your Honor, my client has expressed remorse—"

Bolt waved at him to be seated. "Counselor, the court

has noted your client's statement of contrition. However, remorse expressed after a conviction carries zero significance with this court."

A murmur of approval spread through the courtroom. Bolt's reputation for cutting through legal theatrics and speaking plainly about justice played well in this conservative corner of Florida. The *Naples Daily News* had crowned him "The People's Judge" after quickly making his mark when he took the bench at the relatively young age of thirty-three.

Bolt cleared his throat before saying, "The jury has recommended that the death sentence be imposed."

The court erupted, and Bolt brought the gavel down with authority. "I will not tolerate chaos in my courtroom. I realize this is emotional for everyone, but you must refrain from any outbursts when the court is in session."

Bolt looked directly at Cortez. "The court sentences you to life in prison without the possibility of parole. Mr. Cortez, you are hereby remanded into custody."

As the bailiff cuffed the defendant, Bolt pounded the gavel again.

"This court stands adjourned."

The courtroom erupted into a beehive of activity: reporters rushing for the exit, families embracing, and a handful of spectators applauding as officers led Cortez away.

Bolt gathered his papers with practiced efficiency, pleased that he had taken another predator off the streets. Perhaps the community could sleep a bit easier tonight.

O'Leary approached the bench. "Excellent work, Your Honor. That was exactly the outcome the county needed."

Bolt nodded curtly. "Justice isn't about outcomes. It's

about process. The evidence supported the verdict—the sentence was merely a consequence of the jury's decision."

O'Leary smiled. Bolt never took credit for the sage role he played overseeing the trials in his courtroom.

As he retreated to his chambers, Bolt overheard the conversation in the gallery. "That was perfect. We need more judges like Bolt . . ." "Thank God Bolt isn't afraid to put these animals away . . ." "My sister says she feels safer knowing he's on the bench . . ."

The respect in their voices should have filled him with pride. Instead, as Bolt closed the door to his chambers, he felt only the familiar weight pressing his chest.

He loosened his tie as he contemplated the time he'd spent trying to balance the scales. Years as a prosecutor and now judge, of sending criminals to prison while knowing that the worst criminal of all sat behind the judge's bench every day.

He unlocked the bottom drawer on his desk and slid it open. He reached behind the compartment and peeled back the tape holding a hidden envelope. Bolt pulled a piece of paper out of it and stared at the newspaper clipping he'd kept all these years: "Two Killed in Brazen Jewelry Store Robbery"

He leaned back in his chair and closed his eyes. The faces of Valerie Van Dore and Michael Martinez bounced into his head. They were innocent people who would never get to go home to their families.

Two people he had helped kill during the jewelry store robbery. He tried to allay his guilt by telling himself he'd been just eighteen years old and hadn't tased them. But the excuse never overcame his conscious; he'd planned the robbery and had directed what had turned into a fatal heist.

Bolt shook the image of the store owner and security guard out of his head and opened his eyes. He had to march forward and continue to make a dent in the debt he'd created.

Tomorrow there'd be another trial, another chance to serve justice, another day of trying to atone for the unforgivable.

Outside his window he could see the families of victims who gathered every day with their signs: "JUSTICE FOR ALL" and "TOUGH ON CRIME WORKS." They believed in him. They trusted him.

If only they knew.

Chapter Five

Frank Luca was on his second mug of coffee when his phone rang. The caller ID read DERRICK—his former homicide detective partner in the Collier County Sheriff's Office.

He answered, "Hey, it's kind of early for you. Is everything okay?"

"Good morning, Frank. Everything is good, but I need a favor."

Luca put his cup down. "What kind of favor?"

"It's an old case. A cold one."

"We're retired, remember?" Luca took another sip of coffee and looked out to the pool where Mary Ann was doing her morning laps. "I'm not interested in chasing ghosts."

"Well, it's not really a case, Frank. More like a conversation. There's this woman, Tanya Martinez. Friend of Lynn's from the school she teaches at. Her father was killed twenty years ago, and she's been carrying it around like a weight."

Luca recognized the tone. Derrick had always been the

soft touch between them, the one who couldn't say no to victims' families. "So, tell her to call the sheriff's office. The cold case unit loves reopening old files when they're bored."

"She tried that. Got the runaround. Look, Frank, she just needs someone to tell her straight whether there's anything worth pursuing or if she should let it go. Ten minutes of your time. As a favor to me."

"I don't do many cases anymore, Derrick. You know that."

"I'm not asking you to do a case. All I'm asking is for you to talk to this poor lady. She lost her dad when she was a kid. She thinks she found something important."

"Then she should bring it to the sheriff's office, not me."

"She tried, but they gave her the cold shoulder."

"Why me? Why don't you deal with whatever she has?"

Derrick hesitated. "She won't show me. She only wants to deal with the legend known as Detective Luca."

"Get out of here."

"No, I'm serious. She was talking to Lynn, and Lynn told her I'd been a cop and that we were partners for a couple of years. She knew about the drug money we hunted down and about that crazy case where you went down to Peru as a special agent for the Treasury."

"Well, she shouldn't believe everything she hears."

"Do me a solid and just meet with her. Maybe there's something there."

Luca was quiet for a long time. "I doubt it."

"Come one, man. I'll buy you dinner."

"Okay, but no more than ten minutes," Luca said finally. "That's it. And dinner is going to be at Bicyclette Cook Shop."

"That's a deal. She'll come by your house around twelve."

EXACTLY AT NOON, Luca's doorbell rang. He swung open the door.

"Mr. Luca?"

"Yes." He stuck his hand out. "You must be Tanya."

"That's me."

She stepped into the house carefully, like someone who had rehearsed the moment a hundred times. She held a manila envelope against her chest like a shield.

"Thank you for seeing me. It's about my father."

Luca studied her: mid-thirties, fit, a teacher, the kind of person who dotted every I and crossed every T. Her clothes were department-store professional, and her hair was pulled back in a ponytail.

Luca looked at her eyes. They held a mixture of hope and desperation he'd learned to recognize after many years with the sheriff's office.

"Follow me. We'll talk in my office."

Luca slid behind his desk.

"Have a seat. Derrick said this was about a twenty-year-old case, but I have to be clear, I don't take cases anymore. I'm just here to listen."

You could hear the woman's chest falling. Tanya lowered herself onto a chair, still hugging the envelope.

Tanya cleared her voice and said, "My father was Michael Martinez. He was killed during a robbery at the Van Dores Diamond Showroom in Waterside Shops, May fifth, 2006."

Luca frowned. The date meant nothing to him, but the case name tickled his memory. "I'm sorry for your loss. I remember hearing about the case when I joined the force, but I was still up in New Jersey when that crime happened."

"Derrick told me that, but you've solved many big cases. He told me about the old murder at Wiggins Pass that you solved."

Luca sighed. "That was a long time ago. And cases are all different."

"I understand, but Derrick said you might be willing to just . . . look at something I found. Can you tell me if I'm grasping at straws or if there's actually something there, because I think there is."

Luca shifted in his chair.

Tanya's voice was steady. "I don't need you to take the case. I just need someone with the experience you have to tell me the truth."

"The sheriff's department is filled with competent officers. I'm sure they can help you."

"Do you know what it's like to watch your mother die wondering who killed her husband?"

Luca wanted to tell her about losing his mother when he was a kid, but said, "No, ma'am."

"She had a heart attack less than a year ago. Stress, the doctor said. Too many years of being a single parent, trying to pay the bills. Twenty years of not knowing, of jumping every time the phone rang, hoping it was the police with news." She sniffled. "It was terrible."

"It must have been tough. Why don't you show me what you have?"

She opened the envelope and began spreading papers across his desk: crime scene photos, newspaper clippings, official reports marked CASE CLOSED - NO VIABLE LEADS.

"My father worked two jobs to take care of us. Days at the jewelry store, nights at a warehouse. He wasn't even supposed to be there that day—he was covering for a sick coworker."

Her finger traced the edge of a photo showing a middle-aged man in a security uniform smiling at the camera.

"He was a good man and a great father. He deserved better, as did the lady who owned the store. My father liked her, he said she was good person. But the detective who handled it tried for maybe six months. Then other cases came up, fresher cases with actual evidence, and we got pushed to the end of the line. And then, nothing. It's so frustrating."

Luca nodded as he picked up the crime scene report. Two victims: store owner Valerie Van Dore and security guard Michael Martinez, both died from the effects of being tased.

He remembered that and read on. There had been a substantial loss of jewelry, estimated to be valued at over four hundred thousand dollars. There were no witnesses or viable suspects, and the limited security footage had been taken by the thieves during the robbery.

"Why now?" Luca asked, though he felt himself getting drawn in. "Why not five years ago, or ten?"

Tanya's voice cracked. "Because next week is the twentieth anniversary, and I promised my mother on her deathbed that I'd find the truth. Because I've saved every penny for three years to hire someone like you. And because . . ." She pulled out a small, leather-bound notebook, its edges worn smooth. "Because I found this."

Luca recognized the type immediately—a security guard's logbook. The kind carried by every rent-a-cop and private security officer to document their shifts. This one was marked "M. Martinez - PERSONAL" in faded blue ink.

"Where did you get this?"

"I was cleaning out my mother's closet last month. She'd kept all of my father's things in a box—his uniform, his watch, some photos." Tanya's voice grew softer. "And this. My mother said the police never took my father seriously."

Luca knew the police tended to discount security guards because of their lack of training.

Tanya opened the notebook to a page marked with a yellow sticky note. "My father was observant, Mr. Luca. Maybe too observant for his own good. Look at what he wrote here, it's just two weeks before he was murdered."

Chapter Six

Luca took the book from the security guard's daughter and read the neat handwriting on the page:

Date: April 21, 2006

Time: 4:14 p.m.

Location: Central courtyard

Four white teenagers hanging around outside in the late afternoon. Two boys and two girls who look privileged. They probably go to private school. It's the same group of kids who came around about a month ago.

One boy asked a question about our security system when I told them to move along. Said he was thinking about applying for a job. Seemed too interested in our procedures.

Tonya reached over and flipped to another page marked with an x.

Luca read:

Date: April 28, 2006

Time: 11:07 a.m.

Location: Van Dores Diamond Showroom

Those teens are back again. One of the girls asked Sally

the salesgirl when she went on break, about Mrs. Van Dore's schedule, what time she started and if she only worked the afternoon shift.

"And here," Isabella said, turning to the final entry, dated May fourth—one day before the robbery.

The guard had written:

Date: May 4, 2006

Time: 3:34 p.m.

Location: Van Dores Diamond Showroom

Saw the same group of teens again this afternoon. They're watching the store. Something feels wrong. I'm going to mention it to Mrs. Van Dore tomorrow.

Luca studied the guard's handwriting, his careful observations, and the growing concern evident in the tone of his observations. Martinez had been doing exactly what a good security guard should do—documenting suspicious activity. But he'd never gotten the chance to report it.

"The sheriff's office never saw this?"

"They did. They told Mom that my father was always calling them about suspicious behavior that never amounted to anything. They said they had to focus on the crime scene, the physical evidence. And when the case went cold, they returned his personal belongings, including his notebook."

Tanya closed the logbook carefully. "Mr. Luca, my father knew these kids were going to do something and wrote descriptions of the kids."

Luca was quiet for a long moment. He'd retired from the sheriff's office. Sure, the reward money he'd earned from tracking the drug money contributed to the why of retiring, but the fact was he had burned out from too many cases like this one.

There were too many families left with questions, too many killers who walked away clean. That was why he promised himself to only take cases that interested him, cases where he might actually make a difference.

He looked across his desk. There was something about Tanya Martinez that reminded him of why he'd become a cop in the first place. The way she'd spent three years saving money, the methodical research she'd done on her own, the quiet determination in her voice when she talked about a vow to her dying mother.

"Ms. Martinez, I can't promise you I'll find your father's killer. Twenty years is a long time, and if the sheriff's office couldn't crack it when the trail was fresh . . ."

"I understand. But all I ask is that you try."

Luca looked at the cashier's check again, then at the photograph of Michael Martinez in his security uniform. A working man, pulling double shifts to give his daughter a better life. The kind of victim who deserved better than a file drawer marked UNSOLVED.

"Yeah," he said finally, sliding the check back across the desk. "I'll try. But I'm not taking your money until I find something worth pursuing. Give me a week to review the files and see if there's anything there."

For the first time since she'd walked into his world, Tanya smiled. "Thank God. Thank you, Mr. Luca."

After she left, Luca poured himself another cup of coffee and reread the marked pages in the guard's notebook. He'd told Tanya he would hunt around a bit and talk to his old contacts at the sheriff's office. He hoped that would be enough to give her a definitive answer about whether there was anything worth pursuing.

But as he studied Martinez's careful observations, Luca

felt the familiar itch that had driven him through years of police work. The sense that there was always one more question to ask, one more lead to follow, one more piece of the puzzle waiting to be found.

He picked up his phone and called Derrick.

"And what did you think?" his former partner said.

"The woman's not crazy," Luca said. "Her father documented everything: descriptions, suspicious behavior in the weeks before the robbery."

"Sounds like there's something to work with."

"I've got a couple of things to look into, that's it," Luca corrected.

Derrick scoffed. "Right. Just like that missing person case in Immokalee was 'just a few phone calls.'"

"That was different."

"Right. You need any help with this?"

Luca was quiet for a moment, staring at the notebook entry dated May fourth, 2006. The guard's final observation. It was written less than twenty-four hours before someone electrocuted him.

"Maybe," he said finally. "I might need a favor or two. I'll let you know."

Luca hung up. As he picked up his mug he thought twenty years was not only a long time to keep a secret, it was also a long time for killers to get sloppy.

Chapter Seven

Luca flipped open the notebook to a random page and read the handwritten entries.

Date: March 15, 2005

Time: 2:47 p.m.

Location: Central courtyard near fountain

Middle-aged, Hispanic male observed lingering in front of Ferragamo. He was using what appeared to be a measuring tool along the storefront's perimeter. Subject had small bag of equipment and was photographing the store's security features and window displays. I called Waterside's security office, but the subject left before being intercepted.

Date: March 16, 2005

Time: 11:33 p.m.

Location: West wing, behind the luxury boutiques

Two individuals discovered attempting to access electrical utility boxes that control store alarm systems. Subjects were using small tools and what appeared to be electronic devices near the panel. When challenged, they claimed to be "an after-hours maintenance crew" but no such work was authorized. Both fled toward the perimeter landscaping when backup security announced their presence.

DATE: April 3, 2005

Time: 10:15 a.m.

Location: East promenade walkway

On the way into work, I observed a well-dressed woman carrying a professional camera with a telephoto lens. She was observed documenting store layouts, taking photos of entrance configurations and security camera positions. When I questioned her, she claimed to be doing "architectural photography." She left when asked to produce a permit or authorization.

DATE: April 8, 2005

Time: 1:22 a.m.

Location: North walkway near Louis Vuitton

Black male in dark clothing milling about with a bag of what appeared to be tools. Subject was examining window frames. When a salesperson came out to talk to him, he walked away quickly.

DATE: April 23, 2005

Time: 4:38 p.m.

Location: lululemon

. . .

A WOMAN, with no bag, came out of the store and hurried toward the parking lot. The same individual was observed ten minutes earlier speaking with another woman by the fountain. They appeared to be a team of shoplifters. I alerted the mall's security office.

DATE: May 7, 2005

Time: 7:45 p.m.

Location: Side corridor

Shortly before closing time, an unidentified person was checking trash receptacles and planters, appearing to hide or retrieve small packages. Subject avoided main walkways and stayed in shadows between decorative lighting.

DATE: May 13, 2005

Time: 1:34 p.m.

Location: Inside the Van Dores Showroom

WATCHING the camera feed from the office, a male customer was looking at bracelets. The salesgirl laid four of them out side by side. The subject appeared overly nervous and seemed to be trying to distract the salesgirl as he tried the bracelets on. When he used a finger to drag a bracelet toward him, I jumped out of my seat. I went into the showroom and stood next to the counter. The male left shortly afterward without making a purchase.

DATE: May 19, 2005

Time: 12:20 p.m.
Location: California Pizza Kitchen

WHILE ON LUNCH BREAK, I observed a late-model, tan sedan. Two Hispanic males were in it. They kept circling, and when the driver slowed, the passenger took photos. They did it only when the security guard was not in view. They parked and I followed them. The pair stood in front of the Apple store, pointing and whispering before they left.

DATE: May 20, 2005
Time: 4:33 a.m.
Location: South courtyard near Omega luxury watch retailer
White male subject observed using what looked like a small mirror to examine the underside of outdoor security cameras. The individual appeared familiar with security camera blind spots.

DATE: June 1, 2005
Time: 9:18 p.m.
Location: Main plaza between anchor stores
Two individuals posing as customers were observed conducting detailed surveillance of evening closing procedures for multiple high-end retailers. Subjects had notebooks and appeared to be timing guard patrols and documenting which stores had staff remaining after hours.

. . .

Luca put the notebook down. Waterside Shops wasn't devoid of crime, but Martinez seemed not only overzealous but paranoid.

Luca picked up of the phone and called the sheriff's office to talk to the man who replaced him as the lead homicide detective when Luca retired.

"Homicide, Detective Donovan."

"Hey, Donnie, it's Luca."

"Frank, how are you?"

"Everything is good. How about with you?"

"Thank God it's going well. What's on your mind?"

"I need a little information, it's before your time, and frankly mine as well."

He hesitated. "Okay. Tell me what you want."

"About twenty years ago, there was a robbery at the Van Dores Diamond Showroom, and two people were murdered. The case was never solved, and it went cold."

"Yeah, I remember some of that, but I didn't work on it."

"I know, but the security guard, a Michael Martinez, was killed during the theft. He kept a detailed logbook, and there were notes about some kids he claimed were casing the store."

"Okay. And what is it you need?"

"Can you check the file? I'd love a copy of whatever you can give me in general, but for some reason, Detective Florez seemed to completely discount the notebook. I'd love to hear why."

"I'll see what I can dig up for you."

"Thanks, Donnie."

There was a soft knock on the door. It swung open and Mary Ann said, "How did you do with that woman?"

"It's tough to say. Back in 2005, there was a murder, robbery in Waterside."

"Yeah, that was at Van Dores. It was less than a year before I started working at the sheriff's office. What did she want?"

I told her what I'd learned from the security guard's daughter and told her Donovan was going to pull the file.

She said, "You're going to wait on him?"

"I'll check with the schools. According to the notes he made, these kids were in high school. The robbery happened in the middle of the day. I'll see who was out of school that day."

"That should have been checked into."

"According to the dead man's wife, the detectives handling the case completely discounted Martinez."

"Kmart cop syndrome?"

"Maybe, but based on his notebook, the guard seemed paranoid. How many high school kids do you think call in sick each day?"

"When Jessica was going, I think it was around five percent."

"That seems high."

"Maybe, but there's something like fifteen thousand high schoolers going to Collier high schools now. A lot less back then."

"Geez, I can't believe the growth." He tapped on his phone. "That means there's over three thousand seniors. If the five-percent sick rate is correct, there would be almost two hundred kids out that day. It'd be impossible to check them all out."

"Didn't you say the guard thought they were private-school types?"

"He did."

"Google how many kids are in the private high schools here."

Luca typed into the search bar. "Looks like that would be about three hundred seniors."

Mary Ann said, "At five percent, you've got yourself about fifteen to twenty names, but it's going to be less than that. We grew about twenty percent since 2006."

"You know, you still got it. It's a good thing I kept you around all these years."

Chapter Eight

Luca printed the lists he'd wrangled out of the administrative secretaries at three private schools.

Luca had discovered the Collier public schools were all closed on May fifth , 2006. This made the private school leads the longest of shots, a moon shot.

He scanned the lists. There were twenty-two private school seniors out sick on the day of the robbery and murders.

As a licensed private investigator, Luca had access to Florida's Department of Motor Vehicles database. He quickly ran the names through the DMV and eliminated three blacks and three Asians from the list.

He was left with sixteen names to check into: ten male and six female. Curiously, fifteen of the names attended the Community School of Naples. It was the area's largest private school. He shook his head; it made it tougher as he expected the four robbers to attend the same school.

Looking over the list, Luca's spirits rose; among them

were several familiar names, prominent figures and businesspeople.

Marion Johnson – a weatherwoman for WINK News.

Conrad Bolt – a respected judge

Peter Palmer – owner of three car dealerships

Elena Borelli – the only female to run a major hedge fund in America

Frank Federici – proprietor of six local restaurants.

Barry Seigler – a personal injury lawyer

Luca hoped to cross them off and further narrow the suspect list. Then he could focus on the remaining names on the list.

David Flan

Cindy Clermont

Jillian Vasel

Joseph Serano

Loretta Gulliver

Richard Wanamaker

Vicky Francis

Ernest Rigo

Anthony Crespoli

As had proven invaluable throughout his career, the first thing Luca would do was to check whether any of the names had a criminal record.

Luca was glad he had kept his private investigator license, even though he had taken only one case in the past three years. It allowed him to use a database that contained information on whether someone had a criminal record or a civil judgment against them.

He'd screen the list and concentrate on anyone with a history of criminality or who had lost a notable lawsuit.

Luca typed Marion Johnson in the search bar and wasn't

surprised when nothing came up on the TV personality. Next on the list was Conrad Bolt. The judge was someone who had a stellar reputation and was tough on crime. Luca didn't expect a hit, and nothing came up.

Peter Palmer was the next name he checked. Luca did a double take; there was a restraining order against him. It was granted to his wife eight years ago and had been renewed. There had been no violations of the order. Luca ran through the possible scenarios as he checked the civil system. There were four judgments against Palmer.

Luca sat back. It wasn't unusual for people to sue a car dealership, and lawyers often went after the owners when they filed those suits. It didn't mean Palmer was personally guilty of anything, but combined with the restraining order, it elevated Peter Palmer to the top of the list.

Luca had heard of Elena Borelli. When she was just thirty, she parlayed the gains from investments in the energy sector into semiconductors stocks that tripled. The trades catapulted her fame and fortune, and she opened the first hedge fund owned by a woman. Borelli was often quoted in newspapers whenever the stock market made a large move in either direction.

He plugged her name in, and nothing showed in the criminal system. However, a dozen civil judgments against Borelli populated the screen. Again, he reasoned there was no shortage of investors who'd go to court when the market moved against them.

There were no SEC filings against Borelli or Horizon Investments, the company she had founded. It was reassuring, but Luca made a note to dig into the judgments to determine if a pattern of behavior was responsible.

Luca had eaten at two of Frank Federici's restaurants

and enjoyed their Italian food and relaxed atmosphere. He popped the proprietor's name into the criminal database, and it came up empty.

He moved to the civil system, expecting to discover a couple of lawsuits. Luca told himself to make a reservation when no judgments were found against Federici.

Mary Ann called out, "Frank! We have to leave. Jessica's flight is landing in twenty minutes."

"Okay. I'll be ready in two seconds."

He plugged in the last name he recognized, Barry Siegler. The personal injury attorney didn't have a record. Luca expected there to be civil judgments, and he was right. There were two that had been settled.

He needed more details, but they appeared to be clients unhappy with Siegler's representation. Additionally, Seigler was the only one not to attend the Community School of Naples.

Luca made a tic mark next to David Flan's name. He'd resume the research as soon as he could.

MARY ANN POINTED. "THERE SHE IS."

They got out of the car and met their daughter as she came out of the terminal. Mary Ann hugged Jessica and Frank kissed the top of her head and took her luggage. "So good to see you, Jessie. How was the flight?"

"Good. Way better than driving, but it was packed. Not an empty seat anywhere."

"That's the way it is these days."

Mary Ann said, "Are you hungry?"

"Definitely, I only had a bar this morning."

Frank said, "You want to go to First Watch? We can get a stack of pancakes like we used to."

Mary Ann rolled her eyes.

Jessica said, "Sure. But I'll pass on the cakes. Maybe a Cobb salad, if they have them."

Luca drove straight to the restaurant and grabbed a table by the window. They were handed menus and ordered beverages.

Mary Ann said, "I like the color of your hair. Did you go to someone different?"

"Yes. I tried someone new. He was good but doesn't speak English. I had to use Google Translate to communicate with him."

Frank said, "That's ridiculous. Did he just get here?"

"I don't know, I didn't ask."

"I hope the price was right."

"It was. So, Dad, Mom told me you're back in action, working a new case?"

"I just started on something, but I'm not a hundred percent sure I'm taking it on."

"That sounds like a yes to me."

Chapter Nine

Mary Ann and Jessica left the house to go shopping, and Luca went into the den he used as an office. He logged on to the investigator's portal and typed the next name on the list, David Flan, into the search bar.

Flan had been arrested twice for driving under the influence. It was criminal, but not in the vein Luca was searching for. Flan also had numerous civil judgments against him that were related to a variety of business ventures.

Luca considered whether Flan's troubles were a window into his character before plugging Cindy Clermont into the system.

Clermont had a record: two drug possessions and a shoplifting conviction. Serious but not an ah-ha moment.

Jillian Vasel and Joseph Serano came up clean in both the criminal and civil systems.

Luca was going to move on to the next person when his phone rang. It was Donovan.

"Donnie, what's going on?"

"Lucky for you, Frank, it's been quiet, so I had a chance to pull that old Waterside file."

"Great. I really appreciate it. What's it look like?"

"There wasn't a lot of physical evidence. The store had two cameras, but the thieves must have taken the DVD recording because the machine was empty."

"What about any cameras the mall had?"

"This was over twenty years ago; there were a couple of cameras, but the coverage sucked, and whoever did this knew to avoid them. If this was today, we'd have video of them from various angles."

"Was there any attempt to track the kids based on the security guard's descriptions?"

"There's nothing in the file, but there were two notes about the guard. Apparently, this guy had a habit of calling in threats that never materialized. Finnigan, who took the lead on this back then, wrote, and I'm quoting here, 'Martinez had a vivid imagination, and we basically stopped responding to his concerns unless someone else corroborated it.'"

"The guy took his job seriously; it's a shame nobody else did."

"That's not fair, Frank. The detectives chased down leads and questioned almost fifty people. They might have been teenagers, but they were smart about it."

Luca regretted not looking into the cold case when he was with the sheriff's office. "Not smart enough to avoid killing two people."

"Yeah, they had a decent idea using Tasers, but the owner had a bad ticker, which did her in, and they zapped the guard too long in the chest for his system to overcome."

"Did they check the fences who dealt in high-end jewelry?"

"Yeah, they put out an alert all the way up both coasts, but nothing materialized."

"Are there any loose ends in the file to go on?"

"Nothing that I can see. They ran into dead end after dead end, and there was no movement in the investigation."

"Homicide investigations are like sharks, if there's no movement they die."

"There's a lot of truth in that, especially in the old days. Today, with all the evolving technologies, we can go back and close some of these cold ones. But not this one."

"Can you make me a copy of whatever you have?"

"Sure, if I'm not around when you came by, I'll leave it with the front desk."

"Thanks, Donnie."

Luca stared at the screen. He went over what he'd told the security guard's daughter, Tanya. He'd been careful, not promising anything, and was glad he hadn't. He looked at the list. There were five more names to run.

Next up was Loretta Gulliver. There was nothing in the criminal or civil systems on her. He moved on to Richard Wanamaker.

Wanamaker was a troublemaker. He'd been arrested six times for petty theft and another time for walking out of a Fifth Avenue restaurant without paying his bill. Wanamaker's name drew a blank in the civil system. Luca circled his name and moved on to Vicky Francis.

When he put her name in, an arrest popped onto the screen. She'd been taken into custody for insurance fraud. Luca scrolled down. The woman had burned her home down to collect the insurance proceeds. The felony caught

Luca's attention. It was a high-value crime and elevated Francis to the top of the suspect list.

Luca moved on and typed Ernest Rigo into the system. He sighed when two arrests populated the screen. Rigo had served time for two assaults. One with a deadly weapon. The civil system had nothing on Rigo. Luca wondered whether Rigo's parents regretted spending the money on private school, or was it their last attempt to straighten their kid out.

Anxious to finish going through the list, he put in the next name and got an immediate hit. Anthony Crespoli had been arrested twice for racketeering. One of the charges involved gambling, and the other, drug distribution. Though they weren't thefts, the crimes were interesting because both crimes involved working with others to commit.

Luca shook his head; there were too many people requiring a closer look. How had these upper middle-class kids gone from playing with Cabbage Patch dolls and toy cars to committing serious crimes?

He needed to streamline his approach, or he'd waste weeks interviewing and verifying what he was told.

Luca picked up the guard's logbook and began reading Martinez's descriptions of the kids. He had an idea he hoped would narrow the list down.

He drove down Airport Pulling Road and turned onto Orange Blossom Road. He parked in the county complex and went into the headquarters of Collier's library.

Luca waited until a man with a bushy head of white hair finished flirting with the woman manning the front desk and approached.

"Hi, where would I find the high school yearbooks?"

"They'd be in the reference section."

"Where would that be?"

"What year are you looking for?"

"2006."

"Go straight through those doors and head into the far corner."

"Thanks."

"But you can't check them out. You'll have to go through them here."

"I understand. Thanks."

He snaked his way to the reference area and tilted his head, reading the spines of the books shelved in the section.

Luca bent down and pulled the lone copy of the 2006 edition of the *Knight* off the shelf. He set the Community School's yearbook on a wooden table. Beside it he laid his list of names and the guard's logbook.

He paged through an alphabetized section that contained school photos of each student and cursed under his breath.

Luca was hoping some of the students wouldn't fit the clean-cut description the security guard had noted, but almost all the graduating teenagers listed were well-groomed.

He began to look at the pictures of the six names who had criminal records, starting with Cindy Clermont.

Except for her wry smile, she could have been the proverbial girl next door. Anthony Crespoli was next alphabetically. His short hair and perfect teeth didn't give Luca any clue he'd be committing organized crimes.

Luca quickly looked at the other seniors and came up

with nothing. He flipped the yearbook closed. If he were to take the case, he'd have to start knocking on doors and talking to people.

Pawing his chin, Luca wasn't sure he was up to the grind. He began putting together what he'd tell the security guard's daughter. She was a nice woman, and he'd love to help her, but he was basically retired, and this case would require too much of his time.

His phone pinged with an incoming text. Luca pulled it out. It was from Jessie: *Hey, Dad. You like the blue one or the green one?*

Jessie was holding two pairs of swimming trunks.

He typed back: *I don't need a new one. Save your money.*

I'm buying you one, so pick a color.

Blue.

I'm glad, that was my favorite too. Love you!

Love you, too.

Luca smiled, thinking about how special Jessie was. He glanced at the yearbook, confident that Michael Martinez had thought his daughter was also special. And twenty years later she was hunting for justice for her father.

He opened the yearbook and paged through the photos of events held at the Community School in 2006.

Luca examined the two-page spread for a fundraiser benefiting Avow Hospice. He put a hand on the page and flipped to the alphabetical photos. He flipped between the picture of Anthony Crespoli and the fundraiser.

It was Crespoli. He looked at the girl standing next to him. He had his arm around her waist. He flipped to Cindy Clermont's picture. It wasn't her.

He moved on to Vicky Francis's graduation photo.

It was her. Francis and Crespoli knew each other.

Luca's heart rate sped up. He grabbed the yearbook and shelved it. He had to get home to start a deeper dive into some of the suspects.

Chapter Ten

Instead of starting with Vicky Francis and Anthony Crespoli, Luca pulled up the case files on one of Ernest Rigo's arrests. He stopped midway through the summary.

Luca stared at the revelation: Ernest Rigo had used a Taser during an assault. Rigo had been arguing with a man inside a bar. He had challenged him to fight, and when they stepped outside, Rigo tased him.

Luca didn't believe in coincidences; he called things like that evidence.

He sat back. Was this the break he'd need to solve this Waterside case?

Luca got back to the keyboard. The robbery-murder case had gone cold in 2010. Four years later, the use of a Taser hadn't prompted anyone to investigate a possible connection.

He checked but couldn't find any statistics on civilian Taser use, but Luca knew the Collier Sheriff's Office used them often during arrests, sometimes once a week. It was commonplace, unlike the use of a firearm.

Luca opened the Van Dores Diamond case file. He paged to the list of interviews. Putting his finger on the screen, Luca ran down the list of names. He shook his head; they hadn't talked to Ernest Rigo.

Thinking they could've listed Rigo's interview by his first name, he jumped up to E. It wasn't there. Luca would be the first person to talk to Rigo. A surge of adrenaline shot through him. He navigated to the state employment database and pulled up Rigo's record.

A quick Google search provided him with the telephone number to Tropical Roofing. He punched the number in.

"Tropical Roofing."

"I'd like to talk to Ernie Rigo."

"Uh. Hang on, I think he just got back in from a job."

"No problem, I can wait."

"It's up to you."

The call was put on hold, and an annoying stream of notes began to play.

Luca put the phone on speaker and opened his email inbox.

He blew away four spam messages and opened an email from Collier County. Luca had gotten into the habit of checking the prior day's arrests and still received the daily email with the details.

Luca clicked open the report. His eyes went to the second picture. He read the woman's name. "Holy shit!"

Victoria Francis had been arrested. He jumped out of his chair when he saw the charge: possession of stolen goods.

Luca clicked on the case number and opened the arresting officer's report.

Case Number: 25-0384

Reporting Officer: Officer Robert Z. Blake #217

Location of Incident: 6 Palm Drive, Collier County, FL

On June 1, 2026, at approximately 1645 hours, I was dispatched to 6 Palm Drive along with Officers Meritt, Clemens, and Else. The dispatch was related to a tip received from a confidential informant concerning suspected stolen property being stored at the address.

Upon arrival, I observed a Caucasian female, who identified herself as Vicky Francis, (Victoria Francis DOB: 4/07/1987), exiting the home with a duffel bag. I told Ms. Francis why I was there. Francis attempted to reenter the residence without explanation.

I showed Francis the search warrant and instructed her to stay outside with Officer Else.

Along with Officers Meritt and Clemens, I then executed the warrant. During the search, the following items were discovered:

- Fourteen televisions, seven Samsung and seven Sony, in unopened boxes, each with store security tags still attached.
- Thirty-six designer handbags in original, new packaging (a dozen each of Louis Vuitton, Gucci, Prada).
- Ten cartons of high-end perfumes. Six containing Chanel and four of Yves St. Laurent.
- One large jewelry box containing twenty-seven felt bags holding assorted gold chains, diamond rings, and watches.

Each of the items was photographed in place, tagged as evidence, and have been stored in Property Locker #14C.

Ms. Francis was placed under arrest for Possession of Stolen Property (F.S. 812.019) and Dealing in Stolen Property (F.S. 812.019(2)). Officer Clemens read her Miranda rights, and when asked, Francis stated she understood those rights.

Questioning where she got the items, Ms. Francis claimed they were gifts from friends who had moved out of Naples. Though I asked, Ms. Francis could not provide names or receipts for the items.

Ms. Francis was transported without incident to the Collier County Jail and booked under Arrest Number 25-0384.

OFFICER SIGNATURE:
R. Z. Blake #217

LUCA PICKED UP HIS PHONE, discovering that the roofing company Rigo worked for had hung up. He punched another number into his phone. The call was answered on the second ring.

"Donovan, homicide."

"Donnie, it's Frank."

"Hey, Frank. What's up?"

"Look, last night a woman was arrested for possession and dealing in stolen property."

"And here I thought you were retired."

"Come on, Donnie. This is serious. The woman you're

holding, her name is Victoria Francis, she might have been involved with the Waterside robbery-murder."

"What makes you think that?"

"They found a bunch of stolen jewelry in her house. You should check to see if any of the jewelry came from the Waterside robbery."

"You can't be serious. You're saying she held on to it for twenty years?"

"It could be. None of it ever surfaced."

"I don't buy it. It doesn't make sense."

"Maybe they got scared when they learned two people died, and never fenced the goods."

"And they held on to evidence that would link them to the crime? For twenty years?"

"Criminals aren't the sharpest knives in the drawer."

"Yeah, but holding the jewelry would tie them to the murders. Nobody is that stupid."

"Don't kid yourself. It's possible they hid them and thought it was safe to sell them now."

Donovan didn't say anything.

Luca said, "I know it's a long shot, but can you take a look at what was stolen from Waterside and compare them to the pictures from yesterday's search?"

"Frank, this stolen goods case is being handled by Detective Sloan."

"The Waterside case is a double homicide. It's yours."

Donovan exhaled. "Okay, Frank. I'll check, but I really doubt there's a connection."

"Thanks, Donnie. Let me know what you find out."

Chapter Eleven

Luca called Tropical Roofing, discovering that Ernest Rigo was in the field supervising a job at a condo development in Village Walk. He hopped in his car and drove to the community off Vanderbilt Beach Road.

He shook his head as the gate lifted. He'd told the guard he was with Tropical Roofing, and without checking his ID they let him in. It was nothing more than what he called security theatre. It made the residents feel good, but Luca knew it was next to nothing to keep determined criminals out of gated communities.

Luca scanned the rooftops as he crossed over a bridge. To the left, roofs were stacked with tiles. He weaved around and pulled behind a Tropical Roofing truck.

He checked Rigo's DMV photo before getting out of the car. The Spanish music playing was punctuated with the boom of clay tiles being tossed off roofs into dumpsters.

The truck was idling. Luca peered into the passenger window. Behind the wheel Rigo was talking and laughing on the phone. He swiveled his head and Luca waved.

Rigo ended the call and lowered the window. "Hey, I'm sorry about the mess, but roofing is a messy job."

"That's okay. You're Ernest Rigo, right?"

He tucked his chin in. "Yeah, and you are?"

Luca introduced himself, telling Rigo he had a couple of questions about a case he was working on.

"What kind of case, and what do I have to do with it?"

If Luca was still on the force, he would've told Rigo that he was the one asking questions. Instead, he said, "It's an old case from 2006. You were just a kid then."

Rigo's shoulders dropped. "Yeah, I was in high school. Those were the good old days."

"Before you got into trouble."

"What do you want, dude?"

"Let me come around to the other side. I don't want to mess with your privacy."

Luca went to the driver's side. Rigo slid down the window.

"Look, I ain't got time for this. I'm on the job."

"You like using Tasers, don't you?"

"That dude was in my face. He threatened me with a pool stick."

"But you took it outside, and he didn't take the cue stick with him."

"He was a fucking jerk."

"Why'd you use a Taser?"

"Why not? It did the job."

Rigo didn't say it wasn't deadly. Was that because he knew it was?

Luca leaned into the car, invading Rigo's personal space. "Was it your idea to use Tasers for the Waterside Shops robbery?"

"What are you talking about, man?"

"The robbery that left two people dead in 2006."

"What, are you crazy or something? I had nothing to do with that."

"Where were you on the day of the robbery, May fifth, 2006, at approximately one p.m.?"

"I don't know, man, that was twenty years ago. All I know is I had nothing to do with it."

"You're going to need an alibi."

Rigo put the truck in gear and said, "Go fuck yourself, okay?" as he drove away.

Luca got back in his car. He knew memories faded over time, and in this case two decades had passed. But he felt he had to try and pinpoint where Rigo was when the security guard and jewelry store owner lost their lives.

Adjusting the air-conditioning vent, his phone pinged with a message from O'Leary, a Collier County prosecutor: *Victoria Francis is going to be released against a fifty-thousand-dollar bail.*

Luca put a call into the sheriff's office.

"Homicide. This is Detective Frederick."

"Hey, Joe, it's Frank Luca."

"How are you?"

"Good. Is Donovan around?"

"No, he's at a presentation in Fort Myers."

"Did he mention anything about a Victoria Francis? He was supposed to check pictures of the stolen goods found in her house against the swag taken out of the Waterside Shops murder."

"What Waterside Shops murder?"

"It's from 2006."

"Oh, I didn't move down here until 2018."

"Can you check into this?"

"What's the rush?"

"Francis is being released on bail in the morning, and I don't want her to disappear into the wind."

"I'll see what I can do."

Luca disconnected the call and scrolled through his phone for Donovan's personal cell number. He found it and sent Donovan a text: *This is Frank Luca. I need to talk to you ASAP.*

Five minutes went by without a reply. Luca called the number. Donovan answered on the third ring.

"I'm at a conference. What's so urgent?"

"I'm sorry, but Francis is being released on bail in the morning."

"Who?"

"Victoria Francis. She was arrested for stolen goods. She might be connected to the Waterside—"

"Hold on, Frank. You dragged me out of a meeting for a twenty-year-old case?"

"It was a double homicide. She—"

"This is going to have to wait. Goodbye."

"Wait, wait."

Donovan hung up.

"Damn it!"

There was a knock on the den door.

Mary Ann asked, "Frank, is everything all right?"

"Yeah."

The door swung open.

"What's the matter?"

Luca said, "Nothing."

"Don't tell me nothing. I heard you."

"What, are you spying on me?"

Mary Ann shook her head. "Sometimes you can be a real . . . I was going to the laundry room, if you must know. Okay?"

"Sorry. I guess I'm just frustrated."

"Is it that case?"

"Yes." He told Mary Ann about Vicky Francis and the stolen goods found in her house. He finished with, "I know it happened before I got to Naples, but we're talking about two murders. This could be the link that solves it."

"It's an old case and—"

"That's what everyone is saying, and I'm sorry, but that's just not good enough. We should be jumping all over this."

"Patience was never your strong suit, Frank."

"I'm not going to apologize for trying to get a daughter justice for her father."

"You don't have to. All you have to do is give the sheriff's office a little time. You know as well as I do that they've got a full plate keeping the county safe."

"That's true."

"Jessica wants to go to Gumbo Limbo for lunch. Do you want to come?"

Frank hesitated before saying, "Definitely."

Chapter Twelve

The deeper Luca looked into Anthony Crespoli, the greater his suspicions became. Crespoli had married Maria Dalio in 2015, but the marriage ended in divorce six years ago. They had no children.

His wife didn't have a record and neither did her parents, but Crespoli's family had mob connections. Luca couldn't find any evidence that Crespoli worked or owned a business, so where he made his money was a question.

Luca slowed as he approached the green building housing The Naples Country Club and turned off Route 41 into Naples Park. He slowed down going west on 101 Street. A block off Vanderbilt Drive, stood the two-story house Crespoli called home.

The house was white, in a coastal contemporary style. It was too big for the lot, but that was common in the neighborhood. Luca drove past the home and pulled over. He put the address into Zillow, and the Zestimate came back at just under three million dollars.

He contemplated the home's value for a moment before driving to his meeting.

Luca gave his keys to La Playa's valet and made his way to the pool area. Sitting at the bar was Anthony Crespoli. His body had thickened, but he still had the same short hair and broad shoulders he had in high school.

"Mr. Crespoli?"

"Yeah. You must be Luca, the investigator."

Luca stuck his hand out and Crespoli enveloped it. "Thanks for meeting me."

"No problem."

A pair of kids jumped into the pool behind them. Crespoli shook his head. "They ain't supposed to use this one. Anyway, you want a drink or something?"

"No thanks. Are you a member here?"

"Yeah, it's good but getting too crowded. They're selling too many memberships."

"At the prices I hear they go for, it'd be hard not to."

Crespoli shrugged. "Vanderbilt is the best beach in town."

"I agree with you. What do you do for living?"

"A little bit of everything."

"Like what?"

"What did you want to talk to me about?"

"I was hired by a family to check into something that happened a while ago, and I'm talking to a ton of people who went to the Community School twenty years ago."

"It was a hell of lot smaller back then. It's grown like the rest of Naples."

"It sure has."

"So, what happened back then that you're checking into?"

"You knew Victoria Francis, didn't you?"

"Oh yeah, Vicky. Sure, I knew her, but not so good. We had a couple of classes together."

Crespoli was backpedaling like an Olympian.

"You had your arm around her in a couple of pictures I saw."

"That's not a crime, as far as I know."

Luca leaned in. "No, but racketeering is."

"Look, I don't know what your game is, but I'm not playing." Crespoli got off the barstool and dug a twenty of out his pocket. He tossed it on the bar and walked away.

Luca followed him. "Hang on a second."

Crespoli turned around.

Luca said, "I'm sorry for bringing up the past."

Crespoli took a step toward him. "You gonna tell me what you really want?"

Luca motioned to a quiet spot along the fence. Crespoli followed him there and Luca asked, "You remember the jewelry store robbery where two people got killed at Waterside?"

He tucked his chin in. "Sure, I remember. That was wild."

Luca looked him straight in the eye. "Did you have anything to do with it?"

"Me?" He shook his head. "No way, I was a just kid when it happened."

He seemed to be telling the truth, but answering with a question was a tactic criminals used to buy time to construct an answer.

"Are you sure about that?"

"Damn right I am. Don't tell me somebody gave you some bullshit it was me, because I was nowhere near that place and had zero to do with that."

"What about anyone you went to high school with?"

"A couple of kids thought it could've been Ernie."

Luca was sure it was the roofer he'd talked to. "Ernie what?"

"Ernie Rigo."

Luca knew Rigo had a couple of arrests, but they were for assaults. "Why'd they think that?"

"Ernie made himself out to be a tough guy, you know. Always looking for a fight, that kind of shit."

Luca wanted to steer it back to Vicky Francis. "Anybody else you can think of out of the girls you knew?"

He shrugged. "Not really. Everybody was interested in who the girls could've been, but we thought they didn't go to our school or had dropped out."

Luca blinked. He hadn't thought any of the thieves might have left school. "What about Vicky Francis?"

"I don't know, she was kind of a schemer."

"What do you mean by that?"

"You know, she'd work behind the scenes to get what she wanted."

"Can you provide some examples?"

"Well, like the first day of classes, she'd suck up to the teachers, and she'd get out of doing homework by helping them. That kind of stuff."

Being a teacher's pet was a long way from participating in a killing. "Anything more than that?"

"You know, one time Mrs. Mackenzie had her pocketbook stolen. They had no idea how it happened, but a couple of girls were in the classroom around when it happened, and Vicky was one of them."

"I assume she was questioned?"

"Yeah, but they went easy on her from what we heard because the teachers all stood up for her."

Luca thanked him and left. Crespoli had an affiliation with a mob family out of Chicago, but the gang limited its activities to operating illegal gambling places. There was no record of their involvement in hijacking or robberies.

Luca's hunch had seemingly turned to dust. He'd move Crespoli down to the bottom of the suspect ladder. Luca would investigate the others who had records.

As soon as he got home, Luca jotted down notes from his talk with Crespoli. He read back what he'd written, trying to see if he'd missed anything. He hadn't.

He tossed his notebook on the desk. A lost pocketbook and teacher's pet? That is all he had. Unless something dropped in his lap, the odds of finding who was responsible for the deaths were less likely than finding a phone booth on Fifth Avenue.

Luca stood, it was hopeless. Coming around the desk, he saw the security guard's logbook and froze. The guy had been killed and his daughter wanted justice. Luca couldn't give up so easily.

He sat and opened his laptop. Looking at the list, his gaze bounced between Ernest Rigo and Victoria Francis.

Rigo had used a deadly weapon, putting him behind bars for one of his two arrests. That was enough to start with the man Crespoli said was a tough guy.

Luca pulled up Rigo's arrest records. The first was for beating a man unconscious during a 2010 fight at a Fort Myers nightclub. Rigo had claimed the man had made lewd comments to Rigo's girlfriend. Rigo was given probation for three years, and there were no violations, telling Luca the man could control his animal instincts, if he wanted to.

But the case Luca was interested in was one that put him behind bars for twenty-two months. He clicked on the case file. The assault had occurred in another bar in 2014, just after his probation ended.

Luca leaned into the screen. He read the next line two times. This could be it.

Chapter Thirteen

Two days had gone by.

And two things were bothering Luca: Victoria Francis was out of jail, and Donovan hadn't called to say if any of the jewelry found in Francis's house matched what had been stolen from the Van Dores Diamond Showroom twenty years earlier.

Luca looked out the sliding door. Mary Ann had finished her laps and was toweling off. He stepped onto the lanai.

"I don't know how you do it every morning."

"Believe me, most days I don't want to, but the doctor was right, swimming is keeping the MS at bay."

"And nothing else is as good, like bicycling?"

"Swimming engages just about every muscle, and there's no strain on your frame. Plus, it's good for my lungs. I never get out of breath anymore."

"That's good."

"You should try it."

"Nah."

"You don't have to do a lot of laps. Just start with three and work your way up."

"I'll stick with walking. Let me ask you something."

"What?"

"Do you think it's okay to call Donovan? It's been over two days, and it's like almost four days since I told him to compare the stolen jewelry."

"I'd wait on him. If he gets annoyed with you, he may not help you on the next case."

"The next one? He's not helping on this one."

"If you want to burn bridges, go for it."

Luca smiled. "If he gets pissed, I'll send him flowers."

He retreated to the den. If things got heated, he didn't want Mary Ann to know she was right.

Luca checked the time. It was nine forty-five. He decided to make another call before reaching out to Donovan.

A woman answered. "Rigo residence. Who is calling?"

"Uh, this is Frank Luca, I'm a private investigator looking to speak with Mrs. Rigo."

"What is the nature of the call?"

"It's an old case, and I was looking for background information on the Community School of Naples."

She hesitated. "This is Mrs. Rigo. What would you like to know?"

"Oh, I thought, you might have been a maid or something."

"We've done well, but we live a normal life."

"Would it be convenient to meet in person? Maybe for a cup of coffee?"

"When were you thinking?"

"Whenever it fits your schedule. I'm totally open."

"Hmmm. I've got an appointment in Vanderbilt Collections at eleven forty-five. There's a cute little spot named Angelica's, who have superb, if not sinful, pastries."

"Sounds good. I'll see you there."

The call had lasted all of two minutes. Luca got up and went to the bathroom. He sat on the throne and coaxed the bladder the doctors had made for him after cancer destroyed the one God had made.

It took a long time to empty his bladder, and this time it was okay by Luca. He got back in the den and felt good; it was 10:02 a.m.

He punched in Donovan's number.

"Homicide. This is Detective Donovan."

"Hey, Donnie. It's Frank."

"Hello."

"I hate to be a pain in the ass, but did you get a chance to check out the stolen goods?"

"I sure did."

"And?

"Victoria Francis had nothing close to what was taken from the Waterside case. Like I told you, I can't see anybody waiting twenty years to fence jewelry. It just doesn't happen."

"Okay. It was worth a shot. Right?"

"If you say so."

"I'm sorry, I was just trying—"

"Frank, do me a favor and enjoy your retirement."

Before Luca could say anything, Donovan said goodbye and hung up.

He tossed the phone on his desk. Taking a long shot was worth it. Wasn't it? How else could you solve a twenty-year-old case?

He picked up his phone and went into the kitchen.

Towel wrapped around her waist, Mary Ann was putting fruit into a blender.

She looked up. "How did it go with Donovan?"

Frank shook his head. "There was no match."

As she poured protein powder into a blender, Mary Ann said, "I'm sorry."

"It's okay."

Frank opened the slider as the blender whined. He paced the lanai. Victoria Francis wasn't off the hook. She had stolen jewelry in her possession. Just because the Waterside stuff had been fenced didn't mean she hadn't been involved in that robbery.

<hr>

LUCA SURVEYED Angelica's outdoor space. Half of the outdoor tables were filled with people chatting and sipping coffee. Standing in the shade was a tall, elegant woman he pegged as Eleanor Rigo.

He approached the well-dressed lady. "Mrs. Rigo?"

"Yes. I assume you're Mr. Luca."

"That's me."

He extended a hand, but the woman just smiled.

"Shall we get a coffee?"

Luca glanced at her small, white handbag. It didn't smell of leather, but it reeked of money.

"Yes, ma'am."

He held the door for her, and the combined smell of coffee and baked goods made his stomach growl.

She ordered a croissant and decaf espresso. Luca eyed a creamy hunk of Napoleon but settled for a dark roast coffee.

They sat at an outdoor table. Mrs. Rigo took a nibble and dabbed her mouth. "Now, how may I help you with the Community School?"

"Your son went there, right?"

"Yes, Ernest and both of our daughters, Emily and Emma, attended as well, though it was after Ernest graduated."

Luca couldn't help from wondering what was it about names that started with an E that this woman liked?

"I hear it's a good school."

"The best in the area in my opinion."

"Do you recall the robbery and murders at Waterside Shops about twenty years ago?"

"Of course. We shopped at Van Dores occasionally and knew the owners."

Luca saw the connection he was looking for. "The perpetrators were never caught."

"It doesn't reflect well on law enforcement."

Luca wanted to tell her it didn't put the school in good light either, but said, "We know it was four teenagers who we believe attended the Community School."

"That's surprising. It's the first time I've ever heard that."

"It's true. It's believed they were seniors."

"That's heartbreaking to hear."

Luca lowered his voice. "It must have been difficult to hear about your son's arrests."

"Ernest went through a rough patch dealing with anger, and fortunately, with therapy, he was able to overcome it."

"He used a Taser during one incident, which is what was used in the Waterside robbery."

She set her cup down. "What are you implying, Mr. Luca?"

"You're a smart lady, I'm sure it crossed your mind that your son was involved."

"I'm absolutely confident that Ernest had nothing to do with it."

"How can you be so sure?"

"Because we were in Orlando that day."

"I'm sorry, but it's hard to believe you remember where you were twenty years ago."

"May fifth is our daughter Emma's birthday, and the entire family, including Ernest, went to Disney World to celebrate. We were there overnight, and the next morning I received a call from a dear friend to let me know Mrs. Van Dore- had been killed. We sent flowers to her wake."

"I see. I assume this can be verified."

Eleanor Rigo stood. "If you're so inclined, check with The Floridian. We used to stay there back then. Naturally, we have numerous family photos of the excursion as well. Good day, Mr. Luca."

Watching Mrs. Rigo march away, Luca knew his hopes had been dashed. He drained the rest of his coffee thinking there was a reason the case had never been solved.

He'd talk to Victoria Francis, and if that went nowhere, it was time to tell Tanya there was nothing more he could do.

Chapter Fourteen

Based on Florida's employment records, Victoria Francis had bounced from one retail job to another. Luca viewed it as a red flag. He'd investigated where she lived and found out Francis owned a two-bedroom apartment in the Remington, a beach-front luxury building, which was a part of exclusive Bay Colony.

Putting aside the several million dollars that Bay Colony places went for, Luca knew there was no way you would be able to pay the homeowners fees on what you took home from a retail paycheck.

Where was Francis's money coming from? He couldn't recall a single thief in his career who had been able to live so comfortably. His mind drifted to a jewel thief he'd read about operating in the South of France.

There was enough wealth and showiness in Naples to have a certain type of individual target the moneyed set. But Luca knew pride was important to the success of a theft.

Luca recalled a financial scam that proliferated when he was on the force. A little bit of publicity would have stopped the fraud, but none of the victims wanted anyone to know they'd been duped. Before he caught the swindlers, dozens had been ensnared by the trickster.

Luca turned off Park Shore Drive into Venetian Village. He parked and wound his way to a store called Everything But Water.

There weren't any customers in the store. Vicky Francis was behind the counter scrolling on her phone. She lifted her head and smiled.

With her strawberry blonde hair and light freckles, she looked more Irish than corned beef.

"I'm Frank Luca. We spoke on the phone."

She came around the counter. "Well, hello there."

Her bright pink sneakers matched her lululemon top. But what caught Luca's eye was the necklace she was wearing. He wasn't into jewelry, but it looked more expensive than anything he'd bought for Mary Ann.

"Thanks for seeing me."

"Hey, no problem. We're not exactly busy."

"Things slow down in the summer."

"This off-season is way slower than the last couple."

"It does seem that way."

She smiled. "If you can't control it, you can't worry about it, right?"

"I have to say, for someone who was just released on bail, you're in a good mood."

"It's not worth getting down about things."

She hadn't learned the lesson that crime didn't pay. But maybe in her case it did. "You were caught in possession of a large amount of stolen goods."

"I told them the stuff wasn't mine. I was holding it for a friend."

"You had quite a few pieces of jewelry. Do you know where they came from?"

"No. Like I said, it's not mine."

"Okay. So, how do you like living in Bay Colony's Remington?"

"It's nice and all, but it can be a little too quiet for me."

"It's expensive there."

"Yeah, no doubt."

"How do you afford to live there working in a retail store?"

"I work to keep myself busy." She smiled. "You can't play pickleball all day long."

Was she stealing to prevent herself from watching TV?

"Those condos go for millions of dollars. How did you swing buying one."

"I married well."

"Your husband must have a great job."

"I'm divorced."

"What did he do for a living?"

"Which one?"

"How many times were you married?"

"Three."

She may not have been a magical jewel thief, but she seemed to know a lot about getting men to part with their money.

"You have me beat. I got divorced in New Jersey and ended up marrying my partner when I joined the force down here. What did your husbands do?"

"One of them was a big shot with WCI. They built Pelican Bay along with a ton of other communities down here."

"Is that how you got the apartment?"

She nodded.

"That's a nice necklace you're wearing. Is it new?"

She put her hand on where the necklace met her chest. "I've had it for years."

"My wife's birthday is next week. She'd love something like that. Where do you buy your jewelry?"

"No place in particular. If I see something I like, I go for it."

"Do you remember, in Waterside Shops, there used to be the Van Dores Diamond Showroom?"

"Not really."

"There was a robbery about twenty years ago."

"Who can remember that far back?"

Luca stared into her eyes. "It's hard to forget, especially for the families, that two people were killed."

Here face didn't betray her. "I'm sure it is."

A good thief needed nerves of steel and Francis had them. "You said earlier that when you see something you like, you go for it."

"Yep, that's what I do. Life is too short, so just go for what you want."

"Does that apply to stealing other people's jewelry?"

"Of course not."

"Then how do you explain the jewelry and other stolen merchandise in your home?"

"I told you, I was holding them for a friend."

"That's hard to believe."

"You can believe what you want. Look, I've got enough money, I don't need to steal to live."

Luca knew people stole for the danger and the challenge. It was the same with climbing Mount Everest. People got high off it.

"There's no doubt you're living well."

She smiled. "It sure burns up my exes. But you know what they say, living well is the best revenge."

"You went to the Community School of Naples."

"Boy, you did your research, didn't you?"

"You can find everything on the internet these days. You were a senior when the Waterside robbery happened."

She hesitated. "If you say so."

Luca couldn't tell if the delay was her doing math in her head or if she was thrown by the statement. "You were. I talked with several of your classmates. Everyone said you were a thrill seeker."

"I guess I liked to have fun, but what kid doesn't?"

"You liked to plan schemes, like robbing a teacher's pocketbook, and the time you stole the science test the day before the exam and that you got away with them both times."

She chuckled. "It was harmless fun. They made it so easy, it was hard to resist."

"Was the Waterside Shops robbery easy?"

"What? You think I had something to do with that?"

"What's more thrilling than robbing a jewelry store in the middle of the day?"

"That's way different than what I did in school."

"I don't see it that way. What I see is that getting away with the stuff you did wasn't good enough anymore. They didn't provide the high you got when you started, so you upped the stakes."

"That's ridiculous. You got it wrong. Way wrong."

The door swung open, and a pair of women entered the store.

Francis said, "Good afternoon. If I can help you with anything, let me know."

The ladies said they were browsing and Francis whispered to Luca, "Look, I don't have to talk to you. If you're not going to shop, please leave."

Luca lowered his voice. "I think you had a role in the Waterside Shops robbery, and I'm going to nail you for it."

Chapter Fifteen

Jessie was on the lanai, laying in a lounge chair as she scrolled through her phone.

Luca stepped outside. "Hey, kiddo. What's going on?"

"Hi, Dad. Nothing much, just chilling. Mom went to the doctor. I wanted to go with her, but she said no. Is everything all right with her MS?"

"Yes. She's doing great. She probably just wants you to relax."

"I'm a little bored, to be honest."

"It's your last day here."

She shrugged. "How is that case you're working on?"

"It's been a dead end, but I have one last lead to check out. If it doesn't pan out, I'm going to tell the client that it's hopeless."

She swung her legs off the chaise. "What's the lead?"

Luca told his daughter about Vicky Francis.

"She sounds dicey."

"That's what I think."

"What are your next steps?"

"Well, I've got to take a deeper look at her, check who she was friends with back in high school and see if there are any connections to some of the other students who were out when the murders took place."

"That's a good idea. You're going to talk to the people who went to the Community School back then?"

"If I find something, but I'll start with checking the yearbook that came out when she was a senior. It's the year of the robbery."

"That's a cool idea. Can you imagine nailing a murderer from a yearbook?"

"It's not going to be that easy, but it's the only thing that make sense at this point."

"You're going to check the pictures and see who her connections were?"

"Exactly."

"There's probably a zillion pictures."

"It is what it is."

"I can help you."

"Nah, just relax, I'll get to it after you leave."

"No, it'll be fun. Come on, let's go now."

***

LUCA HELD the library door open for his daughter. He led her to the section that held the yearbooks.

Luca pointed. "Grab that table over there. I'll get the yearbook."

Jessie opened her phone to the photo of Victoria Francis that her father had texted her. It was the formal picture of Victoria Francis taken for the yearbook.

Luca put the book down and sat. "They only had one copy."

She propped up her phone. "That's okay. We'll have two sets of eyes looking at it."

"That's a good idea, having the phone right there to compare."

She smiled. "I learned from the best."

"You're smarter than me and you mother put together. You know that?"

"That's not true, unless we're talking about math."

"Hey, no fair."

"Sorry, Dad. Just kidding."

"I know. Let's get going here."

Luca flipped the yearbook open and paged to the events section. "All right. Let's see if we can find a connection of hers."

There was nothing on the first five pages. Luca turned the page to a book fair to benefit the Galiano Children's Museum and pointed at a girl standing behind a tableful of books with another girl.

"Is this her?"

Jessie put her phone on the page. "No. The shape of her face is different."

"You're right."

They went through all the events featured in the yearbook but couldn't find a picture.

"I don't know what to make of it, but it seems odd that there isn't one picture of Francis besides the formal one."

"It's not that unusual, Dad. Maybe she didn't participate in things."

"Well, I guess it's over, then."

"We should look at the yearbook for the year before."

"Why?"

"The pictures and events are not just for seniors. We might find her in one of them."

"That's a great idea." Luca nudged his daughter. "I'm surprised I didn't think of it."

Jessie chuckled as Luca went to get the prior year's yearbook.

They combed through the pictures and stopped when they came to a photo of an art sale to benefit a veterans organization.

Jessie stabbed the page with a finger. "There she is."

Victoria Francis was in the middle of five other students. "Yeah, you're right. Now we need to check who these other kids are." He pointed at a boy. "This guy looks familiar."

Jessie said, "You look at the formal pictures in that book, and I'll check the other one."

Luca said, "Okay, but I'm focusing on the kids who were out the day of the murder."

"You're the pro."

Luca flipped to the pages with images of seniors whose last names started with an R. He found the one of Ernest Rigo, despite his mother saying he was in Orlando when the robbery occurred. Rigo wasn't one of the kids with Francis. Luca could forget about Rigo.

He thumbed the pages to a photo of David Flan. "Bingo. It's him."

Jessie leaned over. "Yes. There's no doubt it's him. What does that mean?"

"It's early, but he was on my radar."

"You're going to solve this, Dad. I can feel it."

"We'll see. I want to check on the girl next to Francis. Her face rings a bell."

Jessie moved the book closer to Luca. "Dad, look, it's her."

Luca looked at the picture of Jillian Vasel. "Good job, Jessie."

"Do you have something on her?"

"No. She seemed to be clean."

"What do you think it means that Francis and she are together?"

"It may be nothing, but I need to go over Francis with a microscope."

"This is fun. I can help you."

"We still need to identify the other two kids with Francis in the picture."

Chapter Sixteen

Luca showed his credentials for the second time, and the gate into Bay Colony opened. He took the brick-paved driveway to an imposing clubhouse. He sighed when he saw it was valet parking only.

He handed his keys off, and a uniformed attendant swung the twelve-foot-tall doors open.

"Welcome to the club, sir."

He was shown into a wood-paneled room by a reserved woman in a uniform. The emerald-colored grass of the golf course stretched to the horizon.

He followed the maître d' as she approached a man reading the newspaper. "Mr. Hyde, your guest has arrived."

Martin Hyde folded the paper. "Thank you, Belle."

Luca shook his manicured hand, thinking Hyde was a man who ate crepes and caviar.

Hyde swept his hand toward a chair. "Have a seat. Would you care for a beverage?"

"No thanks."

"You wanted to discuss Victoria. Is this related to her recent arrest?"

"I'm collecting background information."

He sat back, folding his hands on his lap.

Luca asked, "How did you meet Ms. Francis?"

"By complete accident. An associate of mine was hosting a cocktail reception to celebrate the opening of a new complex, and Victoria was there. I normally don't attend those types of functions, but I was recently divorced and was attempting to keep myself occupied."

"What do you do for a living?"

"Opportunist investments."

Luca didn't understand what it meant, but Hyde wasn't a suspect. "You're obviously doing well."

Hyde said nothing and took a sip of the reddish liquid in his glass.

"I understand Ms. Francis got the Remington apartment in the divorce."

"She did, along with a tidy sum of cash."

"She seems to like her jewelry."

"Most women do."

"Did you gift her much jewelry during your marriage?"

"I don't believe in jewelry. It's an asset that hemorrhages value before you leave the retailer."

That was a line I had to remember if Mary Ann asked for a piece. "Where did she get her jewelry?"

"From her first husband."

"How do you know that?"

"Victoria told me."

"I'm trying to understand why Ms. Francis would seemingly be involved with stolen goods."

"Victoria is an enigma. She can be enormously engaging,

yet is secretive. I assumed her reticent nature would change over time. However, it never did."

Luca finished up with Hyde and left the toney club. As he waited for his car, the feeling that Victoria Francis was hiding something was taking hold. There wasn't a firm connection to the Waterside Shop murders, but he was getting the vibe that Francis had to be involved somehow.

ALL FIVE OF the bays at Corbin's Tire Center were occupied. Luca stepped into the waiting room. The half dozen customers waiting were glued to a TV watching a *Judge Judy* episode.

Francis's first husband wasn't super-rich like Hyde, but he owned a tire and auto service place. Luca knew the higher customer service they offered in Naples was nothing more than a cover for the inflated prices they charged.

Wearing a tie, a man behind the counter asked if Luca had an appointment before going to get Larry Corbin.

Corbin couldn't have been more different than Victoria Francis's second husband. While the wealthy Mr. Hyde might nibble on canapes, Corbin was more likely to be eating ribs at Michelbob's.

The owner had a firm handshake and was a couple of inches taller than Luca's six-foot frame.

"Come on back to my office."

Luca's claustrophobia caused him to pause before entering the small, windowless space. The walls were covered with travel posters. Corbin moved a stack of papers off a chair next to his desk.

"We're really jammed up today. Two mechanics called in sick. I hope this ain't going to take too long."

Luca sat. "I'll get right to it."

"Good, I guess this is about Vicky getting arrested."

"It's related. Did you buy a lot of jewelry for her?"

"No. Not really. I mean, I got her an engagement ring and a necklace for our anniversary the first year we were married, but my thing was going away. I'd rather spend money on a nice vacation."

"Where did she get her jewelry from?"

"She had connections and got some good deals."

"What kind of connections?"

"I don't know. I didn't get involved."

"She was caught with stolen jewelry, among other things. I don't think it's her first time either."

"I don't know nothing about that. We've been divorced forever."

The whiny sound of an impact wrench being used on lug nuts could be heard as Luca asked, "How did you meet her?"

"We were in school together."

"The Community School?"

"Yeah, we started dating as juniors and got married a couple of years after we got out of high school."

Luca's heart rate sped up. "What can you tell me about her?"

"She's a free spirit, you know, she does what she wants and doesn't care what anybody says. It was fun, but after a while, you know, it got old. I wanted to have kids, but she didn't and we drifted, you know?"

"I understand she was mischievous in school."

"Like I said, back then it felt like fun, but sometimes she'd cross the line, you know?"

"How would she do that?"

"Some of the things she did were mean, and I don't know what word I'm looking for, not delinquent, but something like that."

"You must have been a senior when the Waterside Shops robbery murder happened. Do you remember that?"

"Sure. The cops came and talked to a bunch of kids about it."

"Do you think she had anything to do with the robbery?"

"You mean Vicky?"

"Yes. Do you believe Victoria Francis was part of the team or played any kind of a role in the robbery and murders that happened at Waterside Shops on May fifth, 2006?"

Chapter Seventeen

Larry Corbin looked at the ceiling.

Luca said, "What's the matter? It's a simple question. Do you think your former wife, Victoria Francis, had anything to do with the robbery of the Van Dores Diamond Showroom in Waterside Shops?"

"I'm trying to remember."

"Remember what?"

"It was twenty years ago, man, give me a break."

"You wouldn't forget something like that."

Corbin clamped his eyes shut. He sprang them open and shook his head. "There's no way she was involved."

"How can you be so sure?"

"I was trying to remember when she broke her leg. It was right before the robbery happened."

The sound of Luca's crest falling was audible. "Are you certain about that?"

"Definitely. The school had a junior prom the Friday before, and she and I were volunteers." He smiled. "I remember trying to make her dance with a full cast on."

"And you're positive it was a couple of days beforehand?"

"Yeah."

"How did she break her leg?"

"She was walking across the top of a swing set and fell."

"You were there?"

"Yeah. I swear, you could hear the crack when she hit the ground."

Luca ended the interview and trudged out of the tire dealership. He got in his car, put the air-conditioning on and sat stunned. He'd been certain Francis had played a role in the robbery.

He ran through the remaining suspects. There were no red flags.

Luca had nothing. He'd make sure the timing of Francis's broken leg made it impossible for her involvement. If it turned out she couldn't have been one of the four teenagers, he'd have to tell Tanya he had run out of ideas and would have to walk away from the case.

Luca tossed his notebook on the desk in the den and followed the smell of coffee into the kitchen. Mary Ann was drinking a cup.

She said, "What's the matter?"

"Nothing."

"Come on, Frank. You look like you lost your puppy. What happened?"

"I went to see a couple of Victoria Francis's ex-husbands. She was my last hope to solve the Waterside crimes."

"What did they say?"

"The first guy is a rich businessman. When I asked him what he did for a living he gave me some bullshit like opportunity investing or something. Can you imagine this guy has so much money that he gave her a two-bedroom condo in Bay Colony? Right on the beach."

"Sounds like an expensive divorce. Are you upset he's got money, or did something else happen?"

"He actually gave me the impression Francis could be involved. Oh, and by the way, he said he never buys jewelry because it goes down in value."

"It's not an investment, Frank. You buy someone a piece of jewelry because of its sentimental value."

"Whatever. Then I went to see husband number one, and he said it couldn't be her because she broke her leg a couple of days before the robbery."

"Did you check to be sure it's true?"

Luca frowned. "It's not my first rodeo, Mary Ann."

"You don't have to be snarky about it. I'm just making sure."

"I know. I'm frustrated."

"What are you going to do?"

"I'm going to drop the case. It's been cold for twenty years, and there's nothing I see that is going to change that."

"If that's what you want to do."

"Trust me, I don't want to tell the guard's daughter I can't get her justice. But this one is never going to get solved."

"When are you going to tell her?"

"Today. I don't want this hanging over my head any longer."

"Maybe you should sleep on it."

"Nothing is going to change overnight, but I'll wait until the morning."

LUCA CARRIED his second cup of coffee into the den. He took a sip and made a call.

"Hello. Who is this?"

"Good morning, Tanya, it's Frank Luca, the investigator."

"Oh hi, Mr. Luca. Do you have news for me?"

"Yes, but it's not good news."

"What happened?"

"I'm sorry, but I gave it my best shot, and I don't want to waste your money. I don't see a path to solving your father's murder."

"Are you sure? Did you check—"

"I did my best and checked into almost twenty possible suspects, but they all came out clean."

"And there's nothing else you can do?"

"I'm afraid not."

"I was counting on you. You were my last hope."

"I'm truly sorry. I wish there was a way to help you get justice for your father, but there just isn't."

LUCA TRUDGED INTO THE KITCHEN. Mary Ann was chopping broccoli on the island. She put the knife down.

"You know, if this case is getting you down, just drop it, okay? You don't have to do this anymore."

"I already dropped it."

"Are you serious?"

"Yes. Like I said, first I thought Rigo was going to get me something to work with, but his mother put the kibosh on that. Then all the signs were pointing at Vicky Francis, but she had a broken leg. I've run out of leads and had to tell Tanya I was dropping it."

Part Three

Chapter Eighteen

Judge Conrad Bolt was in his chambers combing through a law book looking for a precedent to deny a motion a defense lawyer had presented.

There was a soft knock on his door. "Your Honor?"

It was his judicial assistant. "Yes, Marilyn."

"There's a call for you on line two."

"Who is it?"

"The woman wouldn't identify herself."

"Please tell whoever it is I'm unavailable."

"Okay. But she's called three times already and said she is an old friend who wanted to surprise you."

Bolt stiffened. "An old friend? That's interesting. Yesterday I was told a lady friend of mine from law school was in town vacationing. It could be her; I'll take the call. Thank you."

The judge stared at the flashing red button on his desk phone. His hand hovered above the receiver. He took a deep breath and answered, "This is Judge Bolt."

He clamped his eyes shut when he heard Cindy Clermont's voice.

"Hey, Conrad."

He whispered, "We're not supposed to call each other."

"Yeah, well, we need to talk. Now."

"That's impossible."

"Meet me in Clam Pass's parking lot in a half an hour."

"I'm in the midst of an important case. I can't just0 leave."

"Unless you're looking for publicity, you better be there."

Bolt's heart skipped a beat as the line went dead.

After waiting ten minutes, the judge slipped out of the rear exit of the courthouse. He got into his car. At the first red light, he took his jacket and tie off.

Mind racing, he drove north on Airport Pulling Road, turning left onto Pine Ridge Road.

Crossing Route 41, Bolt cursed the case management system Collier County used to assign cases to judges.

He was certain Cindy Clermont wanted to talk about a case on his calendar.

Bolt refused to look to his right as he passed the side entrance for Waterside Shops. Had Cindy chosen Clam Pass to remind him of what they'd done?

Bolt slowed as he approached the beach's parking lot. He reached for a ball cap on the back seat and tugged it as low as it would go on his head.

Cindy was standing at the tree line. Bolt parked and Cindy knocked on the passenger window. Bolt unlocked the door and Cindy got in.

"Nice car, Conrad. How much did this cost? Sixty thousand?"

Bolt slid lower in his seat. "You know we're not supposed to make contact."

"Yeah, well, what can I tell you, a little something came up."

"What do you want?"

"I need help on a case."

"You'll need to hire a lawyer for help. I can't do anything."

"You have to help me. My lawyer said he was almost certain I'll be convicted on the drug charges."

"Then you may want to consider a plea."

"The bastards won't give me probation. They want a minimum five-year sentence."

"You should have considered that possibility when you were engaged in the distribution of cocaine."

"You have to help me, Conrad."

"I'm sorry, but there's nothing I can do."

In a firm voice, she said, "I said, you have to help me."

"The only thing I can recommend to you is to turn state's evidence against that boyfriend of yours. He's a career criminal."

"No. I don't have to do anything."

"Then you'll have to face the consequences of your actions."

"You've got it wrong, Conrad."

"Really? Why don't you enlighten me, then."

"It's simple. You're the judge, you can dismiss the case."

"I believe you've been watching too much TV."

"If I go to prison, I swear I'll tell everyone what we did twenty years ago."

Bolt's stomach clenched. "Are you threatening me?"

"I call it my survival plan. I bet they'll make a deal with

me if I tell them that Judge Bolt and the others are no better than any other murderer."

"Don't even say that. Must I remind you that you're the one who tased the guard. It was your fault—"

Cindy smiled. "Come on, you know that doesn't matter to the law. You were there and you're going to be charged with murder."

"You've lost your mind. Do you know that?"

Cindy opened the car door. "Find a way to dismiss the case, or you'll find out just how crazy I am."

Bolt wiped away the sweat on his upper lip and watched Cindy get into a gray Toyota Camry.

CONRAD BOLT GLANCED at his nightstand clock. It was 2:47 a.m. He threw the covers aside and padded into the family room for a bottle of water.

The judge sat in the dark contemplating his options. Should he contact the others? Reaching out would break his own rules, but why should he have to deal with Cindy on his own? Maybe the others could talk sense into her.

But talking sense into someone who could bargain away a long prison sentence was a fool's game. He'd presided over many criminal trials, a dozen involving organized crime. Bolt knew whatever code existed years ago that kept criminals from ratting on their accomplices was long gone.

He paced the room. There were three options: take a chance Cindy wouldn't follow up on the threat, find a way to dismiss the case, or make his own deal and reveal what they'd done.

If Bolt went to the authorities, maybe he could avoid

prison. Doing so would ruin his reputation, and he'd have to step down from the bench. He would also be disbarred and have to find a way to make a living. It'd be tough, but when it was over he could move someplace far away where he wouldn't be recognized. Maybe to the panhandle or somewhere on Florida's east coast.

It'd be difficult, but he'd finally be able to shed the rucksack of guilt he'd been carrying. Who knew what the future looked like? Maybe he'd be presented with an opportunity on the speaking circuit.

Bolt went into the kitchen and put the coffee machine on. As it heated up, the judge retrieved his laptop from his den. There had been several judges who'd come clean about the conspiracies they'd been a part of. Bolt would see how they fared and see if he could use the information to his advantage.

Chapter Nineteen

Elena Borelli looked out the window of her private office. About a mile away the white, sandy beach was nearly empty. It'd been a year since she'd been to a beach in Naples. She preferred the busy, formal beaches of South France, which were minutes from her vacation home in Cannes.

There was a knock on the glass door. She swiveled her chair around, nodding to her right-hand man, Marco Rialto.

"Am I disturbing you?"

"No. Just deep in thought."

Rialto smiled as he took a seat. "Do you have another billion-dollar idea?"

"That's not what I was contemplating, but there are two targets I'd like research on."

"Okay, but let me tell you about the meeting with Continental first."

"How did it go?"

"Excellent. They agreed to give us one board seat so far."

"Keep the pressure on them. Tell them our offer is going

to expire next week and we're going to make a deal with Farro."

"That could work, but they'll check around and—"

"It's already covered. The word is going to start leaking."

"Excellent."

"What about Tivoli? I wanted that deal closed this month."

"They're holding fast at four percent."

Borelli tapped the desk with the tip of her forefinger. "You tell them if they don't sell us twenty percent, we're going to call the loan."

"We might have to be a bit more delicate, Elena."

"I've been dancing with them for eighteen months. They've had four hundred million of our money. And we're not earning what we should on that investment."

"We're getting seven percent."

Elena scoffed. "People who invest in hedge funds like ours do it for the outsized returns, not seven measly percent."

"I can't fight you on that. Under your leadership, we've been in the top three performers for five years now."

"I don't pay attention to the rankings, it doesn't mean anything."

"It helps draw money."

"It does, but in this world, you can go from hero to goat overnight."

"I'm not saying it can't happen, but we've built many safety triggers that'll insulate us in the event of a Black Swan event."

Borelli said, "I don't worry about the knowns; it's trying to discover the unknowns that makes the difference."

"And you're good at seeing around corners."

"I don't know what you'd call it."

"A woman's intuition? We're the only hedge firm run by a female in the top twenty."

"I've got work to do."

Rialto popped out of his seat. "I'll let you know how it goes with Tivoli."

"Don't disappoint me."

"I'll try not to, but they were adamant—"

Elena said, "I'll email the research targets."

She waved her hand and Rialto headed out the door.

Borelli took a cell phone out of her desk and sent a text.

A reply pinged in: *Thirty minutes.*

ELENA WALKED through Robb and Stuckey's living room displays. She brushed off a salesman and went to the contemporary section of the store.

In his late fifties, Bebe Herzog was looking at the price tag on a lamp. Elena walked to the dresser next to him and opened the drawer.

Bebe, an ex-Mossad agent, said, "Can you believe they want six grand for this?"

"Nothing is cheap these days."

"What do you need?"

"We're running into a bit of resistance on a deal we're looking to close with Tivoli."

"You need something to soften them up?"

"Anything that would facilitate a closing would be appreciated."

Bebe nodded, saying, "Leave it with me."

"If you're in the market for lighting fixtures, you should try Wilson's. I bought quite a few there and they were a lot less expensive."

Bebe gave her a quizzical look.

Elena said, "Everyone, especially the wealthy, loves a bargain."

FOUR DAYS LATER, Elena was in her office reviewing a contract. The door to her office was open and Rialto stepped into the threshold.

He said, "Do you have a moment?"

"Sure. Come in."

Rialto smiled. "Tivoli caved! We were able to negotiate for two additional board seats."

"Well done."

Elena wasn't going to tell him Bebe had dug up dirt on the company's CEO. There had been a bawdy party aboard the CEO's yacht, and the former Mossad agent reminded the executive that agreeing to a deal would ensure the festivities remained private.

"Where are we with Continental?"

"We're making progress, but not at the speed I'd like."

The phone sitting on Elena's desk began to vibrate.

She dragged it over. "I've got to get this. Please close the door on your way out."

The door softly closed and Elena answered the phone.

The accented voice on the line said, "Usual place, in an hour."

"Okay."

ELENA SPIED Bebe in the far corner of Robb & Stucky's parking lot. She pulled into a space next to his car and opened the window.

"What is so urgent?"

Bebe said, "Your judge friend met with Ms. Clermont."

"Are you certain?"

He held out his phone.

Elena exhaled and handed the phone back.

"Any idea why they met?"

"He's the judge appointed to oversee her case. It's obviously some kind of blackmail attempt."

Elena stared straight ahead but said nothing.

"Do you want me to intervene discreetly?"

"I'm inclined to say no at this point, but I appreciate the heads-up."

"No problem."

"I'll let you know if there is a change in plans."

Elena put the car in reverse and, before taking her foot off the brake, began to doubt the hands-off strategy she had taken.

She hadn't risen to the top woman in the finance world by sitting on her hands. She lived by astronaut Jim Lovell's quote: 'There are people who make things happen, people who watch things happen, and those who wonder what happened.'

Her cell rang. It was her personal assistant.

Elena answered. "Yes, Vivian."

"I'm just reminding you the Crush Cancer committee is meeting in an hour."

She'd forgotten about the meeting, and as the chair of

this year's event she couldn't blow off the obligation. "It's been a busy day. Is it still on?"

"Yes. I checked before calling you."

"Is everyone attending?"

"That's what I've been told."

"I'll be there."

"Good. I'll resend the agenda and include a summary you can use."

"The event is in two weeks. Where are we in regard to fundraising?"

"We've received one point five to date and have commitments for another one point three."

Elena didn't want anyone to know she would donate a million to the cause. "We need to get close to raising five million."

"That might be a stretch. Last year they barely got half that amount."

"We have to do it."

"I don't know."

"Did we get commitments from Ted Barengat and John Winslow?"

"Not yet."

"Call them. Today. If they hesitate, remind them I've supported their causes."

"I'll get right on it."

"Okay. Thanks."

"Oh, hold on a second."

"What is it?"

"*Gulfshore Life* and the *Naples Daily News* want to interview you about the event."

"You know I don't do interviews."

"Yes, but I think you should do at least one of them. Everyone who's been given the award does them."

She wanted to say that she wasn't everyone. Instead, she frowned.

Her assistant said, "Come on, it'll be good for your image. You know, help to deflect from the 'you're too wealthy crowd.'"

Chapter Twenty

There was a hint of Pledge in the air as the bailiff said, "All rise."

Those in attendance clambered to their feet as Judge Bolt strode into the courtroom. He took his seat, glancing at the gallery. It was the first case of the morning and there was just a handful of spectators.

Bolt shuffled papers as the bailiff called out the case number.

Sheila McNamara rose from her seat at the defense table. "Your Honor, we move to dismiss the charges against Ms. Cynthia Clermont on the grounds of entrapment. The evidence is clear: The state, through its agent, induced my client into committing a crime she had no predisposition to commit."

Prosecutor O'Leary jumped to his feet. "The state strenuously disagrees, Your Honor. The defendant made a choice to sell cocaine. She wasn't forced at gunpoint. She took the money and handed over the drugs. That's distribution, plain and simple. And may I add that the defendant has a history."

Judge Bolt avoided looking at the defendant and stared at her lawyer. "I'll hear the argument. Ms. McNamara, please proceed."

The attorney for the defense stood. "Your Honor, the county's case rests on the actions of an undercover officer, whose name has not been revealed to us, but who presented himself as 'Joey Carter.' Over six weeks, this operative targeted my client, who I'd like to add was struggling to pay her mother's housing and food expenses.

"We contend the undercover officer steered the conversations with my client toward drugs, offering to 'help' her with money troubles. It's our contention that the officer created the crime. It's a classic case of entrapment."

O'Leary scoffed. "The only thing classic about this is the defendant's claim of entrapment. Nobody forced her to sell the drugs. She could have simply refused, and we wouldn't be here today."

McNamara shook her head. "No, Your Honor. The undercover agent exploited my client's financial desperation, her mother's destitution. That's not predisposition, that's coercion. The Supreme Court in Jacobson versus United States made it clear: If the government induces the crime, entrapment bars prosecution. That's exactly what this case is."

Bolt kept his gaze on the rear wall of the courtroom as he spoke. "The law doesn't tolerate the government manufacturing crimes to trap the vulnerable. The officer's pressure and exploitation crosses the line into entrapment."

O'Leary gasped.

Bolt continued, "The prosecution has not shown predisposition beyond the induced act itself. I'm granting the motion to dismiss."

Cindy Clermont hugged her lawyer and left the courtroom smiling. The prosecutor wagged his head and made for the exit.

Bolt wanted to call a short recess to process what he'd just done. Instead, he brought the gavel down. "Bailiff, call the next case, please."

WHEN COURT RECESSED FOR LUNCH, Bolt retreated to his chambers. His judicial assistant raised her eyebrows as he passed her.

Before slipping into his chambers, Bolt said, "No calls, Marilyn."

"Yes, Your Honor."

Bolt closed the door behind him and stripped off his black robe. He loosened his tie and went into the bathroom. He splashed water on his face, terrified at what he'd done.

He toweled his face and averted his eyes from the mirror.

The phone on his desk rang.

Bolt shouted, "I said no calls!"

Marilyn's voice came through the door, "It's Chief Judge Renhaust."

Bolt froze. "Okay, okay. Put him through please."

Renhaust, who supervised Collier County's judges, said, "Conrad, how are you?"

"Good, sir. Can I help you with something?"

"The prosecutor's office is grumbling about the Clermont dismissal."

"It was entrapment, sir."

"You know I don't second-guess my judges. I hope the judgment was made on solid ground."

"It was, sir."

"There's going to be some blowback."

"It comes with the territory."

"Indeed, it does."

A brief silence was broken by Bolt.

"Is there anything else?"

"No. That's all I have. I simply wanted to touch base with you."

"Thank you, sir."

"Have a good afternoon, Conrad."

"You too, sir."

Bolt collapsed into his chair. The dismissal was only two hours old, but the heat was rising already.

CONRAD BOLT DIDN'T WANT to watch the news, but he reasoned that as uncomfortable as it might be, it was better to see what, if anything, the media had to say.

He navigated to WINK News. A reporter was in the field covering a story about a protest over the proposal to build a six-hundred-unit apartment building on Golden Gate Boulevard. The correspondent threw it back to the anchorman, who said, "WINK will follow the developments on this housing proposal."

Seated next to the anchorman was a woman in a blue dress. As the camera zoomed in on her, she said, "Earlier today, a controversial ruling by District Judge Conrad Bolt is raising questions."

Bolt blinked when a picture of him wearing black robes filled the screen.

"Judge Bolt, who has earned the respect of citizens and law enforcement for his tough stance on crime, has many trying to understand a ruling he made this morning. Judge Bolt dismissed drug distribution charges against Naples resident Cynthia Clermont, citing entrapment.

"WINK spoke to Prosecutor O'Leary about the dismissal, and his office issued the following statement:

'In my twenty-five years as a prosecutor, I have never seen a case dismissed on such spurious grounds. The defendant is a drug dealer poisoning our community. There was no entrapment—that is a fabrication.'

"WINK attempted to reach Judge Bolt, but his office issued a brief statement saying the judge stands by his ruling, invoking judicial discretion and declined further comment.

"Let's check in with our legal expert William Bongiovanni. Bill, what do you make of this dismissal?"

"Judge Bolt is undoubtedly a victim's advocate. His no-nonsense approach has earned him the highest rating from the conservative Florida Justice Association. But this ruling is puzzling. Just last week he sentenced a twenty-year-old man to three years in prison for possessing a small amount of marijuana. I'd like to hear what contributed to this decision. Perhaps we're missing something, as Judge Bolt's statement mentioned judicial discretion."

"Thank you, Bill. We're going to keep an eye on this story and update viewers as developments emerge. Coming up after the break: A local school district faces budget cuts, and your weekend weather forecast."

Bolt stood, trying to make sense of how the dismissal was being received. He figured it might get rocky, but they'd mentioned the discretion given to a judge. All Bolt had to do was to hide behind the leeway judges were given. He wasn't up for reelection until two years from now, and he'd use the time to burnish his tough-on-crime reputation.

Chapter Twenty-One

Luca scooped the *Naples Daily News* off the driveway. Padding back into his house, he pulled the plastic bag off the newspaper.

He scanned the headlines and shook his head. Another fatal car accident on Golden Gate Boulevard. He looked at the picture of an overturned car and went back into the house.

Mary Ann was coming out of the master bedroom. "Good morning."

He held up the paper. "Morning. There was another accident on Golden Gate. They have to do something."

"What could they do?"

"Enforce the damn speed limit and stagger the lights."

"Does the sheriff have the manpower for that?"

Luca tossed the paper on the table and went to the coffee maker. "Either that, or they're going to need more hands in the morgue."

"Somebody died?"

"A forty-two-year-old father with two kids."

"Was he speeding?"

As a stream of coffee filled Luca's mug, he said, "The car rolled over. He must've been going at least eighty."

"What a shame. Two kids without a father."

Luca sat, took a sip of coffee, and opened the paper.

He held up the newspaper. "Look at this picture. They had to cut the guy out of the car."

Mary Ann took it. "Oh my God. The top is completely flat."

Mary Ann set it back on the table.

Luca said, "Let's hope they do something to put an end to this."

Mary Ann grabbed her iPad off the counter and sat across from her husband.

Luca's eyes drifted to a headline below the fold: "Surprise Dismissal by Law-and-Order Judge"

He scanned the piece. His eyes zeroed in on the judge's name. Conrad Bolt.

Bolt had been on the list Luca developed for the Waterside robbery case. Luca read on and clenched his jaw when he saw the defendant's name, Cynthia Clermont.

As he finished the article, his heart rate sped up. "Why didn't you tell me?"

Mary Ann said, "Tell you what?"

"Judge Bolt dropped a drug case against Cindy Clermont."

"Who are you talking about?"

Luca picked up his coffee and stood. He walked to the den.

"Frank. What's going on?"

"The Waterside case. Two of the people I was looking at are connected."

"It could be a coincidence."

Luca turned and glared at his wife before he ducked into the den.

He opened his laptop and Googled the Bolt dismissal. He read a summary of the coverage WINK News had done. The synopsis had quoted Prosecutor O'Leary.

Luca checked the time. It was only 7:15 a.m. It was too early to call him. He punched in Derrick's number.

His ex-partner asked, "Frank? Is everything all right?"

"Yes, it's nothing to do with us, but something came up in the Waterside case."

"You had me worried. What's up?"

"I just read about Judge Bolt dismissing a drug case."

"Yeah, he's catching a lot of heat."

"Well, guess what? The defendant was someone he went to school with."

"Sorry, pal. I don't get it."

"I made a list of possible suspects, and both of them were on it."

"Out of how many?"

"You're not getting it. I needed to find connections between students who were out of school the day of the robbery. Both of them were out that day, and now Bolt dropped the case on her. Why? It doesn't make sense unless he owes her something or she threatened him."

"I don't know. That's a hell of a leap."

Luca said, "Maybe, maybe not."

"What are you thinking?"

LUCA WAITED until 8:35 a.m. to call the prosecutor's office.

"O'Leary."

"Good morning. It's Frank Luca."

"Frank, how are you?"

"Good, and you?"

"Besides the traffic, I'm living in paradise. What's got you up so early?"

"I just found out about Judge Bolt's dismissal."

O'Leary exhaled loudly. "Don't get me started."

"What do you make of it?"

"It's out of character for Bolt. He's been a victim's advocate from day one, and he's been supportive of law enforcement whenever there's a gray area. This one doesn't make sense; we had the goods on Clermont."

"He claimed it was entrapment. What do you say?"

"That's nonsense. Look, it's true Clermont needed the money our guy offered, but who doesn't? Does that give her the right to sell drugs? In my opinion, her claim of entrapment, saying her financial condition was exploited, doesn't fit the legal definition of entrapment."

"How reliable is the confidential informant they used?"

"As good as they get."

"Hmmm. This whole thing doesn't make sense."

"Bolt invoking judicial discretion is just a tactic to avoid explaining himself."

"Are you sure there can't be a legitimate explanation?"

"Not in my book. And what's of special concern is the possibility we'll have to curtail the use of informants."

"They've always been a touchy subject with the defense."

"They better be careful what they wish for, or they'll have no one to blame for their clients' actions."

"What about Clermont, the defendant? What do you know about her?"

"A model citizen, she's not. She fits your normal user-dealer profile. In lieu of serving time, she's been sent to rehab twice but is still at it. Tell me why you are so interested in this one?"

"I'm looking into an old case that happened when they were in high school. I cast a wide net and their names came up."

"What case is that?"

Deep down, Luca still enjoyed playing the hero and wasn't going to reveal anything. "You've got too much on your plate already."

"I'll say."

"Besides, it's over twenty years old, and it's too early at this point. If it goes anywhere, I'll turn it over."

Chapter Twenty-Two

The grand ballroom of the Ritz-Carlton Naples sparkled under the lighting from a dozen crystal chandeliers.

Outfitted in gowns, tuxedos, and diamonds, four hundred of Southwest Florida's wealthiest residents were gathered for the annual Crush Cancer Gala.

Elena Borelli, whose pink Yves Saint Laurent gown matched the color of the floral centerpieces anchoring each table, stood at the podium.

The hedge fund mogul smiled graciously as applause filled the room.

"Thank you for the warm reception. I promise to keep this short. I'm truly honored to receive this award and thank each of you for the recognition. However, tonight isn't about me."

Elena shifted her weight. "When I formed Horizon Investments over a decade ago, I reminded myself that success came with responsibility to the community. Like everyone in attendance tonight, I take that responsibility seriously. I'm pleased to announce that due to your generosity, this evening we have raised over five million dollars."

The crowd responded with a thunderous cheer.

"It's high time we found a cure for cancer. And with your help, we're going to get there."

Elena lifted the crystal award—Philanthropist of the Year—and basked in the crowd's adoration. The people attending knew her as a pillar of the community, a woman who'd clawed her way to the top and had given back generously.

If only they knew about the jewelry store.

As the crowd rose to their feet, giving her a standing ovation, she noticed a man in a tuxedo entering the ballroom. Elena forced a smile back onto her face. She shook hands with those on the podium and worked her way over to Bebe.

The ex-Mossad agent took her hand. "Congratulations."

"Thank you." She kept her smile on. "What brought you here?"

Bebe leaned in. "I thought you'd like to know Judge Bolt dismissed the case against Ms. Clermont."

Elena powered through the sharp pain that pierced her gut. She waved to a woman in a sequined gown, whispering, "How was he able to do that?"

"He claimed it was entrapment. The prosecutors are up in arms."

"What do you think will happen?"

"Judges have discretion. But he also dismissed it with prejudice, so they can't charge her on it again."

The coordinator for the gala came up to Elena. "The photographer from the *Naples Daily News* is waiting to take pictures."

"I'll be right with you."

As the woman walked away, Elena lowered her voice and told Bebe, "I need you to keep an eye on Clermont and Bolt. I want to know whatever you find out, even the tiniest thing."

She trusted Bebe, but as she walked toward the podium, she worried he was going to uncover her connection to the pair and her role in the Waterside Shops robbery.

As the photographer snapped pictures of her, Elena reasoned that Bebe was trusted and under her control. Her accomplices in the robbery and subsequent murders weren't.

ELENA ENDED the call and put her cell phone down. Was there significance in the twenty-year anniversary of the robbery? Was the universe conspiring somehow to remind her of the past she'd gone to great lengths to put behind her?

What did David Flan want this time?

She closed her eyes and inhaled deeply and slowly. As she released a breath, she considered what it was that made two of the four who robbed the jewelry store as high school seniors successful and the other two basket cases.

Was it the ability to overcome the guilt and compartmentalize? Or had she and Conrad Bolt come out of the womb as achievers? Flan and Clermont had bounced around, never sticking with anything long enough to make a go of it.

She'd considered the impact of the easy money they'd

made from selling the jewelry, but two people dying had turned trouble-free into an anchor of guilt.

She opened her eyes, knowing it was probably the guilt that separated them. She and Bolt had found a way to set it aside, while Cindy Clermont had turned to drugs and David Flan had lost the ability to focus.

On the call, Flan's voice had been tinged with desperation, but he was probably under financial pressure. Again. It was concerning, but Elena would meet with Flan before deciding whether he was a threat.

Chapter Twenty-Three

Elena parked in a shady corner of the Coastland Mall's parking lot. She scanned the aging structure. It had been years since she'd been inside.

David Flan pulled into a spot next to her.

Elena slid her window down. "Get in my car. And leave your phone behind."

Flan, in a T-shirt and cargo shorts, got into Elena's car. "Wow. I've never been in a Bentley. How much did this cost?"

"You look good, David."

"Thanks, you too."

"Why don't you tell me what's going on?"

"Well, I've got this amazing opportunity. I'm sure you've seen one of the Tide Cleaners that are starting to pop up everywhere."

"Yes. I'm aware of them."

"Well, they're opening up new territories, and I can buy the franchise for the eastern section of Collier County. The area can handle three locations without saturating the others, you know."

"I don't know anything about that particular business, but people don't wear the type of clothing requiring dry cleaners anymore. Especially in a place like Southwest Florida."

"The company said that is turning around. You know how things go in cycles. People are going back to the office these days and need to dress up like they used to."

"As I said, I don't know anything about the dry-cleaning industry, but I wish you luck in whatever you decide to do."

"Well, I need more than luck. I need some help from you. You know, with the down payment and build-out costs."

"And how much would that amount to?"

"The down payment is only three hundred thousand, and to build the store, the right way, it runs around four hundred thousand."

"That's a lot of money."

"I know, but it's a one-of-a-kind opportunity. I'd lock down Eastern Collier County."

"I believe that's what you said about the boat rental business."

Flan shook his head. "That was different."

"And the string of breakfast places you opened."

"If it wasn't for Covid, we would be giving Skillets a run for their money."

She knew it was useless to remind him that the relatively short economic slowdown Florida had experienced during the pandemic was more than made up by the subsequent increase in population.

"You're asking for a substantial amount of money for a

business in an industry that is on rocky ground. A whole slew of dry cleaners have closed in the last several years."

"Yeah, that's the beauty of it. There's less competition. Believe me, you gotta talk to the guys at Tide, they really know what they're doing. They're going to dominate the market in the States. And they're going to expand to Europe, and boy, I'd like to get into that end of it."

"David, I've given you money, sizeable amounts, on numerous occasions. How many times? I believe it was six."

"No, it was only five."

"No, I funded six of your businesses. And each of them required substantial capital to get opened."

"You have to spend money to make money, right?"

"Perhaps you should look at businesses that require a low investment."

Flan looked straight ahead and raised his voice. "No, I want this one. It's going to work, you'll see."

"I'll have to think this over."

"Come on, Elena. You've got the money." Flan smiled. "Don't forget, we go way back. We've got a lot of history together. You didn't forget what we did, did you?"

"When do you need the money by?"

David smiled. "Not for a month or so."

"Who are you using for a lawyer?"

"Uh, I don't have one yet."

"You need someone to look over the franchise agreement and leases. Call Figler and Figler. Ask for Sandy, they'll make sure the contracts are good, and then we'll get this done for you."

"Oh, man. You're the best, Elena. This is going to be a home run, a grand slam! You'll see."

"I'm sure it will be. I've got to be on my way, but call Sandy and engage her to review the contracts."

"Sure thing. Thanks again. I'll call you with updates."

"No! Do not call me. You know we have to keep our distance from each other."

"Yeah, yeah, yeah. So, how am I going—"

"Sandy will let me know how things are progressing, and when things are ready, I'll use her to arrange the delivery of the funds. Then you'll be able to close the deal."

He smiled. "Man, it's no wonder you made it so big. You were always so smart, even back in school."

"I'd appreciate it if you'd get out of my car. I have a busy day to catch up with."

"Sure, sure. Thanks again. Man, we're going to clean up on this one." He smiled. "See what I did there? Clean up?"

"Goodbye, David."

Borelli watched Flan get into his car and drive toward the Golden Gate Boulevard exit. She despised the leech and considered his lack of pride in his repeated requests for money. The amounts were large but nothing in the scheme of things in her world.

It rankled Borelli to hold her tongue over the years, but it had been a small price to pay for the safety it provided. She'd have to weigh the consequences of continuing or not.

Her cell vibrated with a meeting notification. She put the Bentley in gear and left the mall.

Chapter Twenty-Four

Luca pulled out the file he'd started for the Waterside Shops case and scanned the list of students he'd compiled. Luca took a red pen and underlined two names: Conrad Bolt and Cindy Clermont.

He'd given Bolt a pass because of his judgeship and stellar reputation. It was feeling like a mistake not to have dug into him.

Luca was convinced there was something going on between Bolt and Clermont that had led to the dismissal. He needed to determine whether it was just an old friendship or something more ominous.

It was easy to believe judges like Bolt were impartial. But Luca reminded himself Bolt was human. And that meant he could fall victim to temptation and bias. Like most of us, Judge Bolt, against his better judgment and training, could be persuaded to help a friend.

Clermont and Bolt lived in different worlds. Though opposites tended to attract, Luca couldn't see a romantic relationship clouding Bolt's decision-making. Besides, the publicity the dismissal caused would have brought an affair into the public arena by now.

If it was more than an odd friendship, Luca believed the incentive had to be money. His stomach clenched at the idea of Bolt taking a bribe to make the case go away.

The reality was there were too many judges who had violated the oath they'd taken. Given Bolt's stellar reputation, Luca figured if it involved a payoff, it had to be a substantial sum of money.

Since private investigators weren't allowed to access financial records, Luca began to search public databases for assets under Conrad Bolt's name.

Bolt lived in a home located in the Quarry. It was valued at a million and a half dollars and had a three-hundred-thousand-dollar mortgage against it. A condominium in Huntington Lakes was also in the judge's name.

Luca reasoned the three-hundred-thousand-dollar property, which Bolt had owned for nearly fifteen years, had been his home before he moved a couple of miles away. He seemed to own the condo free and clear.

Digging into the Quarry residence, Luca discovered Bolt had bought it right before Covid and that meant he'd paid half of what it was worth now. He considered whether you could save the half-a-million-dollar down payment on the money he earned as a prosecutor before becoming a judge.

Bolt's father, who had died ten years ago, had been a mid-level manager for IBM. His mother, who died a year after her husband, never worked more than a part-time retail job.

Luca got up and went into the kitchen. Mary Ann was playing mahjong on her iPad.

He swung open the door to the fridge. "You're really taking this mahjong seriously."

"It's complicated. If I don't practice, I won't be able to keep up."

He twisted the cap off a bottle of water. "You're going to catch up fast."

She shook her head. "These girls have been playing for years."

"Let me ask you something."

Mary Ann put the mahjong reference card down. "What's going on?"

"It's the Judge Bolt dismissal thing."

"Did you find anything out?"

"O'Leary said it didn't make sense, saying it wasn't entrapment by any stretch."

"Well, Bolt disagreed."

"It's not a legal question. Something is going on. He and Clermont went to school together and both were out on the day of the robbery. The two of them are totally different. If it wasn't a bribe, then I think Clermont threatened she'd blow the whistle on Bolt's involvement if he didn't help her. What do you think?"

"That you're a gold medalist in jumping to conclusions."

Luca frowned. "Ha-ha. Very funny."

Mary Ann smiled. "But seriously, do you really think Judge Bolt was blackmailed or took a bribe?"

"It's within the realm of possibility. Think of why it's never been solved, a judge with an unassailable reputation, a real victim's advocate."

"Did you have any evidence?"

"No, but I checked his financials, and he only has a three-hundred-grand mortgage on a place worth almost two million. And before you say anything, I know prices have doubled, but he put down half a million when he bought it."

"He probably rolled the money from his previous—"

"Nope. He kept it, probably using it as a rental."

"So, he took the bribe now for a house he's lived in for years?"

"I don't have it figured out yet. I'm just spitballing here."

"Just don't forget the possibility that Judge Bolt may really have believed the woman was entrapped."

Luca shook his head. "If I don't follow my gut on this, I'll regret it."

AFTER SHOWING his identification to the gatehouse guard, Luca snaked his way through the Quarry. He turned onto Graphite Circle and parked in front of Judge Bolt's home.

Luca could see a lake behind the two-story house. He rang the bell.

Bolt opened the door and their eyes met.

Luca said, "Judge Bolt, I'm working a case." He held up his identification. "It's an old one. It happened before you got on the bench. I'd like to have a quick chat with you."

"Uh, right this moment?"

"Yes, please. I promise it'll be fast, and I could really use the help."

Bolt tensed. "I fail to see how I can be of any assistance if it concerns a case before my time."

"It's background on someone you know."

Bolt hesitated. "Who might that be?"

"Victoria Francis."

Bolt smiled. "I remember her, but that was a long time ago."

"I realize that, Your Honor."

"Look, I don't have much time, but come in and we can chat for a couple of minutes."

Bolt moved aside and Luca stepped into the home. The judge pointed to a pair of swivel chairs. "Why don't we sit there."

Luca settled into a chair. "From what I hear, you were quite the ladies' man in high school."

"I wouldn't characterize it that way."

"There's no need to be modest. You're not married, are you?"

"No. I'm not."

"Planning on being a lifelong bachelor?"

"There's no plan, if I meet the right woman . . ."

"This is a nice house. Have you been here long?"

"Six or seven years."

"It's not cheap in this community, and they don't exactly pay judges what they're worth."

"It's not about the money; I'm happy to serve."

"You were around thirty when you bought this place. How could you afford the down payment?"

"My parents helped out. Now, what questions did you have for me?"

"Sure. Tell me about your relationship with Ms. Francis."

"We may have flirted occasionally, but there was no relationship. We didn't date or spend significant time together."

"I see. So, you just went to the Community School together?"

"That was the extent of it."

"Do you remember her breaking a leg?"

Bolt pawed his chin. "Yes, I do. I believe it was when we were seniors."

"Were you friends with Ernest Rigo?"

"An acquaintance would be more accurate."

"Is there anything you recall about him?"

"It's been twenty years since high school. Rigo came from a wealthy family is about all I can recall."

"Was he a troublemaker?"

"Nothing in particular stands out."

"Okay. Who were you friends with?"

"No one in particular. As is the case in every school, you socialized with whoever you were in a class with."

"Did you take any classes with Cynthia Clermont?"

Bolt frowned. "Mr. Luca, high school was two decades ago. I can't recall that far back."

"But you did know Cynthia Clermont, right?"

"Yes. I remember the name. But we'll have to end this chat. I have a busy day, which includes ruling on several motions."

"I've seen pictures of you and Ms. Clermont together in the yearbook. Were you dating?"

Bolt stood. "For the record, no. We did not have a relationship. It's time for you to leave."

Chapter Twenty-Five

After letting Luca out of his house, Conrad Bolt leaned against the door. He swallowed a mouthful of bile and headed to the kitchen.

He unscrewed a water bottle and rinsed his mouth. Why had he caved in to Cindy Clermont's demand to dismiss the case against her?

He regretted not finding a way to get himself removed from the case. A recusal would have raised questions, but the dismissal had prompted some kind of investigation. Who was behind the inquiry?

Bolt paced the family room. How and why had this private investigator been interested in talking to him? He told himself he shouldn't have given Luca the time. However, the upside was he'd found out someone was sniffing around.

Bolt dismissed the idea that Collier County had hired Luca. They had plenty of investigators as did the Judicial Qualifications Board. So, who was driving it?

Luca had brought up Cindy Clermont. Her name alone

was a signal that the dismissal had prompted the inquiry, but his heartbeat quickened when recalling Luca's questions about the Community School and the friends he had there.

Bolt told himself to calm down. He needed a plan. He sat and closed his eyes. Trying to concentrate on what to do, his thoughts devolved into the discovery of his role in the Waterside Shops murders.

It'd be a huge story and his undoing. His career of trying to make amends as a tough-on-crime judge wouldn't save him from serving time. The only chance to avoid going to prison was to come clean. Now.

Arranging a plea deal, trading the truth, and revealing the other conspirators would provide the only opportunity to avoid a life behind bars.

There was no way to sidestep the disgrace. For the first time in his life, Bolt was glad his parents had passed away. It was going to be ugly. He might avoid serving time, but it was likely he'd be sued in civil court by the victims and their families.

Bolt's shoulders slumped. He would lose it all. He'd be forced to leave his beloved Naples and start over in a faraway place.

Then he remembered the media. With a juicy story like his, the journalists would probably track him down.

Maybe he could write a book and turn over half the profits to a victim's fund to rehabilitate his image. Bolt knew it was unlikely, and even if it became a bestseller, he'd have to go through years of hell before getting to that point.

Bolt had carried the secret of what they'd done for over twenty years. It was a long time to live with guilt, but it also made solving the murders difficult. He shook his head.

Before Luca had come along, the case had been cold for fifteen years.

Bolt wasn't ready to confess. But the judge couldn't think of a way to influence the investigation Luca was conducting.

He had to do some homework. Finding out who Luca was might create a path to a solution. Bolt sat in his den and signed in to a VPN. He then opened a private window on his browser.

A simple Google search of Luca's name opened with an AI summary of the homicide detective's career. As Bolt read about Luca's achievements, his mouth dried. When his stomach began cramping, he closed the laptop.

He was going to need help. There was only one person who understood the situation and had the smarts and resources to help.

BOLT PULLED the door to USS Nemo open. He was thankful the seafood restaurant had one of the busiest lunch crowds in Naples. He avoided glancing in the direction where Elena Borelli ate lunch every Wednesday.

Bolt went to the bar and paid for the takeout he'd ordered. He pulled his phone out and said hello, even though no one had called. Holding the bag with his lunch, Bolt headed for the side exit.

Ear to his cell, he walked past Borelli's table saying, "Yes, I need to see her." He exited the restaurant and went back to the courthouse.

The following afternoon, Bolt tugged his ball cap as low as it would go and walked down the main dock of the

Naples City Dock and waterfront complex. Passing a fish-filleting station, he continued to scan the flags of the boats docked.

Bolt made a beeline to a thirty-foot skiff flying a Sardinian flag just below Old Glory. A man with four days' worth of stubble held his hand out and helped the judge aboard.

As the captain threw off the lines, Bolt asked, "Where are we going?"

"Please take a seat, sir."

Bolt sat and the boat moved away from the dock. They traveled through Naples Bay, past Crayton Cove and Aqualane Shores. Bolt hadn't seen the mansions from the water since a sunset cruise ten years ago.

Entering the waters of Port Royal, the boat slowed. It pulled up to the isolated dock of a Galleon Drive home. The mansion was set on a double lot, and half a football field away from the water.

The captain threw the bumpers over the side as the boat puttered to the dock. He hopped out and tied up the boat.

Holding his hand out, he said, "Sir."

Bolt took his hand and stepped onto the dock. "Thank you."

"I'll wait here."

"Where am I going?"

He pointed toward the home.

Bolt walked up the grassy slope leading to the home's pool and deck. He squinted as the sun bounced off the wall of glass serving as the rear of the house.

A panel of glass slid open, and Elena Borelli stepped onto the stone decking. She offered Bolt a short wave before sitting in one of the club chairs in a covered area of the lanai.

Bolt said, "I'm really sorry, but I just had to see you."

Elena motioned to the chair next to her. As Bolt settled into a seat, she asked, "What is the issue?"

"An investigator named Luca came to see me. He came to my house under the guise he was doing background on an old case. But then he asked me about Cindy."

"Tell me what was said."

Bolt told Elena what questions Luca had asked and what he himself had said in reply.

"I was rather surprised at the dismissal, Conrad. Frankly, it was unwise."

"What was I supposed to do? She threatened to expose all of us."

"Cindy wouldn't do that."

"I'm sorry, but I think she would. You were always soft on her."

Elena sneered. "Conrad, you made a mistake, a serious one."

"I had no choice."

"You could have dealt with it on the back end. Let it go to trial, see what opportunities arose during the trial for a mistrial, and if there was a conviction, you could have given her a break."

"The State of Florida has sentencing guidelines."

"That's rich, coming from the judge who invoked judicial discretion."

Bolt sighed. "She wouldn't have gone for anything like that."

"I don't want to belabor the point, but reinforcing the fact that she committed a crime and pairing it with a reduced sentence with parole options should have put the issue to bed."

"I don't think it would have worked, she was desperate."

"Again, you're wrong, Conrad. Now we're looking at a potential problem."

"What are we going to do?"

Elena said, "Nothing."

"Nothing? We have to do something."

She shook her head.

"What if this investigator comes to see me again? What do I do?"

"Start with avoiding panic and calmly refuse to speak with him."

"But—"

Elena stood. "I must get going. The boat will take you back."

Chapter Twenty-Six

Luca pulled the car into the garage and popped the trunk. Mary Ann got out and stretched.

"I'm stiff. How are you?"

Luca said, "My butt is killing me. I can tell you, next time we go to Key West, if there is a next time, we're taking the ferry."

"You didn't like Key West?"

"It was okay, but we have great beaches here."

"It's not the beaches, Frank. It's the overall vibe of the place."

He shrugged. "It's got a beachy feel to me. But I guess if you fish, it's a great place to be."

"Your problem is you don't know how to relax."

Luca knew she was right. He had to keep productive. Walking around Main Street with its T-shirt shops and bars wasn't enough for him.

"We'll give it another shot, but we're not driving there."

"Really? We can go again?"

"You like it there, so we'll go."

Mary Ann pecked his cheek. "Maybe we'll go back in two or three months."

"Sounds good."

Mary Ann opened the door of her car and said, "I'm going to Publix. What do you want for dinner?"

"Anything is good by me."

Mary Ann backed out of the garage and Luca went into the den.

He opened his desk drawer and pulled out the file on the Waterside Shops. Looking at the list of students absent from school the day of the robbery, he reviewed the history of each kid he'd compiled.

The Bolt dismissal had brought the judge's relationship with Clermont under the microscope. Whether the ending of her case was based on the legal merits was the question. Luca's belief was that it was either a nod to their school years' friendship or blackmail.

Four kids had robbed the Van Dores Diamond Showroom and killed two people in the process. If Bolt and Clermont were involved, who were the other two?

Luca stuck his list in the security guard's notebook and headed back to his car.

The skies darkened as Luca drove to Orange Blossom Drive and parked in the library's lot.

Drops of rain began to pelt the windshield. Luca grabbed an umbrella from the back seat and jogged to the library's entrance. He closed the umbrella and shook off the water.

Luca went inside and made his way to the same table he had sat at with Jessie. He hung the umbrella on the back of a chair and went to the sections where the yearbooks were stored.

He scanned the shelf. The Community School's year-book for 2006 was missing. He checked six other shelves. It wasn't there. Luca looked for 2005, it was also gone. He couldn't find 2003 or 2004.

Luca went to the front desk.

"Excuse me, but I can't find any of the yearbooks for the Community School for 2003 through 2006."

"They're in the section."

"I know where they're supposed to be, but they're not there. Did someone check them out?"

"We don't allow yearbooks to be borrowed. It's probably misshelved."

"I looked around but didn't see them."

"You'd be surprised where people leave things."

"Don't you think it's strange that four consecutive years are missing?"

She shrugged. "Nothing surprises me. They have to be somewhere, sir. Nobody would take old yearbooks."

"I'll look again."

As Luca scanned the shelves, a bad feeling grew. After checking seven aisles worth of books, he'd come up empty.

He popped open his umbrella and stepped into a tropical storm. He lowered the umbrella to keep the wind from collapsing it, but halfway to his car the umbrella went inside out.

"Damn it!"

Luca ran to his car and tossed the umbrella in the back. He climbed in the front seat and pulled his soaked shirt off.

He took napkins out of the glove box and dabbed his hair with them. Luca pulled his phone out and called the security guard's daughter.

"Tanya, it's Frank Luca, the private investigator."

"Oh, hi Mr. Luca. What's going on?"

"I wanted to let you know that even though I said I was off the case, I've still been looking into things."

"You have?"

"Yes, and though it's early, I have a lead I'm following. It might be nothing, but I wanted to let you know."

"The prayers worked."

"Tanya, did you mention my name to anyone about hiring me to look into this case?"

"Yes. I did. I was really happy that someone so famous, like you, was helping me."

Luca almost laughed at the fame reference. "Okay. I don't want you to get your hopes up. I just wanted to let you know I was looking at it again."

"I can come by and give you a check for your work."

"That's not necessary. If and when I need anything I'll let you know."

"When do you think you'll have some news?"

"That's impossible to say. But I'll be in touch."

Luca disconnected the call and punched another number in.

"Hey, Derrick. Are you free?"

"Yeah, what's going on?"

"I'll swing by your house in fifteen minutes. I got caught in the rain and have to change."

After Luca put dry clothes on, he made his way to Derrick's Grey Oaks home. His former partner's villa was one of the smallest homes in the exclusive community.

Luca pulled onto the driveway and waited for the rain to let up a bit. When it did, he dashed to the front door, where Derrick was waiting.

Derrick stepped aside. "Man, it really came down."

"I got soaked to the bone before."

"Let's go in my office."

The walls were covered with grass wallpaper, and a large golden-colored map hung behind Derrick's marble-topped desk.

"You really did this place up."

"Yeah, why not? I spend a lot of time at home."

"Enjoy it, buddy."

"I am. So, what's going on?"

Luca told him about going to see Bolt.

"How come you didn't tell me?"

"I meant to, but we went to the Keys, and frankly, it slipped my mind. And no old-man memory jokes, okay?'

Derrick chuckled. "I'll give you a pass."

"And here's the thing . . . I went to the library to look over the yearbooks again, you know, to see who was friends with who, like I told you I had been doing."

"Okay."

"And the yearbooks were missing. Not only the one from 2006, but 2003, 4, and 5 as well."

"That's weird. But it could be a filing thing or something."

"No. I don't buy that. Somebody took them. They know I'm on the case, and they want to put roadblocks up."

"Who?"

"I don't know."

"You think it's Judge Bolt?"

Luca scrunched his face. "Nah, he's not the type to sneak out of a library. Besides, he's been lying low since the dismissal."

"You can check the surveillance video."

"Do you know how many people go in and out of there?"

"What about Clermont? She's not afraid of a little thievery."

"You think Bolt told her I'd gone to see him?"

"If they're as close as you say, sure, why not?"

"Hmmm."

"Or it could be one of the other two who did the robbery with them."

Chapter Twenty-Seven

Mary Ann was on the phone when Luca came into the house. She waved hello and he paced the kitchen as she chatted with a neighbor about what to get for a friend's birthday.

Luca went out to the lanai and circled the pool before coming back inside. Mary Ann was still on the call.

He sighed and sat.

Mary Ann said to the neighbor, "I've got to go, Frank is waiting for me."

She ended the call and said, "What's the matter?"

"Nothing. I wanted to bounce something off you."

She put her hands on her hips. "What is it?"

"I went to the library to check the yearbook again, you know, to see if I could establish who was friends with Bolt and Clermont, since we know there's a connection there."

"The dismissal may be suspect, but it doesn't mean they were involved in the robbery."

Luca made a face. "Will you hang on a second?"

"Go ahead. What happened at the library?"

"It's what didn't happen; the yearbook wasn't there."

"And that's supposed to mean what?"

"Somebody took it."

"That's what you were pacing around like a caged lion about?"

"Somebody removed all the yearbooks from the years the robbers were in Community School. 2006, 5, 4, and 3 were all gone."

"Did you check with the librarian?"

"Of course I did. They said it could be misfiled."

"It probably is. How many times did we go with Jessica and a book was out of place."

"Yeah, but all four? And just a couple of days after I went to see Bolt?"

"It's a yearbook, Frank. Not a signed confession."

"Are you going to help me or what?"

"I'm trying to keep you from going off on a tangent."

"This is no tangent, Mary Ann. I'm poking around, and somebody is trying to make things difficult for me."

"I don't know, Frank. It just seems incidental."

"The perpetrators didn't get away with this for twenty years by being sloppy."

"There must be a couple of hundred yearbooks floating around."

"I realize that, I'm just saying they're making me work for whatever I get."

She shrugged. "I guess it's possible."

Luca took his cell phone out. "I'm going to call the Community School. I'll get a copy from them."

Luca came into the house holding up a manila envelope. "These must be valuable. They wouldn't let me borrow one, so I asked them to photocopy all the pictures. They weren't happy about it, so I made a two-hundred-dollar donation to the school."

"That was a good idea."

Luca headed to the den. "We'll see."

He spilled the photocopies on his desk and went through them one by one. He'd look at the informal images and find the student name in individual pictures of each senior. When he identified who it was, he'd write the kid's name on the photocopies.

It was tedious work, but he'd identified eight students who appeared with Conrad Bolt and ten who looked like friends of Cindy Clermont.

He was holding pictures of Bolt and Clermont when Mary Ann called out, "Frank, it's after six o'clock. Put the grill on."

"I'm coming!" He looked at the pictures of the suspects, "After you."

The next morning, Luca cross-referenced the students he'd identified as possible friends of Bolt and Clermont against the list of kids absent from school the day of the robbery.

That comparison narrowed the list to five names: Joseph Serano, David Flan, Elena Borelli, Ernest Rigo, and Loretta Gulliver.

Luca smiled. He drew a line through Ernest Rigo but reminded himself to circle back to Rigo if he ran into walls with the others.

Two of the four remaining names were probable suspects in the twenty-year-old homicide and robbery. Luca knew it wouldn't be easy but felt it was a manageable task to uncover the perpetrators.

The hard part would be to get the evidence necessary for an arrest and conviction. After two decades, memories would have faded, and any evidence collected was at risk of degrading or being misplaced.

Luca pulled up Joseph Serano's DMV record. An image of a man with a headful of snow-white hair and an unlined face came into focus. Though he wore a big smile, his eyes were downcast.

Luca punched Serano's details into the search bar of the criminal database. He drummed his fingers as the hourglass circled. It came up empty, but there was a reference regarding an encounter with the police.

Luca clicked the link and the report came up. Serano had called the police in February of 2011 claiming his car was stolen. After a brief investigation, video surveillance had shown Serano getting out of the car where the vehicle was ultimately located.

Despite the evidence, Serano denied he left the car where it was found. A note in the file had been written recommending the case be referred to a prosecutor for conspiracy to commit insurance fraud.

A surge of adrenaline coursed through Luca's body. Serano had planned to cheat an insurance company. It was proof that Serano had gone for what he considered easy money.

Had Serano been emboldened by getting away with not only the jewelry stolen from Van Dores but the murders as well? Luca told himself it was a pattern.

Luca compared the yearbook picture of Serano with the

one on his driver's license. Though twenty years had passed, besides the white hair, Serano hadn't changed much.

Luca picked up a red pen and underlined Serano's name; he could be the key to the case. He checked the State of Florida's employment records and found out Serano worked for Rogers Accounting Solutions.

He called their Bonita offices but was told Serano wasn't in. He asked for the human resources department and left a message.

Luca looked up Serano's cell phone number and called him.

"Mr. Serano?"

"Yes. Who is this?"

"Frank Luca. I'm investigating one of your neighbors and would like to have a quick chat with you."

"Uh, it's not really a good time."

"I promise I'll be fast, and if I don't submit my report today, it'll raise more questions than—well, you know how it goes."

Serano hesitated. "All right. Come now, but I don't have a lot of time."

Chapter Twenty-Eight

Luca drove west on Orange Blossom and passed the county offices and library. He turned into a community that looked like it had been picked up and moved from Connecticut.

He parked in front of Joseph Serano's brick home. The light color of the brick was the only clue you were in Southwest Florida.

Luca took the brick walkway, hopping over a downed palm frond, and rang the doorbell. Cell phone to his ear, Serano opened the door.

"Can I call you back, Tommy? . . . Thanks, yeah, we'll talk later."

He pocketed his phone, asking, "Detective Luca?"

"Yes. I'm Frank Luca. But I'm actually an investigator."

"Oh. Come in. So, you're not with the police?"

"No. I work for various governmental agencies. They hire us to vet potential candidates for employment."

He smiled. "Like background checks?"

"Yes, but a bit deeper than the normal process of calling a candidate's references."

Luca followed him into the kitchen.

Serano sat on one of the wicker chairs surrounding a glass-topped table. "I guess for important positions like those needing security clearance."

Luca took a seat, saying, "Something along those lines."

"So, who's up for a big job?"

Luca took his notebook out. "We'll get there. First, I've got to document who provides the information."

"Sure."

"It's a little nerdy, so hang in there with me."

"No problem."

"Where did you go to college?"

"Gulf Coast University."

"And high school?"

"High school? Boy, you weren't kidding, were you?"

"I got to fill in the forms."

"The Community School in Naples."

"What do you do for a living?"

"I'm a CPA."

"Where are you employed?"

"Rogers Accounting Solutions."

"Solutions?"

He shrugged. "We do more than taxes."

"What do you do there?"

"Things like accounts receivable and payables for the clients who outsourced it to us."

"How long have you lived here?"

"Five years."

Luca consulted his notes for the name of the person living a couple of houses down the block. "How well do you know Robert Kowlowski?"

"Who?"

Luca repeated the name, saying, "He lives on your street."

"What house?"

"Five doors down, on your side of the street."

"I hardly know him more than to wave hello every now and then."

"And that's the extent of the relationship?"

"There is no relationship. I didn't even meet him in a formal way."

"Okay. Let's move on to Conrad Bolt."

"You mean the judge?"

"Yes. You went to high school with him and were friends there."

"I mean, we knew each and had some classes together, but we weren't close."

Luca sensed Serano backing away from Bolt as if the judge were radioactive. "There are various pictures of the two of you together."

"Who can remember that far back?"

"Who else were you friends with during high school?"

"This is ridiculous. What is this, the CIA or something?"

"How about Cindy Clermont?"

"What about her?"

"What can you tell me about her?"

"This is nuts. I'm sorry, but I've got to go."

"Please, just hang in there for a few more questions and then we'll be done. Were you close to Ernest Rigo?"

"We hung around a little. You know, played some basketball and soccer. He was a good kid, but spoiled, you know."

"It looks like his family was wealthy."

"Yeah, crazy rich. They were living on easy street. And it was all inherited, they had it handed to them."

"Must be nice."

"Tell me about it."

"What do you remember about the robbery?"

"What robbery?"

Luca suppressed a smile. "The one at the Van Dores Diamond Showroom at Waterside Shops. In 2006. You were a senior at the time."

"Yeah, that was something. The cops came around, but I don't think they ever found out who did it."

"Did you have anything to do with it?"

"Me? Are you nuts or something?"

Luca noted a denial was missing. "Did you?"

"No." Serano jumped out of his seat. "Look, I really have to go."

Luca stood. "Okay. I appreciate you taking the time, Mr. Serano. You've been a big help."

Serano stood by the door as Luca got into his car and drove away. As Serano replayed the conversation with the investigator, his stomach clenched. There was no way Luca had come to see him for a background check.

Mad at himself for agreeing to meet with the investigator, Serano closed the door and went into the family room. He fell into his recliner and, shutting his eyes, considered whether he should run.

LUCA'S MIND was pinballing ideas on what to do next. He couldn't settle on a path forward and called Derrick, who answered on the first ring.

"Frank, what's going on?"

"I have to tell you about this meeting I had."

"With who?"

"Guy by the name of Joseph Serano."

"Don't know him, but I'm all ears."

"He went to the Community School and was out the day of the Waterside crimes. I went back over the pictures, and he's friends with both Conrad Bolt and Cindy Clermont."

"There's nothing connecting Bolt and Clermont to the robbery."

"I know."

"Does Serano have a record?"

"No, but years ago he lied about his BMW being stolen for insurance money."

"Did they file charges against him?"

"No. They let it go."

"That doesn't leave you much to work—"

"If I get a chance to tell you what he said . . ."

"Okay, okay. Tell me."

"He was tense when I first got there, tried to avoid meeting me when I called, but when I gave him some bull that I was doing a background check on a neighbor, you'd have thought he was sipping cocktails on a Caribbean beach."

"Now, that's a scene I can get into."

"When I mentioned Bolt, he got all goosey and said he hardly knew him, despite all the photos. He got even more nervous when I asked about Clermont."

"Interesting. Maybe there is something there."

"Then when I asked him about the Waterside robbery, he got cagey. So I asked him if he was involved, and he wouldn't answer the question."

"What did he say?"

"He mocked outrage, asking me if I was nuts. Then he said he had to go."

"It's not an admission, but why not say no?"

"I think I just caught him off guard. I was switching subjects on him so fast he couldn't keep up."

Derrick chuckled. "I remember those days."

"There's something there, but, and I'd only tell *you* this, I don't know what to do next."

"You need to come up with some kind of evidence."

"After twenty years, it's not so easy. Do you have any ideas?"

Derrick said, "When we used to hit dead ends, you used to say we had to go back to the fundamentals."

"True, but what?"

"I can see that knocking on doors two decades later would be a waste of time. Who would remember anything more now than when it happened?"

"I know, when you are involved in something traumatic, people seem to either remember things vividly or draw a blank."

"What about the physical evidence?"

"There's not much. They checked for DNA, but the collection procedures back then didn't pick up any."

"This is a tough one."

"I think the only way to pursue this is by focusing on who might have been involved."

"That could be any kid who was around seventeen to nineteen at the time."

"No. I narrowed it down."

"That's not scientific."

"Who needs science when you have my instincts?"

Derrick mocked, "Do you really think that's going to work?"

"No. But I have nothing else. If I keep pushing, maybe I'll catch a break."

"And if you keep buying lottery tickets, you might win."

"Yeah, but there is something going on with Serano. If I can tie him to Bolt or Clermont . . ."

As Luca's voice trailed off, Derrick said, "I don't know, buddy. If I was you, I'd bail out on this one."

"Says the man who told the daughter to call me."

"I was just trying to see if you could help her."

"And I gave my word that I would."

Chapter Twenty-Nine

Luca cut out a picture of Rigo from the photocopies he'd made of the yearbook. He used a small piece of scotch tape to secure it to the wallboard alongside pictures of the other students on the list.

He put Rigo in the second line, which also had Elena Borelli. Rigo's mother had given him an alibi, but loved ones had been known to fabricate covers for family. Borelli was the most successful woman South Florida had ever produced, but Luca couldn't give her a pass like he originally did with Serano and Bolt.

Luca needed to prioritize, but he was going to look each of them in the eye and see what he could get from them.

Luca's glance settled on Serano. He silently begged the image to give him a message. Despite his pleas, nothing came. He had just visited him and felt something was there but shifted his gaze onto David Flan.

Luca paged through his notes. Flan was currently unemployed and didn't have a criminal record, but there was no shortage of civil lawsuits against him.

Luca scanned several of the legal actions brought by numerous plaintiffs. All of them were related to failed businesses where Flan had ownership interests. The vast majority of the claims were made by investors who'd lost the money they'd given to Flan.

After reading the court filings, it was clear Flan's rosy projections were not grounded in reality. However, the legal protections his lawyers crafted prevented him from losing a single accusation that he'd committed fraud.

Luca sat back and considered the information. Flan had controlled a dozen companies, and not one of them had succeeded. Were the operations a front to skim or launder money?

After looking up Flan's number, Luca left him a voicemail.

Luca looked at the last picture of those on the suspect list: Loretta Gulliver.

He checked her background, and the woman appeared to be a nun. She was married with two children and lived in Estero. Luca located her phone number, and it went to voicemail. When most people saw a call from a number they didn't recognize, they let it go to voicemail rather than risk being presented with a 'once in a lifetime' opportunity. He left Gulliver a message.

Luca looked at the image of Elena Borelli. The high-profile woman didn't have a record and wasn't married. He found the number and called the financier's office.

Luca was politely told Ms. Borelli was busy. They asked for his number and the reason for the call. Luca gave his number and told the receptionist it was related to an investigation of a former colleague.

Luca didn't like to wait and was surprised when his phone vibrated.

"Hello, this is Frank Luca."

"Mr. Luca, I'm Regina Carter, the human resources manager at Rogers Accounting Service. You called our office regarding a former employee."

Luca hesitated. "Former employee? Doesn't Joseph Serano work there?"

"No, sir. We relieved him of his duties yesterday."

"Oh. May I ask why?"

"That's confidential, sir."

"I realize it may be sensitive, but I'm a licensed investigator and the information could be critical."

"Without getting into specifics, all I can say is that we uncovered financial improprieties with the accounting services of the clients he managed."

"Money has gone missing?"

"We believe improper payments were made to individuals and entities unrelated to the clients' businesses."

"And you think Joseph Serano was responsible for them?"

"He had no explanation for the unauthorized payments."

"Have you notified the police?"

"As I'm certain you're aware, this is highly sensitive, and we're having an internal discussion over the best way to handle this. We've reimbursed those involved but haven't decided on whether to pursue charges."

Luca wanted to tell her they had to file a complaint to deter others. "I'm sorry to hear this and wish you well."

He ended the call and pumped his fist. "Yes! Yes! Yes!"

Carrying an armful of laundry, Mary Ann heard her husband shouting. "Frank, what's going on?"

He met her in the hallway. "I got a break in the Waterside case."

"What happened?"

Luca told him about Serano.

"Wow. Great work."

"It's the break I've been hoping for."

"You made your own break with this guy."

"I might be a one-man band, but I can still hit the high notes." Luca started to sing in falsetto.

Mary Ann rolled her eyes. "The dogs in the neighborhood are barking."

"Seriously, I feel like I'm on my way."

"What's your next move?"

"I'd love to confront Serano, but I want to talk to a couple of the others, see what kind of intel I can dredge up."

"Sounds like a plan. I'm going by Terry's to play mahjong."

As he said, "Have fun," Luca's phone rang. He grabbed it off the desk and checked the number. It was a restricted number. He was going to swipe it away but thought it could be someone returning his call.

"This is Frank Luca."

"Stop sticking your nose in places you shouldn't."

"Who is this?"

"Never mind who this is."

"Is this about Serano?"

"Who?"

"Joseph Serano."

"Don't know who that is. But you better listen to what I'm saying, stop your private investigator bullshit or you'll be sorry."

"Who is this?"

The call disconnected.

First, the yearbooks had gone missing, and now somebody was threatening him. Someone wanted him off the Waterside case. But who was it?

Chapter Thirty

Derrick swung open the door to his Grey Oaks home. "Come in, Frank."

Luca said, "I'm sorry, but I needed to bounce some things off you."

Derrick's wife came into the foyer. "Hi, Frank."

"Hey, Lynn, how are you?"

"Good."

"Where's the little angel?"

"She's napping. She was in the pool before nine, and between the swimming and the heat, she's exhausted."

"You have to be careful with the heat. Make sure she's hydrated."

"We try. How's Mary Ann?"

"Good. She's out playing mahjong again."

"She really likes it, huh?"

"I think so. She's always playing it on her iPad."

"My neighbors want me to play. They have a group that meets at the clubhouse."

Luca fibbed. "I've been thinking of giving it a try."

"We have to make a dinner date."

"Definitely, it's been too long. But do me a favor and leave this guy behind. He's a conversation killer."

Derrick said, "And you came here for my help?"

Lynn laughed and walked away, saying, "You boys behave yourselves."

They settled into chairs in Derrick's office. Luca's ex-partner kicked off his flip-flops and rested his feet on a gray ottoman.

"So, tell me, Frank, what's going on?"

Luca explained the threatening call he'd received.

Derrick said, "You think it might have been Serano, even though they said no?"

"I thought about that. It's certainly possible. But it didn't sound like him."

"There's all kinds of tech being used to disguise voices today."

"Tell me about it. But that doesn't explain the yearbooks that have gone missing. And that was before I spoke to Serano."

"Hmmm. And you're not working any other cases?"

"No, this is it."

"Then it's got to be the Waterside case."

"There's no doubt in my mind, someone wants me off the trail."

"Did you say anything to Mary Ann about the call?"

Luca shook his head. "No. I wanted to wait until I got more information."

"Do you think it's something more than just a bullshit attempt to scare you off?"

"Honestly, I don't know. But if Judge Bolt is involved, he's got access to plenty of rough characters."

"And he can dangle a light sentence in return for doing what he wants done."

"Yep, and there's no telling who else is involved and what kind of resources they have to intimidate me."

"Let's hope it's just an intimidation attempt."

"I'm with you. Protecting a dangerous secret hardens the heart."

"That's why you have to take the threat seriously."

Luca nodded.

Derrick said, "Why don't you just drop the case? Tell the security guard's daughter you ran into a dead end and be done with it. You don't need the money."

"I'm not doing it for the money."

"The case is twenty years old. Tell her between the lack of evidence and deteriorating memories, it's unsolvable."

"I can't."

"Why not?"

"Because I got a shot at getting justice for her."

"You're the best detective I ever knew, but come on, Frank, do you really think you can solve this?"

"I do, and apparently whoever is threatening me thinks so as well."

LUCA WAS WATCHING the five o'clock news when Mary Ann returned home.

"How was mahjong?"

"Good. It's taken a while, but I've got the hang of it. I even won a round."

"I knew you would because you put the time in."

"I still get confused sometimes. I'm going to get dinner started."

"Come here first."

Mary Ann came into the family room. "What's up?"

"I just wanted to let you know, but there's nothing to worry about."

"You're making me nervous."

"It's nothing, but I got a weird call."

"From whom?"

"I don't know, but the caller said for me to stop working the Waterside case."

"What did they say?"

"That I should stop investigating or I'd be sorry."

"Did you call the sheriff's office?"

"No. There's no need to panic. It could even be this guy Serano I was telling you about."

"The accounting guy who was stealing from clients?"

"Yeah, he thinks I'm looking into him and who knows what other scams he's running."

"But you think he's connected to the Waterside case, don't you?"

"I'm hoping he's the key to it."

"I don't know, Frank. Maybe you should turn it over to the sheriff."

Luca stood. "There's nothing to turn over. I need to go a little further, or it's just going to stay in the bottom of a cold case bin."

"You have to do something."

Luca patted his wife's shoulder. "There's no need to panic. Just keep your eyes open, and we'll be fine."

"What about Jessica? We have to tell her."

Luca's stomach dropped. "I'll call her."

"I can't believe this is happening."

"Come on, Mary Ann, don't get hysterical on me. You know most of these threats are just hot air."

"I don't care about most cases. I don't want anything happening to Jessica or us."

Luca put his hands on his wife's shoulders. "I will never let anything happen to our family. If this gets hot, I promise I'll bail out."

"You better keep me in the loop with everything. No hiding anything."

"Absolutely. Don't forget, Jessie is in Orlando, so I don't think we have to worry about her any more than we already do."

"I don't care if the risk is under one percent, we can't take chances."

"You're right."

"Call Jessica. Now."

"Okay."

Luca took a minute to think about what he was going to tell his daughter. He weighed the threat again, making sure he hadn't missed anything before dialing her number.

"Hey, Jessie. How's things in Orlando?"

"Hi, Dad. Is everything all right?"

"Yes. How is the job going? You bringing law enforcement into the modern world?"

"I like the job, the company, and the people, but I miss Naples."

"Nothing is forever. You get the experience and the contacts, and you'll find something here."

"I know. I guess I'm a little homesick. How's Mom?"

"She just came back from mahjong. She won her first game."

"Cool. I'll call her later."

"Are you still working on that project to integrate and sort the databases?"

"Yes. Now we're using an AI tool to generate profiles for unsolved felonies across the state."

"That's interesting."

"There's so much going on, and the changes with tech are coming a gazillion miles an hour."

"I guess it's good I retired when I did."

"The data can't solve anything without the fundamental work law enforcement does."

"Was that a backhanded compliment I just heard?"

"You were, are, the best detective Collier ever had."

"Are you angling for a better Christmas gift this year?"

She laughed.

"I miss that laugh of yours. When are you coming home again?"

"Mom said you guys were going to take a trip here."

"Yeah, we talked about it when we were in Key West. We just have to check some dates."

"Let me know."

"We will."

"I have a meeting in five. I'll talk to you later."

"Hang on a second, I want to tell you something."

"What?"

"You know I'm working that old case, a robbery and murder that happened over twenty years ago at Waterside."

"Yeah, What about it?"

"Well, I'm making progress, and I got a call telling me to back off or I'd be sorry."

"Dad, you better be careful. You of all people know there's a ton of nutjobs running around."

"Don't worry. I don't think this is anything serious, and it could be related to someone I spoke with who may not even be involved in the Waterside crime but who was stealing from clients."

"Oh."

"Anyway, your mother and I thought we should tell you about it."

"Okay, thanks."

"Just be careful. Keep your eyes open, and let me know if you see anything."

"Why would I see anything?"

"I don't know, but that's what parents do; we think of our children first."

Luca finished the call.

Mary Ann said, "How did she sound?"

"Good. Same as always."

"I don't know, Frank, I'm getting a bad feeling about this."

"That's because you're worried about Jessie. Meanwhile, she's hundreds of miles away, and we have no idea if there's even something to worry about."

Chapter Thirty-One

The obvious place to start was Joseph Serano. Luca believed that Serano stealing from clients was part of a pattern that dovetailed with the Waterside jewelry heist.

Serano's background didn't have any clues that he could be violent. Luca believed the teenagers who robbed the Van Dores Diamond Showroom, using Tasers, hadn't planned to seriously hurt anyone. But he knew the thing about armed robbery was that anything could go wrong. And many times, it did.

And with Waterside, it had gone terribly wrong.

Given the guilt of killing, in this case, two people, Luca couldn't rationalize how they'd kept their involvement secret for so long. The only explanation was that they all had ironclad discipline or a leader who kept the participants in line.

Wondering how long Serano had been stealing from clients, Luca placed a call to the thieving accountant.

He listened to it ring before it went to voicemail. Luca left a message.

Then he put a call into David Flan. It also went to voice-mail, but Flan's mailbox was full and Luca couldn't leave a message. Luca tapped out a text, but there was no response.

He left the den, sweeping his car keys off the hallway table.

Fifteen minutes later, he rang Serano's doorbell. Through the glazed sidelight, Luca saw somebody move toward the door then stop. Serano lived alone.

Luca pressed the bell two more times. But the figure disappeared.

Pounding his palm on the door, Luca said, "I know you're in there. Open the door. I just want to talk."

He waited a second before saying, "If you don't answer, I'm going lean on my car horn. I'm sure the neighbors will come out."

Through the closed door, Serano said, "Go away or I'll call the police."

"Go right ahead. The neighbors will enjoy the show."

After a brief pause, the lock clicked and Serano cracked open the door. "Look, my lawyers reached an agreement, and I'm going to make everybody whole. Nobody is going to lose any money."

"Good, but I'm not here about that."

"What do you want with me?"

"The Waterside robbery twenty years ago."

"I told you I had nothing to do with that."

"Yeah, and you told me you were still working at your job."

"We were trying to work things out. I—"

"Look, I don't give a crap about what you stole from your clients. But Waterside is another matter. Two people lost their lives."

"How many times do I have to tell you? I didn't have anything to do with that."

"Who was in charge? I bet it was Conrad Bolt, or was it Cindy Clermont?"

"I hardly knew them."

"The yearbook pictures paint a different picture. So, tell me, who was the fourth person? I know it was a girl. Which one was it?"

"I swear I had nothing to do with that. I would never do something like that."

Luca held up a hand. "Man, that's rich coming from someone who stole from his clients."

Serano's shoulders sunk. "I screwed up, okay. I admitted it and I'm trying to make it right. But I'm not some armed robber. Nobody got hurt from what I did."

"Is that what you tell yourself? That your crimes didn't hurt anybody?"

"You know what I mean. There's a world of difference in what I did compared to holding up a jewelry store."

"In my book, you cross one line, the other ones get awfully blurry."

"I didn't do it."

"I'm going to piece this together, and you're one of the pieces."

As Luca headed for his car, Serano said, "You'll see, I had nothing to do with it."

LUCA FOCUSED on trying to tie Serano to some of the others on his list.

No one had returned his calls, raising his suspicions.

He punched in David Flan's number and was surprised he answered.

"Hello?"

"Mr. Flan?"

"Yes. Who's this?"

"Frank Luca. I left a message yesterday."

"Oh. Right. What do you want?"

"I'd like to meet with you. I'm a private investigator, and we're looking at someone you knew."

"Who are you talking about?"

"I'd rather disclose that when I see you. When are you available?"

"Uh, I have some family in town this week."

"It won't take long. All I need is a half hour at most."

"I might have time the day after tomorrow. Can I call you that day if I do?"

"That'll work."

Luca wasn't sure what to make of the phone call with Flan. On the one hand, Flan had originally tried to avoid meeting with him. But when Luca said it wouldn't take long, he seemed to warm to the idea.

Luca had spoken to several of the students he suspected of being involved in the Waterside robbery. Wouldn't they tip off anyone else involved that a private investigator was asking questions?

What if they talked among themselves and had reinforced whatever their playbook was? Was their gang that good? And if they were, the chances they had pulled other jobs was high.

Luca pushed out of his mind the idea that these thieves and murderers were some kind of special group and put another call into Elena Borelli.

Once again, the receptionist claimed Borelli was in meetings the rest of the day. Luca left his number and was about to call Loretta Gulliver when his cell rang.

He recognized the number. It was Joseph Serano. Luca hesitated before he answered, using the time to try to figure out why he was calling. Settling on the call as a way to throw him off his trail somehow, he answered, "This is Frank Luca. Who's calling?"

"Mr. Luca, it's Joe Serano."

"Hello, Mr. Serano. What can I do for you?"

"It's about the Waterside robbery."

Luca smiled. "What about it?"

When Serano started talking, Luca couldn't believe what he was hearing.

Chapter Thirty-Two

Luca flung open the slider. The bang and rebound startled Mary Ann, who was reading on the lanai.

"What's the matter?"

"I can't frigging believe it."

"What?"

"Remember I told you about Joseph Serano?"

"That's the guy who was stealing from his job and you said was involved in the Waterside crimes, right?"

"Yeah, but I was wrong."

"Can you say that again?"

"Don't be a wiseass."

"Sorry, I couldn't resist."

Luca wagged his head. "I was so damn sure he was involved."

"What did you find out?"

"On the day of the robbery, Serano and his mother were rear-ended at a light near Coconut Point. They were taken to Lee Health by ambulance and released at two fifteen p.m."

"He told you that?"

"Yes. He said he was telling his sister that I was bothering him about it, and she remembered it was the same day they got in the accident."

"And you verified it?"

"Of course I did."

"Now what?"

"I have no frigging idea. I got to say, I'm this close"—Luca held his forefinger a hair away from his thumb—"to walking away from it. I don't need to be banging my head against a wall."

"You tried, Frank, that's all that counts. Some cases never get solved, and this one is twenty years old."

"I know. I hate giving up, but I'm going to tell the daughter I hit another dead end and that's it."

"And we won't have to worry about the threat you received."

"I didn't think it was anything, but yeah, that's over too."

Mary Ann reached for her phone. "I'm going to text Jessica to tell her."

"Okay. I might as well call the guard's daughter and get it over with."

Luca retreated to his den and was scrolling for Tanya's number when a call came in. He recognized the number but couldn't place who it was.

"Hello, this is Frank Luca."

"Mr. Luca, this is Amanda Clark, I handle Elena Borelli's calendar. She asked me to reach out to you in regard to setting up a call or meeting with you."

"I appreciate the callback." Luca was going to tell her there was no longer a need to meet, but he hedged. "I'm a bit swamped, you can tell her I'll get back to her."

"Wonderful. She'll wait to hear from you. Goodbye, Mr. Luca."

The call disconnected, and Luca found the number for the security guard's daughter and called her.

"Tanya, it's Frank Luca."

"Oh hello, sir."

"Look, I've run into another dead end with the case."

"Oh no. You said you had a good lead."

"I thought I did, but it didn't pan out."

"Darn. What else do you have?"

"Here's the thing, Tanya, I don't have anything to follow."

"You'll find something. You're the best detective, right?"

"I'm sorry if I gave you the impression that I'd be able to solve it. I tried everything I know and put a lot of time into this."

"I'm more than happy to pay you."

"It's not the money, Tanya. I want justice for what happened to your father as well, but I can't see a path to getting there."

"You'll find a way."

"Unfortunately, this case is twenty years old, and there's really no physical evidence, and memories have faded during that time. I can't see how to change that."

"What are you saying?"

Luca exhaled. "I'm sorry, but I can't work this one any longer."

There was a long pause before Tanya whispered, "Damn it. My one and only shot to get Dad justice is gone."

Luca finished the call and opened his desk drawer. He grabbed the bottle of Tums and tapped out two. He sat back and closed his eyes. There had been very few cases he hadn't been able to solve. It bothered him, but what gnawed at his stomach was letting the daughter down.

Part Four

Chapter Thirty-Three

Elena drank her morning coffee on the terrace off the master bedroom. The generous balcony was one of three in her Gulfshore Drive home. She took a sip of her dark roast and looked at the sparkling Gulf of America.

She loved the way the morning sun bounced off the water. Elena picked up her iPad and began reading the first of five newspapers she made it her business to review each day.

After going through *The Wall Street Journal*, *The Financial Times*, and *Investor's Business Daily*, she navigated to the *Naples Daily News*.

She glanced at the front page. A picture at the bottom of the page caught her attention. Above the image of a destroyed vehicle was the headline:

"Fatal Crash Kills Naples Man"

NAPLES — A 38-year-old Naples man died Wednesday evening after his vehicle crashed into the median and overturned on Livingston Road, according to the Collier County Sheriff's Office.

David Flan was pronounced dead at the scene after his 2018 Ford Focus struck the median near the intersection with Pine Ridge Road around 8:15 p.m., deputies said.

The vehicle flipped multiple times after impact, coming to rest on its roof in the southbound lanes. Flan was trapped inside and had to be extricated by Collier County Fire Rescue personnel.

"The driver appeared to have lost control for unknown reasons," said sheriff's office spokesman Deputy Philip Grey. "No other vehicles were involved in the crash."

Traffic investigators closed southbound Livingston Road between Golden Gate Boulevard and Marbella Lakes Drive for approximately three hours while examining the scene and clearing debris.

The Florida Highway Patrol is assisting with the investigation. Officials have not determined what caused Flan to lose control of his vehicle, and toxicology results are pending.

According to public records, Flan, who was unemployed, lived in the Pelican Bay area.

This marks the fourth fatal traffic accident in Collier County this month.

Anyone who witnessed the crash is asked to contact the Collier County Sheriff's Office at (239) 252-9300.

Elena put the iPad down and poured herself another cup of coffee. She added a teaspoon of Benefiber and, as she stirred it, decided to make a call.

THE HOT, reddish sun was two feet off the horizon. Walking along the water's edge, Elena skipped toward safety as a wave rushed in. As she tugged the wide-brimmed hat she was wearing, Bebe sidled up to her.

The ex-Mossad agent said, "Look at the color of the sky. It's going to be a beautiful sunset."

"Sunsets are something I never take for granted."

Bebe said, "You know, people think money makes you happy. You get the money and then you're grateful. But being grateful is the key to happiness. If you're grateful, you're happy. It doesn't matter if you have money or not."

She smiled. "That's true, but money certainly removes many of life's annoyances."

"I see what you did there. That's clever of you."

"Speaking of money, the compensation agreement for your family, should anything happen to you while under our employ, is ready for signature. I'll have it sent to you."

"I plan on being around for a long time, but it's appreciated."

"You've earned it."

"Thank you."

"And after careful consideration, I think we should bring you inside the organization sooner rather than later."

"Whatever you decide is fine."

"Good. So, did everything go well?"

"Perfectly. You have nothing to be concerned about."

"Excellent."

They walked along the edge of the water for a few moments before Elena said, "I'm sure you would have said something, but is there anything new on Judge Bolt?"

"No. He's kept to himself, and the blowback on the dismissal has completely died down."

"It's nice when things go as expected. But that's what good planning ensures."

"Yes. But there is something related that needs watching."

Elena stopped in her tracks and turned to Bebe. "What now?"

"Ms. Clermont's boyfriend was arrested in Lee County two days ago."

As she began walking, the financier said derisively, "No surprise there. I'm sure it was drug related."

"It's more serious than that. Perez was charged with first-degree murder."

Elena shook her head, disgusted by the same charge she had dodged. "Keep an eye on this."

"I was intending to."

Elena stopped walking. "I assume the cretin is in jail. What is his bail set at?"

Bebe studied her face. "A million. Is there something I need to know?"

Though it was a stretch, Elena was concerned Clermont would try to blackmail her for the bail money. "No. But the Clermont-Bolt drug case has put just about anything in the realm of possibility."

"That's true. Is there something you need regarding this new development?"

"At this time, I want you to monitor this. Personally."

Bebe nodded. "I'll keep a close watch on the situation."

"Where are we with that investigator who was poking around?"

"I believe he's gotten the message."

"Good. Keep an eye on that as well."

LUCA PULLED INTO HIS GARAGE. "I'm looking forward to a cup of coffee."

Mary Ann got out of the car. "Me too. I'm glad we went to the beach early."

Luca had his hand on the doorknob when Mary Ann said, "Take off your flip-flops."

"I washed them off."

"Come on, Frank, two weeks ago you tracked sand all over the house."

He kicked them off and used his hand to brush off granules of sand. "I'm going to jump in the pool, have my coffee, and read the paper. You coming?"

"No. I'm showering."

Luca hit the power button on the Nespresso machine and went onto the lanai. He stripped his T-shirt off and jumped in the pool.

He swam around for a minute then got out. After he toweled himself off, he went inside and made a cup of coffee. He set it on the outdoor table and was about to sit when he slid open the door and grabbed the *Naples Daily News* off the kitchen counter.

Luca snapped open the paper and picked up his mug. He scanned the top story. A meeting of the county commissioners had gotten ugly when they approved a multi-building apartment complex on Vanderbilt Beach Road.

Wondering how bad the traffic was about to get, his eyes settled on a picture of a mangled car. He shook his head, wondering how fast the driver had to be going to do so much damage in the deadly accident.

He turned the page and reached for his mug. He shifted his hand to the paper and flipped it back to the front page.

When his eyes caught the name of the man who died in the fatal car crash, Luca said, "Holy shit!"

Chapter Thirty-Four

Luca read the article twice, then checked the address he had for David Flan. It was in Pelican Bay. It was the same David Flan from the list of former students he'd compiled for the Waterside Shops robbery.

There was no mention in the article that the crash was suspicious. Luca grabbed his phone and made a call.

"Homicide, this is Detective Donovan."

"Hey, Donnie, it's Frank Luca. How are you?"

"Good. What's up?"

"Last night there was a fatal accident on Livingston."

"Yeah, I heard about it."

"Was there anything suspicious about it?"

"Suspicious? Not that I know of. Why are you asking?"

"The dead guy might be connected to something I'm looking into."

Donovan sighed. "Is this another one of your hunches?"

"It's more than that."

"I'd like to help, Frank, but my plate is full."

"Can you find out if they examined the car?"

"Sure."

"Thanks, I appreciate it."

Luca punched in another number.

"Medical Examiner's Office."

"Hey, Melissa. It's Frank Luca."

"Hi, Frank. How are you doing?"

"Everything is good. And with you?"

"Thank God. We're all fine."

"Is Dr. Bilotti in?"

"Sure. I'll get him for you."

A moment later the medical examiner said, "Hello, Frank. How are you?"

"Good, Doc. How about you?"

"Life is a gift, my friend. The sooner we recognize it, the happier we'll be."

"You're a thousand percent right, but I'm still working on the recognizing part."

Bilotti chuckled before saying, "I'm assuming you called for a reason."

"Yeah, well, I can use a little help with something."

"What is it?"

Luca told him about the auto accident, and Bilotti said, "The body is in the morgue. I haven't seen it, but Stacey said impact appeared to be the cause of death."

"Are you going to autopsy it?"

"We're waiting for the investigating officer's report before making a decision on conducting one. Is there something you're aware of?"

"Not specifically, but I think it's a good idea to do an autopsy in case he was drugged or something else shows up."

Bilotti didn't say anything.

Luca said, "All I'm saying is you have the authority to decide to do one, and I think with everything I learned about the dead man, I'd do one."

"What exactly have you learned?"

"Well, for starters, he was one of the people on a list of suspects I developed for the Waterside Shops robbery and murder case."

"What case is that?"

Luca explained the twenty-year-old case.

Bilotti said, "Neither of us were here when that occurred. What other information on the deceased do you have?"

"Nothing concrete, just a lot of innuendos. But they're talking to me, Doc."

Bilotti chuckled. "Perhaps you need another kind of doctor, one who specializes in psychiatry."

Luca moaned. "I walked straight into that."

"You certainly did, and I couldn't resist."

"But seriously, this one is raising more flags than an honor guard. We worked on a ton of cases together, and I really think this is worth looking into."

"I imagine we'll see if you still have the magic, Frank."

"You're going to do it?"

"You and your history support the case for an autopsy."

"When do you think you'll get to it?"

"I realize you're lacking in the patience category, Frank. Fortunately, we're not particularly busy, and I'll make it my next order of business."

Luca opened his front door, and as Derrick stepped inside, he said, "I'm sorry to pull you over here, but I couldn't wait."

His ex-partner smiled. "You never could, could you?"

"Everybody is a comedian today."

Derrick followed Luca to his den. "What's going on?"

Luca picked the newspaper off his desk and handed it to Derrick. "Read the article on the car crash."

Derrick browsed the text and said, "And what's another accident on Livingston mean?"

"The guy who died is David Flan."

"I saw that, but—"

"He was on the list I developed of the suspects for the Waterside robbery."

"I thought you were done with that case."

Luca made his best impression of Al Pacino in *Godfather Three*. "Just when I thought I was out, they pulled me back in."

Derrick smiled. "I had a feeling you'd get back on it. So, where are you now?"

"That's what I wanted to brain drizzle about. There's no doubt Conrad Bolt, the judge, and Cynthia Clermont are connected somehow. The dead guy, David Flan, went to school with them as well, and they all seemed to be pals."

"You never got a chance to talk to him, right?"

"No. I was going to, but the lead crapped out and I dropped the case."

"Who else is on the list?"

Luca opened the center desk drawer and took the security guard's notebook out. He pulled his list out of it.

"Elena Borrelli, the wealthy financier, Loretta Gulliver,

and though his mother provided an alibi, it feels like Ernest Rigo had something to do with it."

"You can't trust alibis from family, especially a mother. Remember that case where the mother said her son was with her painting her house and we got video from an Uber driver showing him outside the bar, right after the assault?"

"Yeah. I felt bad for her. She'd lost her daughter a month before. What a mess."

"Proves my point. You can't discount Rigo's involvement."

"Trust me, I'm not."

"And what's the story with Gulliver?"

"I never got anywhere with her, but she doesn't have a record. With no flags, I figured I'd wait to talk to her and see what kind of vibe I get."

"She was friends with the others?"

"There are a couple of pictures of school events where Bolt, Clermont, and Gulliver are together, but nothing more."

"You always said eliminating a suspect is progress, right?"

Luca sneered. "What did you do, talk to Mary Ann?"

"What do you mean?"

"Throwing what I say back at me."

Derrick smiled. "Boy, somebody is sensitive."

Luca forced a smile out. "Get out of here, will you? I got to track down Gulliver."

"What about Borelli? Have you spoken to her?"

"Her secretary called me for an appointment right after I bowed out."

"You should talk to her."

"I plan to, boss."

"Did you tell the security guard's daughter you're back on it?"

"Not yet. But I'll let Tanya know if I get something from the autopsy. Is there anything else, boss?"

Derrick stood. "I got to get going. I was on my way to pick up some supplies for a school project when you called."

"I remember the days. Savor them, buddy."

After showing Derrick out. Luca put a call in to Elena Borelli and was dialing Gulliver's number when his phone started buzzing.

It was Detective Donovan, the man who'd replaced Luca when he left the force.

"Hi, Donnie. What's going on?"

"I spoke to Officer Childs, he led the response team for that fatal accident you called me on."

"What did he say?"

"It was an accident."

"The guy was speeding?"

"I don't know the details, but it was ruled an accident."

"Okay. Thanks, Donnie. I'll see you around."

Luca leaned back in his chair. He wanted to speak to the officer himself and look at the pictures. He was no expert on traffic deaths, but he'd investigated his share of car crashes. In the process of those inquires he'd discovered two that turned out not to be accidents but homicides.

Luca tried to envision David Flan being drugged before getting behind the wheel. But he was unsure how the perpetrator could ensure it'd end in Flan's death.

As he ping-ponged ideas, his phone buzzed again.

It was his friend and medical examiner Dr. Bilotti. Luca answered the phone, hoping the coroner would confirm his suspicion about the death of David Flan.

Chapter Thirty-Five

Luca tried to act nonchalantly. "Hey, Doc."

"Hello, Frank. Do you have a minute to talk?"

"For you? Anytime. What's up?"

"It's concerning the vehicular fatality. The cause of death was blunt force trauma resulting in hemorrhagic shock due to internal bleeding."

"Got it. Did he have anything in his system?"

"I ordered a full tox panel, but there's no evidence of any alcohol or illicit drugs present."

"All right. Let me know when that comes back."

"Absolutely."

"I really appreciate you going the extra mile for me."

"It's my pleasure, wine drinkers have to stick together."

Luca laughed. "We sure do. I wanted to tell you about a white wine from Sardinia that I found. We love it, especially when it's hot."

"I'm sure it's a Vermentino."

"Can't I introduce you to any wines?"

"It's simply a function of drinking too much."

Luca laughed. "You had a head start, you should give me a handicap or something."

Bilotti giggled. "Which Vermentino did you have? Was it is a Vermentino di Sardegna or Vermentino di Gallura?"

"Gallura doesn't sound familiar."

"It's a bit more expensive, but those particular wines are more expressive of the Vermentino grape."

"No surprise, it's more money."

"It's not much more. Next time we get together, I'll open one up."

"I'll talk to Mary Ann and set up a barbecue at our place."

"That would be wonderful."

"I'll let you know."

Luca hung up. The wine talk had distracted him from his dejection over the lack of suspicious results from the autopsy.

Sitting around waiting for Elena Borelli and Gulliver to return calls wasn't in Luca's DNA.

He made a brief call and left the den.

Luca grabbed the cars keys off the foyer table and headed for his car.

LUCA TURNED into the driveway for the Collier County Sheriff's Office. He automatically headed to the employee lot before realizing his mistake and pulled into a visitor space.

The desk sergeant smiled when he saw Luca come through the doors. "Well, look who's here."

"How are you, Mack?"

"Doing well, and how's retirement treating you?"

"Ah, it's not all it's cracked up to be. Half the time I'm bored out of my mind."

"You should take up golf."

"No thanks, buddy. I have enough frustration in my life."

The sergeant smiled. "Who are you here to see?"

"Officer Childs. I called him beforehand."

Two minutes and more small talk later, a skinny, uniformed officer sporting a buzz cut walked into the foyer.

"Mr. Luca?"

Luca extended his hand. "Officer Childs. It's nice to meet the new guard."

Childs scoffed. "I'm just starting out, sir. If I can do half of what you did, I'd consider my career a success."

"You will. Let's talk outside."

Stepping into the sunshine, they both put on mirrored sunglasses. Luca said, "I like the glasses."

Childs chuckled. "So, what's up?"

"You responded to the fatal accident on Livingston the other day."

"Yes, sir. I was the first on the scene."

"What was your initial impression of the scene?"

Childs tilted his head. "Well, to be honest, I figured the driver had been texting and gotten distracted. There were no skid marks, and it looked like he turned sharply to avoid hitting someone in the intersection. Witnesses say he had a red light, and he hopped the curb and slammed right into the utility pole."

"You examined the auto at the impound lot?"

"Yes, sir."

"Was there anything concerning?"

Childs narrowed his eyes. "You believe the vehicle was tampered with?"

"I'm working a case, and the victim is a party of interest in a larger conspiracy."

"A conspiracy?"

"Yes, I'm not at liberty to discuss the details at this time, but my gut is sending signals, if you know what I mean."

"I do, sir."

"Was there anything about this that might tell me it's not an accident?"

"Well, uh, now that you say it. They put the car on a lift, and the brake lines were severed."

"I knew it."

"Hold on a second. I asked about it when I saw it, but the mechanic said it happened when the car went off the road. He said he'd seen it before."

"Did you see brake fluid at the scene?"

Childs shrugged. "I can't say for sure. When I got there, I went to see if I could help the driver, and it was pretty chaotic and . . ."

"I've been there myself."

"I should've looked for that, but I wasn't—"

"Don't beat yourself up. Learn from this, is all you can do."

Childs hung his head. "Yes, sir."

"Did you file your report on this?"

"I was going to get to it this afternoon."

"Look, in my opinion, this car shouldn't be released. It needs to be looked at with an eye that it wasn't an accident. Can you make that happen, or do you need me to call a favor in?"

"No worries. I've got this, sir."

"I know you do. I don't want to butt in, so go through

the normal chain of command, and when you have something, I'd appreciate it if you'd let me know."

"Absolutely, sir."

They shook hands and Childs went back inside. As Luca considered whether to say hello to Homicide Detective Donovan, his phone rang. He didn't recognize the number but answered.

"This is Frank Luca. Who's calling?"

"This is Elena Borelli's office. We're returning your call."

"Oh, thanks for calling back. If you remember, you called me to set up a meeting a couple of days ago."

"Yes, I recall the conversation."

"Well, it turns out that I'm going to need to speak to Ms. Borelli after all. When is she available?"

"Let me check her schedule and get back to you."

As he hung up, a woman walked past him holding a cup of coffee. The aroma made him want one but not the kind they served in the station's cafeteria. He headed to his car.

Driving north on Airport Pulling Road, his phone rang. Luca smiled, it was his daughter.

"Hey, Jessie, how are you?"

"Good, Dad. I was just outside trying to grab a late lunch, and this man on a motorcycle came up to me."

Luca stiffened. "What did he want?"

"He was weird."

"What did he say?"

"He said he knew you and to tell you to watch your back."

A car skidded to a stop, avoiding Luca, who'd run through a red light. Luca swerved and pulled over. "What did the man look like?"

"I don't know, he had a helmet on."

"Did he look or sound familiar?"

"No. I have no idea who he was. What did he mean by watching your back?"

"I'm not sure. But I want you to be extra careful. There are a lot of nuts out there."

"Dad, you're making me nervous."

"Don't be scared. Be on your toes. It's probably some cretin I put away years ago."

"How would they know I was your daughter?"

"I don't know, but these bastards get obsessed when they're put away."

"Can't you find out who it is?"

"I'm going to try. In the meantime, promise me you won't go anywhere by yourself. Okay?"

"I won't. I promise."

Chapter Thirty-Six

Luca's mind raced as he drove home. Who was threatening him? It had to be related to the Waterside Shops case. Or was it some thug he'd put away?

Going through the Rolodex in his head, Luca thought of two possible men he'd arrested during the last five years that he was on the force.

The first one that came to mind was Herman Welke, who was charged and convicted of assault and battery. Welke was sentenced to two years in jail. But the charges also resulted in him losing all privileges he received from his divorce in regard to contact with his children.

Welke, like many convicted criminals, never took responsibility for his actions. Instead, he blamed Luca for the loss and even wrote a letter from prison vowing to get revenge.

The other possibility was Afrika Nemen, a gang member Luca had arrested for assault with a deadly weapon. Nemen served just under three years of his five-year sentence before being released a year ago. The word on the street at the time of his conviction was that the gang was going to seek retribution. But nothing had happened, and the talk died down.

As he hit the remote to open his garage door, he realized the immediate problem was going to be Mary Ann.

He rolled into the garage, and the interior door to the house opened. Hands on her hips, Mary Ann was waiting for him.

He TOLD himself to act calmly as he stepped out of the car. "Hey."

"You better tell me what's going on, Frank."

Luca hit the remote and the garage door lowered. "Let's go in."

Mary Ann led the way, and when they got to the kitchen, Luca said, "I guess you talked to Jessie?"

"I did. Now tell me, what the hell is going on?"

"I don't know. I swear. It doesn't make sense."

"Well, you had better figure it out and fast. If something happens to Jessica—"

"Stop panicking, Mary Ann."

"I'm not panicking. Someone is threatening our daughter, and I want it to stop."

"They didn't threaten her. It's me they're trying to scare off."

"The fastest way to get to anybody is through their kids. They're sending a message that they know how to get to Jessica."

She was dead right. "I'm going to reach out to the Orlando PD."

"What are they going to do?"

"Come on, Mary Ann, you were on the force, you know we look out for our own. Besides, my old buddy, Gerry Simpson, is a lieutenant up there."

"Gerry Simpson?"

"Yes. You remember I told you about him? He used to be with the Middletown force, then he moved over to the Colts Neck force before leaving Jersey for Florida a couple of years before I came down."

"Kind of. But what do you think they're going to do for something like this?"

"I'll make sure they patrol her neighborhood and where she works."

"That's not enough. I think I'm going to go up there."

"That's crazy."

"I don't want to take a chance."

"Neither do I, but we don't know if the threat is credible."

"I can't wait for that, it could be too late."

"Jessie's got her own life going on. She doesn't want her mother around twenty-four seven."

When Mary Ann glared at him, he said, "You'll cramp her style, is all I'm saying."

Mary Ann stormed out of the room and Luca called after her, "Okay, if you want to go, be my guest. Just go right ahead. Just be sure to talk to her first."

When the door to the master bedroom slammed, Luca took his cell out and called his old friend in Orlando.

Luca knocked on the door before stepping into his bedroom. Mary Ann was putting an armful of clothes into a piece of luggage. His gaze settled on the pistol and holster laying on the bed.

"I just spoke to my buddy in Orlando. He said they're

going to ride by her building and office every hour. We got lucky because both places are in a patrol zone that Gerry supervises."

"That's good, but I'm still going."

"I get it. You'll get to spend some time with Jessie. Maybe you'll go to Disney when you're up there."

As she stuffed a toiletry bag into a wheely, she said, "I'm dreading the ride."

Hoping she'd say no, he said, "You want me to come? We can stay at a hotel or something for a couple of days."

"No. I'll stay with Jessica."

"There shouldn't too much traffic this time of day."

"There's always traffic."

After Mary Ann pulled out of the driveway, Luca called Derrick.

"Hey, I may need some help."

"What's up, Frank?"

Luca told his ex-partner what had happened.

Derrick said, "Geez, I mean I don't like it, but it really was a veiled threat at best."

"That's what I told Mary Ann, but she freaked out."

"Lynn would react the same way, but you can't take chances with this."

"I'm not. I called a buddy I knew from Jersey who is running a division in the Orlando PD, and he's going to run patrols by Jessie's apartment and job."

"That's good, real good."

"I'm trying to understand who's behind it. You think it's some bastard we put away?"

Derrick said, "I don't think so. The sheriff's department is pretty good at letting us know when a cretin gets out of jail."

"They do. But what about that jerk Herman Welke? He wrote that letter saying he was going to come after me."

"Which led to him having to serve the full sentence. He got out, what, eighteen months ago?"

"Yeah. I know the timeline doesn't fit. What about Afrika Nemen?"

"The gang member?"

"Yes."

"The sheriff's got two or three informants. We would've heard something if he was going after you."

"Is there anyone else you can think of?"

Derrick said, "No. It's got to be related to the Waterside case."

"That's what I thought, but I wanted to be certain I didn't miss something."

"You didn't, there's no other explanation. Whoever they are, they have to be the most diligent crooks in history."

"No doubt. They got away with it for twenty years, they're good."

"Ruthless might be a better word."

A chill traveled down Luca's spine. "One of the names on the list was David Flan, and he died in a car crash a couple of days ago."

"Was it suspicious?"

"That's the zillion-dollar question. No skid marks, and he wasn't on the phone. Bilotti said he died on impact, and the initial findings were negative on alcohol and drugs."

"Maybe something will show up on the toxicology report."

"If you have time, I could use some help."

"Of course, are you crazy? Nobody messes with my niece."

"Thanks, pal. Maybe you could call the lab."

"I'll call Mack and ask him to prioritize it."

"He always liked you better than me."

"I hate to break it to you, my man, but he wasn't the only one."

Luca snorted. "You dog."

"What else can I do?"

"I have to be honest, this threat has sidetracked my thinking. I have to review things first."

"Sure. Let me know, and we'll get together or something."

"Thanks again, buddy."

Chapter Thirty-Seven

Luca pulled his copy of the Waterside case file out of his desk and began reading though it. He lingered on the interview the police had done at the time with Ernest Rigo. There was something about Rigo that wouldn't go away.

Maybe Derrick was right and Rigo's mother had lied about his whereabouts to protect her son. It wouldn't be the first time Luca had come up against a lying family member. When he added the fact that Rigo's parents were wealthy and that there was no shortage of rich people who believed they could outsmart law enforcement, his doubt bordered on conviction.

Luca paged through the file and found the note where he'd scribbled Mrs. Rigo's phone number. Luca called and left a message for the mother.

He put his cell down and it started vibrating. He checked the number but didn't recognize the caller.

"This is Frank Luca. Who's calling?"

"Mr. Luca, it's Officer Childs. I wanted to tell you we went over the vehicle very closely."

It sounded like bad news was coming. "And did you see anything suspicious?"

"We did."

Luca pumped his fist. "What did you find?"

"Well, the brake line was torn up when it hopped the curb and went off the road. There didn't seem to be any doubt that it happened without any, uh, assistance. But I inspected the entire lines and found two holes in both lines by the wheel wells. The mechanic said he believes they were intentionally punctured."

Luca jumped to his feet. "I knew it."

"I don't know how you did, sir. The mechanic said the loss of brake fluid and bubbles in the line caused the brakes to fail and, unfortunately, cost the driver his life."

Derrick's use of the word ruthless rang in Luca's head. "Could someone have made holes in the line without putting the car on a lift?"

"Yes, I asked him and he said sure, you had to know where to look and all that, but if the vehicle was parked, someone could tamper with it right in a parking lot."

"Did the mechanic say anything about how long it would take to lose the ability to brake?"

"I asked him if someone could time it. And he said roughly that they could, but it depended on how fast they were driving and how often they had to brake and stuff like that."

"Are you going to refer this to homicide?"

"Yes, sir."

"Great work, Officer Childs."

"Thank you, sir, but if it weren't for you, whoever did it would be getting away with it."

"All I can say is to never accept what you see at first; you've got to go a layer or two deeper."

"I'm going to remember that, sir."

Luca hung up and sat down. He mulled over the fact that Flan's car had been tampered with. That made the crash intentional. What was unknown was whether the intention was to murder Flan or just to scare him.

His thoughts went to Jessie. He was glad she had continually turned down his offer to get her a car. There were a lot of things Luca didn't like about Jessie's generation, but preferring city living and using Ubers was now off the list.

Luca grabbed his phone and called Derrick. He filled in his ex-partner on what had been uncovered with Flan's car.

Derrick said, "If you didn't push Childs, nobody would've known."

"Maybe."

"No maybes, Frank. Good work, but I have to say, it's got me worried."

"What do you mean?"

"Whoever these people are, they aren't screwing around."

"They're pros, but they'll mess up. They always do."

"I'm not talking about that. I'm talking about you and Jessie. We can't let something happen."

"My buddy is running patrols by Jessie's place and job."

"Do you think it's enough?"

"I hope so, and Mary Ann is on her way there."

"She's going to Jessie's?"

"Yeah, she freaked out and didn't think the patrols were enough."

"I hope to hell she's wrong."

"Me too."

"She's still carrying, isn't she?"

"Not all the time, but she took her piece with her."

"Good. Let's hope to hell she doesn't need it."

"It's going to be all right."

"What can I do?"

"I know it's probably not related to the Waterside case, but can you dig in a little on Africa Nemen?"

"Sure. What about the other guy, Herman Welke? You want me to check out the bastard?"

"I'm going to look into him."

"Okay, let's get moving."

Luca hung up, and before he could make another call, his phone buzzed.

The number was vaguely familiar.

"This is Frank Luca. Who's this?"

"Hello, Mr. Luca. This is Vivian from Elena Borelli's office."

"Hi, thanks for the call. When can she meet with me?"

"Due to a cancellation, Ms. Borelli has a small window open this afternoon. If that doesn't work for you, it'll have to be late the following week, but there are no guarantees on next week."

"I can make it today. What time and where?'

"Four p.m. at our offices. Do you need directions?"

"No, I know where you are."

"Great."

"Tell her I'll see her later."

Luca disconnected the call and checked the time. It was ten minutes before three. Borelli either had a sudden opening in her schedule, or the financier was hoping Luca couldn't make it. Luca was betting it was the latter.

Luca hated to waste time and believed whatever success

he'd achieved went mostly to his obsession over not wasting time. He had just under an hour. Luca picked up his phone to call one of the prosecutors who had worked on the Herman Welke case.

Before the call connected, Luca hung up. He needed to concentrate on the meeting with Borelli. This woman was obviously brilliant, and Luca would need every ounce of focus he could muster to stay even with the financier.

Chapter Thirty-Eight

The lobby's guard barely picked his head up as Luca dug his identification out. Before he could show it, he was waved toward the elevators.

About to push the button to call for a ride up to the fourth floor, he looked to his left. He had been too preoccupied to exercise the last several days. He hesitated for a second and headed for the stairs, taking them two at a time.

Luca stood at the landing and took a second to slow his breath. He set himself and pushed open the door to the fourth-floor lobby.

Horizon Investments was spelled out in large, gold letters on a plexiglass sign. The space was airy and professionally furnished. A half-moon-shaped desk defined the reception area.

Luca announced himself to the receptionist.

"Welcome to Horizon Investments. Please have a seat while you wait. Can I get you something to drink?"

"No, thank you."

Luca settled on a low-profile, white leather couch. The

glass coffee table had a copy of *Gulfshore Life* and *Forbes*. Both had pictures of Elena Borelli on their covers. Luca felt it was showy and checked the dates of publication. They were both current editions.

He picked up *Forbes*. He hadn't looked at the magazine in years but knew it was much thinner than it used to be.

He checked the table of contents and thumbed to page thirty-eight. A full-page picture of Elena Borelli greeted him. It's headline read: "The Queen of Wall Street South."

Luca wondered if Borelli had an office in Miami, which he thought was referred to as Wall Street South. Or was the lady a bigger deal than he imagined?

A perky but professional woman in a powder-blue pantsuit approached. "Mr. Luca. I'm Casey, Vivian's assistant."

Luca stood, trying to process the fact that there was an assistant to the assistant. "Hello."

"Please follow me, sir."

Luca trailed behind as she asked, "So, how is your day progressing?"

"Pretty good."

"Well, I hope your meeting pushes it into an excellent one."

Luca quickened his pace to keep up with her. "That would be nice."

She pivoted in front of a glass door. "This is you. Ms. Borelli will be with you shortly. Can I get you a cup of coffee? We have a special blend of Black Ivory coffee."

"Black Ivory? I never heard of that."

"It comes from Thailand, where elephants eat the beans and they undergo fermentation in their digestive systems. The coffee isn't at all bitter and is chocolatey."

"I'm sorry, did you say the coffee beans are digested by elephants and then made into coffee?"

She smiled. "I know it sounds gross, but trust me, it's the best in the world."

Luca paused as he considered how different the super-rich were before saying, "No thanks, but I'd appreciate some water."

"Sparkling or still?"

"Still."

"We have Fiji and Acqua Panna."

Luca couldn't suppress his smile. "You don't have any water made from ancient icebergs?"

Without missing a beat, she said, "We used to have Berg. But it became impossible to keep in stock."

"Either the Acqua Panna or the Fiji is fine."

"I'll be right back."

She stepped out and Luca surveyed the room. The only thing on the finely grained wood table was a futuristic-looking communications hub. Each of the buffets anchoring the sides of the room had flower arrangements. He reached out to one. They were real.

He walked around the table to the bank of windows. A sliver of the Gulf was visible. He heard the swish of a door opening.

"Here you go, Mr. Luca."

She set a tray on the table, cracked open a bottle of Acqua Panna, and poured a glass.

"Would you like ice?"

"No thanks."

She handed the glass to Luca and left the room.

Luca took a sip, trying to see what difference there was from Naples' finest tap water.

The door opened. Luca recognized Elena Borelli. Her perfect teeth radiated a gigawatt smile. The financier's knee-length dress barely hid her toned body. Money had helped slow Father Time.

"Mr. Luca, I apologize for keeping you waiting."

He came around the table. "No need to apologize, ma'am."

He extended his hand, and she enveloped his with both of hers. "Please, call me Elena."

Luca processed the softness of her hands, and said, "And please call me Frank."

"If you insist. Please, take a seat."

Luca scurried to the opposite side of the table and sat in one of the leather chairs.

Borelli said, "Is there anything we can get you?"

He raised the glass of expensive water. "No. I'm fine, thanks."

"Excellent."

"You've built quite a business. One in a man's world."

"Thank you."

"It couldn't have been easy."

"I enjoy what I do and don't mind working hard to accomplish my goals."

"I have a daughter who just graduated college. What advice could you give her?"

"Find a field you love and apply yourself to the task at hand."

"What would you say is the secret to your success?"

"There is no secret, but an important component is to go deeper than is necessary, no matter the subject or target. They say the devil is in the details, but I say that's where the advantage is."

"I like that. I'll tell her what you said."

"Why don't we sit over there?" Borelli pointed to the far end of the table.

Luca stood. "Sure."

Borelli pulled out the armed chair at the head of the table. Luca settled into a chair to her right. Luca suppressed the urge to smile at the power play Borelli had acted out.

She set her cell phone in front of her and said, "Now, how can I help the sheriff's office?"

"I'm not with the sheriff's office. I used to run the homicide division."

She recoiled. "Homicide? Oh my. That sounds like distasteful work."

"At times it was. At the moment, I'm looking into an old case for a client."

"Oh right, you're a private investigator."

"I am."

"I'm sorry, but I don't understand your interest in speaking with me."

"You were close to several people that I'm looking into."

"Who might they be?"

"Conrad Bolt."

"The judge?"

"Yes."

"We went to school together years ago. It might have been middle school, or was it?" She looked at the ceiling. "High school?"

"It was the high school at the Community School of Naples. You were close friends then."

"I don't like saying it, but that was over twenty years ago. It makes me feel old." She smiled. "However, I wouldn't characterize our relationship as close. At that age, you consider your friends as vital to your existence."

"When is the last time you saw or spoke to Mr. Bolt?"

"Hmmm." She looked up again. "I believe he and I both attended a fund-raising event at the hotel where the new Four Seasons has been built."

"When was that?"

"They knocked down the old hotel before Ian slammed into us. The hurricane hit in 2022, and before that was Covid. I'd say it was in 2018 or so. I can have my assistant check the calendar."

"Sure, have them check."

Borelli tapped on her phone and set it back down. "Is there anything else?"

Luca looked directly in Borelli's eyes, saying, "Cynthia Clermont."

The financier didn't show anything. "You're taking me on a trip down memory lane?"

"What was and is your relationship to Ms. Clermont?"

"I don't have a relationship with her. We simply went to school together many years ago."

"Along with Conrad Bolt."

"Yes. We went to high school together."

"And the last time you spoke to her or saw her in person was?"

"You have me at a disadvantage. My memory is good, but the last time I saw her was probably at our graduation ceremony."

"You never saw or spoke to her since then?"

Borelli raised her shoulders. "I can't swear to it. We reside in the same town."

"How do you know she lives in Naples if you haven't seen her?"

Borelli frowned. "With all due respect, Mr. Luca. It was an assumption, and you're insinuating that, well, never mind. I have no knowledge where she is or has been since we graduated."

"What about David Flan."

She pulled her phone closer. "I read about the car accident a couple of days ago. It appeared he might have been texting." She shook her head. "How terribly sad for his family."

"You went to school with him as well."

She tapped her phone and said, "I did."

"When is the last time you saw or spoke to Mr. Flan?"

"Again, it's been years."

The door to the conference room swung open. Vivian pointed to the watch on her wrist. "I'm sorry, but you've really got to leave now. You'll still be late but only by five minutes."

Borelli stood, snatching her phone off the table. She said, "Sorry to have to cut this short, but it's a critical meeting. We have a large holding in an exciting start-up company, and the founders just flew in for the meeting. They don't have much time, as they're heading out of Miami for Berlin tonight."

Chapter Thirty-Nine

Bothered by the abrupt ending to his meeting with Borelli, Luca took the stairs and replayed the last part of his interview with the financier. She had reached for her phone when he brought up David Flan.

Had there been an incoming message that prompted her, meaning the timing was coincidental? Or had Borelli hit send on a prepared message, signaling her assistant, in a prearranged way, to rescue her?

Luca knew time was valuable to someone like Borelli, but using the phone when Flan's name was mentioned, followed by her assistant bursting into the room, felt staged.

As soon as he got home, he made a cup of coffee and went into his den. His phone pinged with a text from Mary Ann.

He called her. "Hey, how is it going in Disney country?"

"It's a lot busier in Orlando than I remembered."

"There's something like three million people living in the metro area."

"Remind me never to complain about the traffic in Naples."

"It's been bad up there for twenty years. Remember the time we were stuck on Route Four for three hours?"

"I'll never forget. So how is my bachelor doing?"

"I'm busy. I just came back from Borelli's. You should see her office. It smells of money."

"She was on the cover of *Gulfshore Life*."

"I know. I wonder how much she's worth."

"I'm sure it's hundreds of millions."

"Probably. How's Jessie?"

"She's working."

"At the office?"

"Yes. Today she had to go in for some meeting."

"What have you been doing?"

"I went shopping for groceries. Her fridge is empty."

"How nice to have Mommy around."

"I don't mind. It's good to spend time with her, but since she is out today, I'm bored."

"Since you can't do your laps, go for a walk."

"I already did. I might take a yoga class later."

"Have you seen patrol cars making the rounds?"

"Yes."

Luca asked, "How long are you going to stay up there?"

"I don't know. You haven't heard anything, right?"

"Nothing. We're checking out two guys I put away, to be safe."

"You have to find out who is behind these threats."

"I will. Look, I'll call you later, I have to get going."

Luca ended the call and dug into David Flan.

LUCA SWUNG OPEN his front door. Derrick said, "This better be good. I don't cancel my tennis lesson for just any old thing."

"I think I've got another piece of the Waterside puzzle."

Derrick stepped inside. "What is it?"

"I'll show you. You want anything to drink?"

"A water would be good."

Luca got two bottles of Poland Spring and handed one off. They went into the den and Luca slipped into the chair behind his desk.

He opened his laptop, saying, "I went to see Borelli, and when I brought up David Flan, the guy who was killed in a supposed car accident, she cut off the meeting."

"I can't believe she'd be so obvious about it. She'd know it'd raise suspicion."

"Borelli tried to cover it by having here assistant barge in."

"How'd she time that?"

"I'm pretty sure she sent her a text. One she prepared in advance."

"I don't know, Frank, she'd have to be some kind of different animal."

"She's a billionaire, the top female in a business domi-nated by men. How do you think she got there?"

"That's true."

"And if she was involved in the Waterside robbery, she's the one who made sure they never got caught."

Derrick smiled. "We finally ran into a criminal mastermind."

"Look at this." Luca turned his laptop toward his ex-partner. "These are the businesses started by David Flan. Every one of them failed."

"The guy was a serial entrepreneur."

"More like someone hoping one idea would work."

"It takes a lot of money to start a business"—Derrick pointed a finger at the laptop—"especially a chain of restaurants and a car wash."

"Exactly. And here's the interesting thing, every one of these businesses was owned by an LLC."

Derrick said, "That's pretty normal these days."

"Yes, but I dug into them. The partners were David Flan and another LLC called Brightway Enterprises. Guess who owns Brightway?"

"Borelli?"

"Bingo. She put up the money for Flan."

"And Flan lost it."

"Exactly."

"But I can't believe, with all her money, she'd kill him."

Luca sighed. "Not kill him, but giving him the money to keep him quiet. Don't you see? Flan was one of the kids who pulled the Waterside job."

"She paid him off to keep his mouth shut?"

"Exactly, and maybe she got tired of paying him off and had him killed."

"That sounds way outside of her style. It's too dangerous."

"More dangerous than getting exposed as part of a gang who killed two people during a robbery?"

"That's a good point. She'd lose everything and end up in prison."

"Borelli would not only do anything to prevent that, but she also has the money to do it."

"That's a scary thought."

"Tell me about it."

"I don't want to exaggerate, but if Borelli is behind the threat you've received, Jessie could be in real danger."

Luca wagged his head. "It's keeping me up at night."

"How can I help with all this?"

"I don't want to wear out my welcome at the sheriff's office."

Derrick smiled. "And they like me better."

Exhaling, Luca said, "Yeah, they do."

"What do you need me to do?"

"If we can find any evidence from the car crash that killed Flan, we'd be on our way. Why don't you see what's going on with the investigation, check and see what forensics turned up."

Derrick stood. "I'll get right on it."

After his ex-partner left, Luca dialed a number.

"Good afternoon, Horizon Investments. How may I help you?"

"Elena Borelli, please."

Luca was transferred to Borelli's assistant and asked for another appointment to see the financier. He hung up after being promised they'd check her availability and get back to him.

Luca got up to make a cup of coffee and his phone chimed a reminder.

He looked at the screen. "Shit."

Luca was due at his oncologist's office in thirty minutes. He swiped the car keys off his desk and headed for the garage.

Luca groaned as he stepped inside the doctor's office. He spied the last empty chair before checking in for his annual visit.

Fifteen minutes passed without a patient's name being

called. Luca thought of blowing the visit off. He'd had no problems with the bladder the doctors had fashioned after removing his cancer-ridden one.

But knowing there'd be hell to pay if Mary Ann found out he'd skipped the visit, he picked up a copy of *National Geographic* and began paging through it.

Bored with an article on chimpanzees, Luca checked the time. It was twenty minutes past his appointment time.

Luca took a deep breath and closed his eyes. His phone startled him. All eyes were on him as he checked the caller. It was Mary Ann.

He answered with a whisper, "I'm at the doctor's."

"It's Jessica! They're trying to kidnap her."

Chapter Forty

Luca shot out of his chair. "What? What happened? Is she okay?"

Mary Ann's voice cracked. "They tried to force her into a van."

"But she's all right?"

"Yes, but the poor thing is scared out of her mind."

As he ran out of the doctor's office, he said, "Was she hurt?"

"No, just scared."

"Did she see who it was?"

"No. They came from behind her, but she was able kick her heel into the guy's shin and she got free."

Luca had taught his daughter that defensive move. "But she's okay, right?"

"Yes, just shaken up."

"You're in Jessie's apartment?"

"Yes."

"Stay there. I'm coming up."

"Don't bother. We're coming home."

"Did you call the police?"

"Yes. I think they just got here."

"Good. Let me call my buddy."

"After they interview her, we're going to pack and get out of here."

"I can't freaking believe it."

"They're at the door."

Luca heard the sound of a lock opening. "Call me when you're done."

The call disconnected and Luca jumped behind the wheel of his car. His mind raced with thoughts: Who the hell was doing this? Screwing around with him was one thing, but Jessie?

As he drove home, Luca vowed to ferret out the cowards who were using his daughter to shut him down.

Luca slid behind his desk. His laptop was still open. He hit the enter key and the screen came to life. His eyes settled on the information he'd uncovered about Borelli's investments in Flan's businesses.

Borelli. He had called her less than two hours before the kidnapping attempt. Was she behind it?

He put the thought on hold and called his friend in the Orlando Police Department.

"Hey, Gerry, did you hear what happened to my daughter?"

"Yeah, Frank. I'm really sorry. The patrol was minutes away."

"Can you get to the apartment? I know your guys are

there, but I'd feel more comfortable if you were there with them."

"I'm already on my way."

"Thanks. I appreciate it. My kid is scared, and I doubt she knows who you are, but I'll text my wife that you're coming."

"You got it, Frank. I'm glad she's not hurt or anything."

"You and me both."

"We're going to canvass the area and see about any witnesses."

"Good. Let me know if anything pops up."

"Frank, you must have an idea about who might have been behind this."

"I kinda do, but I need to be certain."

"Frank, you have to give us whatever you have."

"Let me have some time. I've got another call coming in. Call me when you get there."

Luca jogged down the hallway to the garage. He got in his car and sped to Elena Borelli's office.

As soon as the elevator doors parted, Luca stormed up to the receptionist.

"I'm here to see Elena Borelli."

"Do you have an appointment, sir?"

"No. Tell her Frank Luca is here, and I'm not leaving until she sees me."

"I'm sorry, sir, Ms. Borelli is unavailable. She is in a meeting."

Luca raised his voice. "I don't care what she's doing. I want to see her. Now!"

"Please try and remain calm, sir. Or I'll have to call security."

"Tell Borelli I'm here!"

The receptionist swiveled her chair and called her boss's office. She whispered into her headphones before turning to face Luca.

"Ms. Borelli is unable to see you today, but her assistant said she has a time slot available next week."

"I'm not waiting a damn week!" Luca looked in the direction of the conference room he'd met Borelli in before. He started down the hallway. "Elena Borelli! Where are you? It's Frank Luca."

A security guard called out from behind, "Sir. You're going to have to leave."

"Borelli! Get out here!"

The guard grabbed Luca's arm. "Sir, come with me."

"Get your damn hands off me!"

At the end of the corridor, a door opened and Borelli stepped into the hallway. "That's okay, Bruno. I have time to see Mr. Luca now."

"Are you sure, ma'am?"

"Yes. Mr. Luca, why don't we go into the conference room?"

Luca followed her into a different room than when they'd met before. Luca said, "You're lower than I thought. All this money, and you're nothing but a thug."

"Excuse me?"

"Don't act like you don't know what's going on."

"I have no idea what you're referring to or why you're so upset."

"You tried to have my daughter kidnapped? Have you lost your—"

Borelli put a hand on her chest. "Someone tried to kidnap your daughter?"

"Someone? It was you."

"You may think whatever you like about me, but I'd never stoop so low as to endanger a child. I serve on the boards of two charities that help children. Why would I contradict those efforts?"

"To get me to stop looking into the Waterside robbery."

"I can assure you, Mr. Luca, that I have nothing to do with either that or what happened to your daughter. Was she hurt?"

"No. She's just scared."

"Of course. Poor child. Do the authorities have any information on who it might have been?"

Luca scoffed. "You'd love me to tell you, wouldn't you?"

"I can't stop you from making outrageous assumptions, but I can offer help in finding whoever was responsible for this outrageous attempt."

"I don't need your help."

"I'd be happy to put a reward, say fifty, no, make it a hundred thousand dollars for information leading to an arrest on who did it."

"I said I don't need your help."

"Money is an effective motivator for people to come forward. Let me help, please, I insist."

"No."

"Well, I'll call the sheriff then, he's always receptive."

"It didn't happen in Collier."

"Where did it happen?"

"In Orlando."

"Orlando? What was she doing up there?"

Luca wasn't sure if Borelli was pleading ignorance or was genuinely trying to help. "She lives there."

"Oh. She's employed by Disney?"

"No."

"I'm sorry she had such a traumatic experience. If she is anything like you, she'll recover quickly. The important thing is she wasn't hurt physically."

Luca found himself agreeing. "You're right."

"Now, please accept my help in trying to find the people who did this. I want to make sure they're never able to do such a dreadful thing to anyone else."

The door to the conference room swung open and a man in a dark blue suit said, "I'm sorry, Elena, but they're getting a bit anxious."

"I'll be right in."

The man left and Borelli said to Luca, "I know it's nothing compared to what happened to you and your family, but I support a program out of Gulf Coast University, and five of their best students were in the midst of a presentation when you, uh, arrived."

Luca stood. "I'm sorry to have barged in."

"Though I never had children, I completely understand. Please take me up on the offer to fund an award."

"I just might do that."

"I'd be happy to help."

"I'm going to need to speak with you again, not about the kidnapping, but the Waterside case."

"Whenever you're ready, I'll do my best to accommodate you."

Luca avoided looking at the receptionist and took the stairs down to the parking lot. As he walked to his car, his phone buzzed. It was his cop friend in Orlando.

"Hey, how is she?"

"She and your wife are fine, but I wanted to tell you we got a lead."

"You do?"

"Yeah, we have an eyewitness who gave us a partial plate number."

"Holy shit. That's great."

"It is. It was a white van, so we're running the possible combinations. It shouldn't be too tough to narrow it down."

Chapter Forty-One

Luca called Derrick to let him know about the kidnapping attempt.

"Holy shit, Frank. This is crazy."

"Trust me. I'm wracking my brain over who's behind it."

"I thought you were sure it was that finance woman connected to the Waterside job?"

"I thought so, but I went to see Borelli right after Mary Ann told me what happened, and Borelli kind of convinced me she had nothing to do with it."

"What did she say?"

"Nothing exactly, it was just the feeling I got."

"Your gut's good, but we're talking about Jessie and—"

"Borelli even offered to put up a hundred thousand as reward money to find the person who did it."

"She could be covering up, trying to deflect attention from herself."

"I know, I know, but that's not the vibe I got. She seemed really surprised, and I got the feeling she felt something like that crossed the line."

"You need to take a step back. There's too much emotion around."

"I know how to separate my personal feelings."

"Come on, Frank, we're talking about your daughter. You're not a frigging robot."

"I guess you're right. But they got a lead up there, a partial plate and vehicle type. They should be able to piece it together, and then we'll see who the bastard is."

"Man, that would be sweet. If it's Borelli, I'd want to see the look on her face when they take her down."

Another call came into Luca's phone. "I got to go, Mary Ann is calling."

He switched calls and said, "How'd it go?"

Mary Ann said, "Pretty good. They debriefed Jessica."

"How did she do?"

"She's a rock. I mean, I know she was putting on an act, but she is strong."

"She takes after her mother."

"I don't know about that. I was the one crying when they tried to grab her off the street."

"Every parent's nightmare."

"And how. It feels surreal."

"Did they tell you about the lead they have?"

"Yes. I want to look right in that animal's eyes when they catch him."

"They ought to give us ten minutes alone with him."

"That would be nice."

"Let me talk to Jessie."

"She just jumped in the shower. We'll call you from the road."

Four hours later, Luca heard the garage door go up. He

hopped out of his recliner and went to greet Jessie and his wife.

Jessie got out. "Hi, Dad."

Luca embraced his daughter. "I'm sorry you had to go through all that."

"It's okay, Dad. I'm all right."

"No, it's not okay. We're going to hunt down who did this. They're going to prison for a long time."

"I know you'll get them, Dad."

Luca kissed the top of his daughter's head. "Go inside. I'll get the bags."

Mary Ann popped the trunk open and headed into the house. "I've got to use the bathroom."

Luca put Jessie's bag in her room and rolled his wife's into their bedroom. Mary Ann came out of the bathroom. The two of them embraced.

Mary Ann squeezed her husband. "I can't imagine what she went through, it's so scary."

"It makes me sick thinking about it."

"I never thought something like this would happen to us."

"She seems better than I expected. She'll bounce back."

Mary Ann dropped her arms. "Who did this?"

"I don't know."

"Frank, you have to tell me. Is it the Waterside case?"

"I don't think so."

Luca told his wife he'd gone to see Borelli and felt she wasn't involved.

"Then who could it be?"

"We're going to find out."

"This all started with you working the Waterside job."

"I know, but—"

"Don't be fooled by this Borelli character. I'm sure she's got her act together."

"Don't worry. Everyone is a suspect."

"Okay. I'm starving."

"You want me to pick something up?"

"Sure. Ask Jessica what she wants."

Mary Ann called the order in, and before going to pick up the food from USS Nemo, Luca disappeared into the master bedroom.

He came out holding a pistol. "Jessie, this is for you."

"I don't need a gun, Dad."

"You sure do. Look what just happened."

"I wouldn't have used it. I'm not comfortable with guns."

"Well, we're going to fix that. You're a single woman, and that makes you a target."

Mary Ann said, "Frank, do we have to do this now?"

Luca shrugged. "I'm just worried."

Mary Ann said, "I have mine, so we're going to be fine."

Luca nodded. "Okay. But think about it, Jessie. I can take you to the range as many times as you need to get comfortable with it."

Mary Ann glared at her husband.

"Okay, okay. I'll go get the food."

Sitting at a red light on Pine Ridge and Route 41, Luca shot a text to his Orlando buddy.

"What's going on with the lead you had?"

The light turned green, and as Luca hit the gas, a reply came in. He hit the read-back button on his dash: *We've got ten names. We're running them down.*

Chapter Forty-Two

The sun was an hour away from rising, but Luca was on his second cup of coffee. He'd considered every possible suspect he could imagine but kept returning to one probable person.

It wasn't the person who physically tried to take Jessie but the mastermind behind it, Elena Borelli.

He hated to admit it, but Derrick was right, he'd let his emotions cloud his judgment. Borelli had money and a network. He knew it from the get-go but allowed Borelli to convince him she had nothing to do with it.

She was a formidable foe.

Setting his mug in the sink, Luca vowed to never allow Borelli to manipulate him again. He checked his phone, but Gerry, his Orlando buddy, hadn't replied to his text. He reminded himself it was early and retrieved his sneakers from the garage.

An hour later he used the garage pad to get into the house. Coffee cup in hand, Mary Ann put her finger to her lips and shook her head.

Luca whispered, "What's the matter?"

"Jessica is sleeping. You know she's a light sleeper. You shouldn't have went through the garage."

"I was quiet."

The door to Jessica's room opened.

Mary Ann said, "Yeah, right."

After yawning, Jessica said, "Good morning."

"Good morning. Did you sleep well?"

"Oh yeah, I slept like a baby."

Luca looked at his wife and grinned. "Get some coffee. I'm going to take a shower."

Jessie and Mary Ann were both on their iPads when Luca came into the kitchen.

He said, "Jess, we can go to the shooting range whenever you want. A guy I used to work with manages the Alamo gun range on Vanderbilt, so anytime works."

"I don't know, Dad. Even though both of you were cops, I'm not really into guns."

"It's not about being into weapons, it's a life skill, one that you'll never know can save your life or someone else's."

"Dad's right. You have a right to defend yourself, and we'd both sleep easier if you learned how to handle a firearm."

"They're dangerous. Some five-year-old kid shot his little sister last week in Kissimmee."

Luca said, "That sounds like someone was irresponsible and didn't lock the gun up. You'd get a safe and use your fingerprint to open it."

"Let me think about it."

"You have to learn to protect—"

"Frank! All right already. She'll think about it."

"Okay. I just want you to be safe. That's all, honey."

"I know, Dad."

Luca's phone pinged. He looked at the screen and pumped his fist into the air.

"All right! They got him."

Mary Ann said, "Who'd they get?"

"The guy who tried to kidnap Jessie. His name is Mark Dewey, a thirty-eight-year-old punk from Fort Myers."

"Fort Myers?"

"Yeah. I have to make a call."

Luca retreated to his office. He mulled over the fact the kidnapper was from Fort Myers. The implication was a connection to the Waterside Shops crime. It wasn't surprising, but it meant his actions on the case had put his daughter at risk.

He pushed the idea of complete retirement out of his mind and called his buddy Gerry in Orlando.

"Hey, I was just gonna call you. We got the bastard."

"Thanks, I know it just happened, but when are you going to grill him?"

"He's in a room now, but he's saying he's not talking and wants a lawyer."

"Damn. What did he say when you busted him?"

"They said he didn't put up a fight, and it seemed like he expected it. Oh, they found the hood, really a cloth bag, he used in the van."

Luca shuddered at the thought that Jessie had barely escaped. "I didn't look him up, is Dewey violent?"

"No, but he's got a long rap sheet, all of them drug and theft related."

"He's an addict?"

"I don't know how bad, but a user for sure."

"I'm working a case that involves powerful people, and this Dewey character has got to be a hired hand."

"We'll see if he coughs anything up, but we're going to have to wait until the court appoints an attorney for him."

"Keep me posted on everything, okay?"

"Yeah, man, of course. This one was too close to home. When I know something, you'll know it."

Luca disconnected the call and put Mark Dewey into the state crime database. Dewey had been in trouble since his teenage years. He had been arrested seven times: three for possession and four for theft.

The new arrest was a significant upgrade in seriousness. Luca suspected Dewey had been enticed by a large payday. Money wasn't a problem for Borelli, but there was a sloppy element to hiring a small-time crook. One a person like Borelli wouldn't engage in.

Luca believed Borelli outsourced it to someone she trusted, and it was that person who cut corners. Luca wanted to make a note to send to that someone—and he'd find out who it was—a Christmas gift.

Luca called Derrick and updated him on the capture of the would-be kidnapper.

His ex-partner said, "I hope this clown spills his guts."

"I hope so. At this point he's waiting on a lawyer."

"They'll cut a deal, don't worry."

"My head says yes, but money talks, and Borelli has a ton of it. What if they made some kind of agreement, like give him a million bucks, if he has to serve time?"

Derrick said, "Kidnapping carries a long-assed sentence."

"You're right. A deal with the prosecutors will probably be made."

"It will. And then we'll find out who was running it."

"I'm not waiting for that."

"What are you talking about?"

"I'm going to see Borelli now. She's probably in early, and I want to surprise her."

"I don't think that's a good idea, Frank."

"I can't sit on my hands."

"You're interfering, pal. Let it play out."

Luca hesitated. "Maybe you're right. I'll think it over."

As soon as he ended the call, Luca pocketed his car fob, said goodbye to his family, and headed to see Borelli.

Chapter Forty-Three

The parking lot was nearly empty. Luca pulled into a spot and went inside the building housing Borelli's firm. The guard looked up from his phone and nodded.

Luca took the stairs two at a time, spilling onto Borelli's floor. The reception area was dark.

He shouted, "Hello! Elena Borelli, it's Frank Luca!"

He walked down the corridor to the door he'd seen Borelli emerge from on his last visit.

"Elena Borelli! It's Frank Luca."

A young man in a gray suit with peg-legged pants stepped into the hallway, closing the door behind him. "Please, keep it down, sir. Ms. Borelli is on a conference call with London."

"How long is it going to last?"

"It's winding down now."

"I'll wait here."

"Ms. Borelli is completely booked today."

"She is going to have to fit me in."

"But—"

"No buts. You tell her I'm not leaving until I speak with her."

"Sir, you have to understand—"

"No, you go tell her I'm here."

The man frowned and went back into the room he came out of.

Fifteen minutes later, the door opened and the young man stepped into the hall. He stuck his arm out. "You may go in, sir."

Borelli was sitting behind a large glass desk. "Good morning. Did you change your mind about my offer to help?"

Luca marched up to her desk. "I have two words for you: Mark Dewey."

"I'm sorry, I don't understand."

"Don't play dumb with me. It doesn't suit you."

"I'm not. I have no idea who Mark Dewey is."

Luca leaned over the desktop. "You hired him to kidnap my daughter."

"I certainly did not."

"You may not have directly interacted with him, but one of your minions did."

"They did no such thing."

"This will all go a lot easier if you just admit your role. No thousand-dollar-an-hour lawyer is going to save you this time."

She looked him in the eye. "I don't know what led you to make such an outrageous accusation, but I can assure you, I nor anyone at my direction had any role in the kidnapping attempt on your daughter, or anyone else for that matter."

"You can deny it all you want, but you're not going to get

away with it. The man who did it, Mark Dewey, is in custody, and we'll get him to talk."

"That's wonderful news. You'll find out I had nothing to do with him."

Luca scoffed. "Yeah, right."

"I don't know why, maybe it's my net worth or the industry I'm in, but you don't have much respect for me." She frowned before continuing, "That's fine, you're entitled to your opinion, but accusing me of taking part in a heinous crime can be considered malicious slander. I realize having a daughter at risk is emotional, so, I'll let the slander go, but please consider an accusation before verbalizing it."

"You think you're hot shit, don't you?"

"Mr. Luca, I have an extremely busy day ahead. I'd like you to leave now so I can get on with my agenda."

"Well, I wouldn't go too far if I was you. It'll look like you're fleeing and compound your problems."

Borelli's jaw dropped, and Luca turned on his heel and left.

When he stepped into the parking lot, Luca took a couple of deep breaths to slow his heart rate. He got into his car, and a text came in from Orlando. His friend Gerry wrote: *Dewey isn't talking, but a judge just signed a warrant for a search of his apartment. It also covered his phone and cell records.*

Luca smiled. They'd get the truth. He couldn't wait to see the look on Borelli's face when they slapped cuffs on her.

Driving home, Luca considered what kind of a deal Borelli might be able to strike to come clean for the Waterside crimes. A conspiracy to kidnap was a major crime, and in the most egregious cases you could be sentenced to life in prison. Was there a trade to be made between this charge and the Waterside murders that would get to the truth?

Mary Ann was swimming her laps when Luca got back to the house. Jessie was on her iPad.

His daughter asked, "Where'd you go so early?"

"Just following up on a lead."

"About what happened to me?"

"Yes. How are you doing with all this?"

"I'm fine, but I want to get back to Orlando."

"You just got here."

"I just can't leave my job."

"All I hear about is everybody is working remotely. Why can't you do that?"

"They don't really allow it."

"You told them what happened. Can't they make an exception? It's not forever, just until this blows over."

"How fast do you think it's going to be?"

"They're collecting evidence, and as soon as we know all the players in the conspiracy, it'll be safe to go back."

"How long is that going to take?"

"I don't know, but not too long. What's the matter, don't you want to hang out with your old man?"

"That's not it, I love spending time with you guys, but I'm just starting to make friends up there and—"

"So, what's his name?"

Jessie rolled her eyes. "That's not what I'm talking about."

"So, there is a guy."

"Daaad!"

"Okay, okay." Luca motioned toward the pool. "I can't believe your mother does so many laps, and every day."

"She knows she has to."

"She's got discipline."

"So do you, Dad."

"I don't know about that."

"You do."

Luca's phone vibrated. He looked at the screen. It was Detective Donovan from homicide.

"I have to grab this."

Luca swiped his phone and said, "Donnie, how are you?"

"Hey, Frank. I just heard about what happened to Jessie. Is she okay?"

"Yeah, she's fine. She's here with us now."

"Damn. That must have been scary as all hell."

"It was surreal. The Orlando PD has someone in custody. A guy from Fort Myers named Mark Dewey."

"A Lee County man?"

"Yes. I believe it's part of a conspiracy to shake me off the Waterside case."

"Really?"

"Yes, and I expect a high-profile arrest to be made in Collier County."

"Who would that be?"

Luca was about to say Borelli's name, but said, "I don't want to slander anybody at this point, but they got warrants, and they're moving fast up there."

"As damn well they should."

"If you don't mind, if there's going to be an arrest down here, I'd sure like to be there when it goes down."

"You can't be involved, Frank."

"I just want to be there. You can take them down, and after they're in cuffs, I want to look the bastard in the eye."

"Okay, I can make that happen."

Chapter Forty-Four

Luca waited as long as he could. He punched his Orlando buddy's name into his phone and hit the call button.

"Hey, Frank. I was just going to call you."

"You got something on Dewey?"

"They searched his apartment and found a burner in a cereal box. Dewey was using it to communicate with another burner. There was only one number. We triangulated the cell tower data, and using a new AI tool we got from the Israelis, nailed down the location to a property in your neck of the woods. I just got off the phone with Donovan."

"You talked to Donovan?"

"Yeah."

"When?"

"Seconds ago."

Another call came into Luca's phone. "Donovan's calling me. I got to go."

"Hey, Donnie, I just heard."

"Get on your horse, Frank. We just got a warrant, and

we're heading to 11989 Whitaker Road. It's east of Santa Barbara."

"Thanks for clueing me in, Donnie."

"Anytime. You going to make it there?"

"Wouldn't miss it for anything. Whose place is it?"

"It's owned by a towing company. The owner is a woman, Carlie Johnson."

"Does she have a record?"

"No. She's clean."

"Who the hell is it?"

"There's three structures on the property. Our warrant covers all of them as well as any vehicles on the premises."

"When are you conducting the raid?"

"The team is getting ready now. We should be on the move in thirty minutes."

"I'll see you there."

"Okay, but don't approach, stay back until I give you the go-ahead."

"Sure, I'll hang back, just don't forget that I'm out there."

LUCA SPED down Goldengate Boulevard making a turn onto Santa Barbara. He slowed as he came up to Whitaker Road and turned onto it.

A mile ahead, a patrol car was parked diagonally across the road, blocking access. Luca came to a stop, and a young officer spun his finger in the air.

"Police activity. The road is closed. Please turn around."

Luca explained why he was there, and the officer radioed Donovan. The officer backed up his car, and Luca parked in front of the targeted property behind other patrol cars. A tilted mailbox bore the names of Johnson and JR Towing.

Luca kept his phone in hand, waiting for a text from Donovan. After twenty minutes passed, Luca got out of his car. He scanned the property. On it was a one-story home, a shed, an old Airstream RV, and a trailer.

The trailer had three tow trucks parked in front of it. Luca surmised it served as the office for the towing company.

The door to the Airstream swung open. A uniformed officer stepped out of the rounded, aluminum travel trailer. As he lit a cigarette, Luca sent a text to Donovan.

"Hey, Donnie, what's going on?"

Twenty seconds went by before a reply pinged: *You here?*

Yes.

Donovan replied: *Come over to the RV, you got to see this.*

Luca started jogging. The officer put up a hand and Luca said, "Donovan told me to come over."

"Hold on there!"

Donovan popped his head outside the door. "He's with me. Come on, Frank."

Luca stepped into the RV, and Donovan said, "Over here."

Donovan stood in front of an opening that led to a small bedroom. "You sure got under somebody's skin, Frank."

"Borelli?"

Luca paused at the threshold. The lighting was dim. He stepped into the sleeping quarters.

"What the hell?"

"Quite the shrine, isn't it?"

The wall to his left was plastered with photographs of Luca. Some were grainy shots from a distance, others closer and intimate. Luca in his car in front of Publix, Luca walking alongside Mary Ann into a doctor's office.

His eyes drifted to a picture of himself, Mary Ann, and Jessie walking to the entrance of a church. It was from last Christmas. Then he saw the picture of Jessie walking out of her apartment building.

Blood thudded in Luca's ears. "Who the hell lives here?"

"Herman Welke."

Luca felt as if he'd been punched in the gut. "Where is that motherjumper?"

"We've got a team in transit to where he works."

"Where is that?"

"Let us handle it, Frank."

Luca took a step toward Donovan. "That bastard tried to kidnap my Jessie!"

"I know, Frank. You gotta calm down. We should have him in custody any minute now."

"Tell them to pump lead into the bastard's head!"

"The important thing is we're going to nail him, and he's not going to get out this time."

"You better be right about that."

Donovan's phone rang. He answered it and after a short conversation hung up.

"They got Welke. He didn't resist."

"I can't believe he came after my daughter. Christ almighty!"

"It's going to be okay, buddy. Go home. I'll keep you posted."

Luca took a long look around the RV and left.

Trudging to his car, he considered the potential charges Welke would face. They carried long sentences, but judges had latitude.

His mind careened to Judge Bolt and the questionable dismissal he'd granted. Then Borelli crashed into his thoughts.

Luca shook his head. He had been certain the financier was behind the attempted kidnapping. It was the second time he was wrong about her.

He got in his car and exhaled. Luca pounded the steering wheel. His focus on Borelli had blinded him. He'd discounted Welke, and it almost cost him everything. He inhaled deeply and steadied himself.

Twisting the rearview mirror, he took a long look at himself. He'd gotten lucky, and relying on luck was dangerous.

He straightened the mirror and called Mary Ann, letting her know the threat had been eliminated.

Luca took his time driving home. He tried to focus on the fact Welke was in custody but couldn't excuse the mistake he'd made in not following up on a man he knew had vowed to get revenge.

He mustered all the positive energy he could summon but still found himself faking it as he entered his home.

Mary Ann met him in the hallway. They embraced.

She said, "I'm so glad this is over."

"I told you not to worry."

"Where's Jessie?"

"She's taking a shower. I told her we'd go out to celebrate tonight because she's leaving in the morning to go back to Orlando."

Luca felt he should be going to confession, not to celebrate. "She's going back so soon?"

"That presentation she was going to do over Google Meets, she'd rather do it in person."

"Where do you want to go?"
"Jessica wants to try that new place in Mercato: Violi."
"It's Greek, right?"
"Yes, and everyone said it's good."

DURING DINNER LUCA tried hard to stay in the present moment, but it wasn't easy as his mind kept drifting back to the close call. He excused himself to use the bathroom.

He made his way to the restroom, admiring the transformation the restaurant had undergone. He glanced at the bougainvillea hanging in the corner and did a double take.

Sitting in a booth with three other diners was Judge Bolt. Luca slowed his walk down, knowing the Waterside case was now front and center. Again.

Chapter Forty-Five

Luca parked in the Alamo's lot and walked from the shooting range to the white building housing the Butcher. A row of exotic sports cars and two baby-blue Bentleys were parked outside the members-only dining club.

As Luca approached the entrance to the exclusive retreat, the door opened. Out stepped a man whose biceps stretched the fabric of his dark suit.

"Welcome to Butcher, Mr. Luca."

Surprised they knew his name, Luca nodded.

"This way, sir. Ms. Borelli is in the Crystal Lounge."

Luca stepped into an opulent foyer. It reinforced his belief that it was hard to show you made it when you lived in Naples.

A cascade of "Good evening, sir" followed him into an artfully lit lounge featuring crystal lighting fixtures. The room felt like something out of a movie.

Elena Borelli was sitting in a corner club chair. She smiled and set her reddish cocktail on the mirrored table.

Luca sarcastically said, "Good evening."

"I assume you haven't been here before."

"No, ma'am. But I got to say, this place is swanky."

A bow-tied server approached. "What is the gentleman having this evening?"

"A seltzer, please."

"Wouldn't you like to experience one of our signature cocktails, sir?"

"No thanks."

The server nodded and left.

Luca said, "Thank you for seeing me."

"It's my pleasure. Would you like to stay for dinner?"

"No, ma'am."

The server set down a tall glass of sparkling water and left.

Luca was tempted to dig into one of the bowls of nuts and dried fruits inches away from his drink when Borelli said, "I had my assistant do a little research on you, and you built quite a reputation before retiring."

"I was just doing my job, ma'am."

"It's more than that, isn't it?"

Luca shrugged.

"You take it personally, don't you?"

"I have a vision, and though I know it reads like a Hallmark movie, I believe we can live in a supportive community where the biggest crime is some kid taking another's ball."

"It sounds idyllic."

"It's the goal."

"How is your daughter?"

"She's fine. I'm sorry about the things I said but . . ."

"No apologies necessary. I realize how emotional it must have been."

"Thank you. Look, I wanted to ask you about David Flan."

She took a sip of her drink. "What about him?"

"How do you know him?"

"I'm one of the rare ones, someone who was actually born in Naples. There's not many of us, and I met David in middle school, though it may have been grammar school."

"You went to Community School together."

"We did, but I must say, we weren't the best of friends."

"The last time I asked about him you cut off our conversation."

"Are you certain about that? It feels like you're implying something."

"Maybe it was a coincidence, but it felt like you were hiding something."

"I don't recall what precipitated the end of our chat, but I can assure you there was no agenda behind it."

"You said you weren't the best of friends with Flan."

"That's true."

"That is at odds with the investments you made in several businesses he started."

Borelli exhaled and leaned forward. "Allow me to explain it, but first, let me use you as analogy."

"Go right ahead."

"When you recovered the drug money in the case right before you retired, you received a reward. I believe it was around ten million dollars."

"That's close enough."

"I'm willing to wager that you received more than a few requests from friends for monetary assistance. Am I right?"

"There were a couple."

The server swooped in. "May I refresh your drinks?"

Borelli said, "No, thank you."

As the waiter left, Borelli said, "I'm a local girl who made good. There is no shortage of ultra-wealthy residents in Naples, but few who were born here. I've exceeded my expectations, and maybe some of it is guilt, but I find it difficult to turn down requests. Especially from childhood friends."

As Borelli picked up her drink, Luca said, "And what other childhood friends have you helped?"

Drink in midair, Borelli paused before recovering. "Some would say my philanthropic efforts haven't gone far enough, but I'm comfortable with the contributions I've made and continue to make."

"You're a super successful businesswoman, right?"

"I've done well."

"I just don't understand why you'd continue to give and lose money to Flan."

"As I said, it could be guilt playing a role. David never achieved much."

"But over and over again? It doesn't make sense."

Borelli smiled. "The media portrays me as an ice queen, but I'm more of a softy."

"Why did you try to hide your investments in his businesses?"

"Hide? I don't believe that is accurate."

"You created a web of LLCs."

"They were the workings of our legal team to protect me from possible lawsuits."

"David Flan was involved in the Waterside Shops robbery."

Borelli looked Luca in the eye. "Is that so? I've never heard that before."

"David Flan and three fellow students at the Community School committed the robbery and killed two in the process."

"Since Mr. Flan has passed, may I ask why you believe he did something that frankly is out of character, as far as I know him?"

"I'm not going to comment on an active investigation."

Borelli checked her watch. "I'm famished. I didn't have an opportunity to have lunch today, and this drink is having an effect. Are you sure you don't want to join me?"

"No, ma'am."

Borelli stood. "It was nice to see you and good luck with the case."

Luca sat in his car replaying the conversation with Borelli. The woman was good, nearly flawless. She didn't give him anything, but the feeling she was involved in the Waterside murders hadn't gone away.

Borelli had a weakness, and it was hubris.

Chapter Forty-Six

Luca sat behind his desk. He reasoned that he only needed to crack one of the four people who pulled the robbery job. If Flan had been one of them, he was left with three others.

There was something fishy going on between Judge Bolt and Cindy Clermont that kept them in the running. Borelli, successful and self-assured, had the smarts and means to stay undetected for twenty years and couldn't be discounted.

Ernest Rigo fit the profile but had an alibi Luca needed to vet. Loretta Gulliver appeared to be lily-white, but Luca had never spoken to her. All he knew was the woman lived like a nomad. Gulliver lived aboard a forty-foot sailboat, constantly traveling along the coastline as far west as Texas and up to South Carolina.

Gulliver's mother had died fifteen years ago. The death had shaken the woman out of her surveying job. Gulliver quickly sold the family home, bought the boat, and began drifting from one seaside town to another.

Luca put another call into her number and promised

himself he'd write a note and mail it to the post office box she kept in Bonita Springs.

Conrad Bolt plated the scrambled eggs he'd made and put them on the table. After sprinkling them with salt and pepper, the judge tapped his iPad and opened the *Naples Daily News* app.

The lead story covered the expected opening of the new Naples Pier. It had taken a year longer and was slightly over budget.

Bolt hadn't visited the pier in years and had no plans to check out the new design. He scooped up the last of his eggs and scrolled to the next story.

Bolt shoveled the eggs into his mouth and read the headline above the next story:

"Livingston Fatal Accident Ruled Possible Homicide"

Bolt's fork clattered to the floor when he read the first line:

The fatal accident that took the life of David Flan has been declared a possible homicide.

Bolt swallowed and continued reading:

The Collier County Sheriff's Office has opened an investigation into the deadly accident. The one-vehicle crash was deemed suspicious after an examination of the auto revealed a possibility the auto was tampered with.

Judge Bolt shoved the iPad aside. Mind racing, he considered that if Flan had been murdered, who killed him? And why?

Bolt had gone away for college and law school and had purposefully avoided most of his old contacts. He hadn't spoken to or seen Flan in over fifteen years. He had no idea what kind of life his old schoolmate had led.

He'd heard Flan had started several businesses and none had been successful, but other than that, he had no idea if Flan was using drugs or had run with the wrong crowd.

Bolt assured himself Flan's death was unrelated to what they'd done as high school seniors. He put away his iPad and went to get ready for another day on the bench.

An hour later, he greeted his secretary and went into his office. Sitting in the center of his desk was the day's docket.

Bolt read the list of cases he'd preside over. His gaze lingered on a sentencing hearing for a man convicted for distributing drugs. Unless something dramatic was presented by the defense, Bolt would assess a prison term in the upper range of the guidelines.

The intercom beeped. It was his secretary.

"You have a call, Your Honor."

"Who is it?"

"Frank Luca."

A lump formed in Bolt's throat.

"Shall I pass him through?"

"No. I don't have the time. I need to finish writing a ruling."

"Okay, sir."

Bolt collapsed into his chair. What did the investigator want? Had the former detective come up with something on the Waterside case? Maybe Luca discovered he and Flan were friends and wanted to talk to him about David Flan's suspicious death.

Bolt tried to assure himself that interviewing friends of a murder victim was protocol, but it was difficult to ignore the pit in his stomach. If things were truly unraveling, the window to cut a deal was closing.

There was a knock on his door.

"It's time, Your Honor."

Bolt slipped into his robes and tried to steel himself for another day on the bench.

THE SUN HAD STARTED its descent when Bolt turned onto his street. A car was parked in front of his house. The judge slowed down. Who was it?

As he got closer, he said, "Damn."

The private investigator was behind the wheel of the car. Bolt quickly dismissed the idea of driving past the car, and turned into his driveway. As his garage door rose, Bolt looked in the rearview mirror; Luca had gotten out of his car.

Bolt released his grip on the steering wheel and told himself to be calm. He stepped out of his car.

Luca was waiting on the driveway. "Hello, Judge. I need a couple of minutes of your time."

Bolt frowned. "I really don't have the time."

"It'll only take a minute."

"I've got to be somewhere." As soon as the words tumbled out, Bolt knew it sounded lame. "Oh, all right, but please make it quick."

"Thanks."

"Follow me."

Luca stayed behind Bolt as the judge went into the house through the garage. The alarm beeped and Bolt tapped on the keypad, quieting the system.

"We can sit where we talked before."

"Sounds good. I promise to be quick."

They sat opposite each other. Bolt said, "What can I do for you this time?"

"I'll get right to it."

Bolt stiffened. "Okay."

"You knew David Flan."

"I did, but it was a very long time ago."

"When you went to the Community School."

"Yes, the good old days."

"Your other friend, Elena Borelli, also knew him, as did Cynthia Clermont and Loretta Gulliver."

"We were all classmates. I'm sorry, but I don't see the relevancy in a twenty-year-old association."

"David Flan was killed in a car crash."

"What a terrible tragedy."

"He was murdered."

"I saw something in this morning's paper about the accident being suspicious, not a homicide."

"All the details of the investigation have not been made public."

"What happened?"

"His brakes were tampered with."

"Oh my God. Who could have done something like that?"

"That's what I'm here to ask you. Who do you think could be behind it?"

"I don't know anything. I haven't seen David since we were teenagers."

"What about anyone else you know?"

"I really don't have any ideas on who or the why for that matter."

"What about Elena Borelli?"

"Elena? I'm sorry, but that seems preposterous. Borelli operates in a completely different world than David did."

"Not really."

Bolt could feel the blood draining from his head. He cleared his throat. "What are you implying?"

"Elena Borelli put up the money for each and every one of Flan's failed businesses."

Bolt leaned forward. "She did what?"

"Borelli gave Flan the money to start the businesses he did. She set up LLCs and used them to funnel money to Flan. The question is why."

"She has more than ample resources to fund a friend's, uh, old friend's business ventures. It shouldn't matter to her if they fail."

"Do you think it's possible she had him killed?"

"What? Why in the world would she risk everything she has achieved when she could simply refuse to give him any more money?"

"To protect a secret."

Bolt's Adam's apple bobbed as he said, "Well, I don't know anything about any secret, or who—or for that matter, why—anyone would want to harm David."

"Are you sure about that?"

"Absolutely." Bolt stood. "I've got to go, I have early dinner plans on Marco Island."

Luca got up. "Okay. Thank you for your time."

Bolt opened the front door and Luca stepped outside. As the door closed behind him, Luca put his hand on the door and pushed it back open.

He looked Bolt in the eye. "If you know something, now

is the time to come clean. You wait any longer, you won't be able to make a deal."

Chapter Forty-Seven

Bolt swung his legs off the bed. He'd been lying there ruminating for hours. He didn't put a light on and padded into the kitchen.

He blinked as his laptop came alive, and navigated to the Gemini AI app. Bolt paused as he considered what to ask.

The judge typed into the prompt box: *If a person who participated in a twenty-year-old crime where someone was killed came forward, could they get leniency if they identified the others involved?*

Bolt held his breath as the AI tool began to respond: *Yes, in the United States, someone who participated in a homicide from twenty years ago could still face prosecution, as murder generally has no statute of limitations under federal law or in any state. However, by coming forward and providing information to identify and prosecute others involved, they could potentially negotiate leniency through a cooperation agreement with prosecutors.*

This might include a plea deal for a reduced charge (e.g., from murder to manslaughter), a lighter sentence, or in rare cases, immunity, depending on factors like the value of their testimony, their level of involvement, the jurisdiction, and the prosecutor's discretion.

Such deals are common in criminal cases, including cold homicides, to secure convictions against higher-priority targets, but there's no guarantee of leniency—it's ultimately up to the authorities.

He read it twice, pausing at the word homicide. Then he read the last line twice. Bolt knew plea deals were common, but this was a homicide, and as it stated, there was no guarantee and it was up to the people in charge.

Bolt had an excellent relationship with the law enforcement community, and that would help. However, the wild card was whether there would be any fallout from Bolt's betrayal. He was sure some would want him to burn in hell for the deception he'd engaged in.

The judge clicked on the dialog box offering examples of plea deals. The first two were Mafia cases involving "Sammy the Bull" Gravano and Henry Hill from the *Goodfellas* film. Following that were a couple of high-profile political cases.

Bolt's spirits lifted when he read a heading for cold cases and homicides but plummeted when he saw that cooperation deals in long-unsolved murders were less common. There were a couple of cases cited, but those deals highlighted how prosecutors prioritize securing evidence against "bigger fish." It clearly stated the outcomes varied based on the value of the cooperation, the defendant's role, and prosecutorial discretion. Depressingly, it stressed that leniency was not guaranteed.

Bolt was deflated. But he remembered a cold case that had just been solved. Joseph Godcharles had been murdered in 2012, and the case had remained unsolved, but advances in DNA had led to the arrest of Julie Krinisky in December of 2025.

Though no one had come forward to make a deal, Bolt took solace in the celebratory mood the solve provided. The parade of public officials looking to associate themselves with the persistence shown by a detective reminded Bolt that the system loved to close cold cases, especially homicides.

Bolt knew the chances of reaching a plea agreement where he didn't have to serve time was slim. The thought of going to prison, where he'd have a bullseye on his back, was frightening.

He tried to summon the discipline he'd shown in law school to focus on researching cases he could cite when negotiating a deal, but it was a battle, and he was losing.

LUCA STEPPED into Loretta Gulliver's apartment. He pointed to a photograph on the wall of a bear who'd just snagged a fish in midair.

"That's some shot."

Loretta Gulliver said, "It was taken by Thomas Mangelsen. His work is magical. It captures the essence of nature."

Luca nodded, wishing he had some of the patience the photographer had.

Gulliver touched a finger to the frame and tapped it gently. She shook her head, adjusting the picture by an unnoticeable increment. She headed to the tiny kitchen, fiddling with a pastel drawing as well.

"Would you like something to drink?"

"A water would be nice, thanks."

She opened the refrigerator. Water bottles were shelved in a line the Chinese Army would be proud of.

Luca thought this was a woman who'd break out in a sweat if she found a sock on the floor. He also knew it was a sign of being organized to the point of OCD, which was something useful if you were hiding your involvement in a crime.

As she handed off the bottle of Poland Spring, Luca gave a thought to Gulliver being the one to craft the plan to rob the Van Dores Diamond Showroom.

Luca sat in a wooden bistro chair that could have been designed by McDonald's; it became more uncomfortable the longer you sat in it.

"You said you wanted to ask me about people I went to school with."

"Yes. I'm working an old case, and the names of a few people you went to the Community School with came up."

She frowned. "That was quite some time ago."

"Tell me about it. I've been out of high school a lot longer than you."

"Well, you don't look it."

Luca smiled. "Flattery is underrated."

"How did you come to find me?"

"From pictures in the yearbooks."

She nodded slowly.

"When did you go out of town?"

"A couple of weeks ago."

Luca roughly calculated that it was a week after he'd started his investigation. Had she gone out of town to avoid him?

"You've been away for a while."

Another nod.

"Where'd you go?"

"To a retreat in California, outside of San Francisco."

"Sounds nice. What kind of retreat? Like a spa thingy?"

"No. A retreat to help with self-conscious feelings that prevent you from leading a full life."

"Like worrying what other people think?"

"Not really, more like dealing with painful emotional feelings."

"I'm sorry for asking so many questions, but I'm interested. What kind of feelings?"

"Like remorse."

Luca rolled the word around; it was another word for guilt. Was the guilt from taking two lives the root of her unhappiness?

"Well, I commend you for working to improve yourself. I could use an examination, but I'm afraid of what I'd find."

She giggled. "It's something everyone should do on a regular basis."

"I'll keep it in mind. You were close with Cynthia Clermont in high school."

"Not that close. We're very different people."

"In what way?"

"This is going to sound terrible, but Cindy is a small-town girl, you know, more interested in gossip, and lacks an imagination. I hear she got into drugs, and frankly, I'm not surprised. It was the only way for her to get her thrills."

"And what did you do for thrills?"

"It's a big world. I like to test myself, try things I never did before."

Instead of asking if that included participating in a

daring robbery, Luca said, "I'm not much for getting outside of my comfort zone."

"You should try harder."

"Trying hard, I do. I just stick to what I know how to do."

"Well, you had to be uncomfortable when you were first learning how to do what you do."

"I'm from a different time. We just toughed it out, but enough of the New Age stuff. What about Conrad Bolt?"

"He's a judge these days."

"Yes. How did he get along with Cynthia?"

"Oh, they were as black and white as it gets."

"But they seemed to be close in high school."

"I guess so."

"What about Elena Borelli?"

"She's superrich."

"She is. How was she in school?"

"Bossy."

"Do you remember the Waterside Shops robbery?"

"No. What was that?"

"You don't remember two people getting killed during a robbery when you were a senior?"

"No. I don't dwell on the negative."

"Why did you leave Naples after graduating high school? You didn't go to college, so why the move to live on a boat and move around?"

"I had my reasons, and they're none of your business."

"Did you have anything to do with the Waterside robbery?"

Gulliver stood. "It's time for you to leave."

"Answer me, were you involved?"

She palmed her phone. "Please leave, or I'll call the police."

Luca got into his car and called Derrick.

"Hey, I need a little help."

"What do you need?"

"I finally got to talk to Loretta Gulliver, and I'm not sure anything is there. Do you have the time to dig into her?"

"I got it. No worries."

Luca drove off, wondering if there would ever be a time when he had no worries.

Chapter Forty-Eight

After a second sleepless night, Bolt made a call.

A receptionist answered on the first ring. "Good morning, Horizon Investments. How may I assist you?

Bolt deepened his voice. "Elena Borelli, please."

"Who may I say is calling?"

"Mr. Bojangles."

"Ms. Borelli is extremely busy this morning, is she expecting your call?"

"Yes."

"Hold on, sir."

The receptionist used the intercom to contact Elena.

"Ma'am, there's a Mr. Bojangles on the line for you. He said you were expecting his call."

Elena froze. "Mr. Bojangles?"

"Yes, ma'am."

It was the song Conrad Bolt had sung in a junior high school play and their code word.

"Please get a number and I'll call him back."

"Yes, ma'am."

Later that afternoon, Elena unlocked a cabinet and took a burner phone out. She punched in the number Mr. Bojangles had left.

Bolt answered the call. "This is, uh, Mr. B, I mean, Connie. Is that you?"

"I'm going to a novena at St. Agnes. Six o'clock sharp."

"Uh, okay."

Elena hung up. She realized Bolt was scared, and people who were afraid made mistakes.

BOLT SCANNED the cavernous main church of St. Agnes. A group of women were scattered over the pews closest to the altar. In the second-to-last row of the left section he spied Elena Borelli.

Bolt walked along the rear of the church, estimating it could hold three thousand or more parishioners. The judge shuffled into a row and sat next to Borelli, who was wearing a black veil.

She reached for the kneeler, pulled it down and kneeled.

Bolt followed her lead, whispering, "I'm sorry, but there's been several developments."

"Do we need to step outside?"

"I think it's best we do."

"I'm parked to the right of the main entrance. Wait before coming out."

Borelli made the sign of the cross and slipped out of the pew.

After waiting five minutes, Bolt left the church and got into Borelli's Maserati.

He said, "Again, I'm sorry, but this couldn't wait."

Borelli silently stared out the windshield.

Bolt said, "That investigator Luca came to see me again. He was asking about David. He said it wasn't an accident and that somebody murdered him."

"I read about that."

"He wanted to know if I knew who could have murdered him."

"And?"

"I said I had no idea. But then he said you had given David money to start every one of his businesses. I was shocked. How come you never told me that?"

"It's none of your business."

"Come on, Elena, why would you do that? I don't understand why. It's a red flag, and now Luca is asking questions."

"I do what is necessary to protect us. Just like you did with Cindy."

"That's different. I had no choice but to dismiss the charges against Clermont. She said she was going to the police if I didn't."

"It was a foolish move, Conrad. It established a connection for the world to see."

"What was I supposed to do? Cindy isn't stable. She's a drug user and they'll do anything."

"Conrad, you should let me handle things."

"But I told you and you didn't—"

"I said let me handle things."

"But what about her boyfriend, that cretin Perez is up on murder charges, and the state's evidence is compelling, to say the least. Cindy said if I don't—"

"Did you hear what I said?"

"Yes."

"Did you understand what I said?"

"Okay, okay. I'll let you handle it. But what about Luca, the investigator? He's on to us."

Borelli frowned. "You're trying my patience, Connie."

"I'm sorry, but I need to know what you're going to do about everything."

"Goodbye, Connie."

Bolt got out of the car and Borelli motored away.

Chapter Forty-Nine

The fluorescent lights of Cell Block D hummed. It was the middle of the night, but Willie Perez was sitting on the edge of his cot. He wondered if his girlfriend, Cindy, was going to be able to smuggle the money he needed for the drugs that made the dungeon tolerable.

The three a.m. shift change was always orchestrated chaos. A few cells down the line, a prisoner was screaming about needing his meds.

The electronic noise of the unlocking of Perez's cell door was something Perez wasn't expecting for another four hours. He turned to the opening, expecting to see an angry guard.

Instead there stood a large man in an ill-fitting uniform. He was wearing gloves. The toothbrush in his hand was unmistakable.

Perez jumped to his feet. "Hey, man. Leave me alone."

The man moved with lightning speed. He slammed a hand into Perez's throat, pinning him against the cinder block wall.

Perez jerked as the sharpened toothbrush entered his abdomen. Perez flailed as the man repeatedly stabbed him. As his vision began to speckle with white stars, he dropped his arms.

The man stepped back and speared Perez in the heart area. As Perez slid to the floor, the assassin slipped out of the cell.

***

Bolt had to reread the petition before him. He was having trouble concentrating since receiving a call from Luca a few hours ago. He didn't answer it, and the investigator had left a message asking to meet again.

Bolt was afraid to talk to Luca. He knew the current state of things were dangerous. He hadn't settled on how long to give Borelli to manage the crisis before taking the unpalatable step to act on his own.

There was a soft knock on his office door. "Your Honor."

It was his secretary. "Come in."

She stepped inside and set a document on his desk. "Here's next month's calendar. It's been revised."

"On such short notice?"

"I questioned it but was told a defendant died and an assault and battery case was reassigned from Judge Williams to fill the slot. Poor Judge Williams, I hear his cancer is back."

"I spoke to him yesterday. He's confident they caught it early enough."

"That's good news."

"It is. What defendant passed away?"

"I can't recall the name, but it was a homicide case."

The phone in the outer office began ringing, and the secretary said, "I have to get that."

She closed the door behind her, and Bolt picked up the document. His gaze went straight to a date starred in red ink.

The judge smiled when he read the name marked deceased.

It was Willie Perez, Cindy Clermont's boyfriend.

Bolt couldn't believe his luck and whispered, "Thank you, God."

The judge wouldn't have to worry about Clermont threatening him if he didn't find a way to dismiss the case against her boyfriend. And it was a good thing, because the evidence against him was substantial.

Bolt sat back, reveling in the good news. Wishing he had someone to tell, he thought of Borelli. She'd be pleased to know this problem had resolved itself.

Bolt stiffened when he wondered how Perez had died. Had Borelli played a role? It was far-fetched. Borelli had resources, but not the kind needed to reach someone in prison.

The judge had ample contacts in the Collier County Corrections Department. He picked up the phone and made a call.

"Corrections."

"This is Judge Bolt. I'd like to speak to Chris Roberts."

"Hold on, sir."

The head of the corrections department answered. "How are you, Your Honor?"

"Good. I understand one Willie Perez, an inmate at Immokalee, passed away late last night. Was it a natural death?"

"Yes. No, it wasn't a natural death. Perez was murdered. We're investigating this as we speak."

Bolt belched up some of his lunch. He swallowed and said, "Was it at the hands of another inmate?"

"Frankly, we're not sure. The surveillance cameras haven't given us anything to work with. It happened during an early morning shift change, and though I hate to think it's true, it appears coordinated."

Bolt's mouth was dry. "Did Perez have any encounters with other inmates?"

"He was previously assaulted. We're interviewing several prisoners to see if this is related to the prior incident."

"Keep me posted. The integrity of the judicial system must be maintained."

Bolt held his head in his hands. Based on what the head of the corrections department said, this was not a beef between inmates. The fact the video surveillance system hadn't identified who the culprit was meant that it was a professional conspiracy that had been responsible for taking the life of Perez.

The knot in his stomach began to tighten. Bolt had to act.

Chapter Fifty

Valise in hand, Lieutenant Casper was shown into Judge Bolt's chambers.

Sporting a military haircut and piercing blue eyes, the head of the sheriff's investigative unit took Bolt's hand. "Your Honor, it's always nice to see you."

"The pleasure is mine. How is the family?"

"Good. Billy is a senior now, so we only have one more year of paying for college."

"Liberation Day is approaching."

Casper smiled. "It sure is, but boy, time is flying a little too quickly for me."

"For me as well." Bolt looked at the briefcase Casper had set on a chair. "Were you able to get what is needed?"

"Yes, sir."

Bolt lowered his voice. "I'd appreciate if this stayed between the two of us. I don't even want my office to know about it."

"You don't have to worry about me, sir."

"Of course, if a bribe is offered, then it'll become a

matter of public record, but I don't want to besmirch anyone's reputation based on innuendo."

"We're on the same page, Your Honor."

"Excellent. Shall we get started?"

"Please remove your shirt."

As Bolt unbuttoned his white shirt, Casper opened the briefcase. "I brought one of the new-generation recorders. It's self-contained, and the audio quality it captures is excellent."

He held up a little rectangular device smaller than a credit card.

Casper pointed to a chair. "Why don't you sit here?"

Bare-chested, Bolt eased himself into a chair.

Casper took a roll of medical adhesive tape and said, "I'm going to tape this high on your sternum, just below the collarbone."

"As long as it's not visible."

"It won't be."

Casper held the recording unit in the V of Bolt's chest and taped it in place. "That should do it."

"That was quick."

"Put your shirt on and we'll test it for printing."

"Printing?"

"To see if the device causes a bulge you can see through your shirt."

Bolt buttoned his shirt and tucked it into his pants.

Casper said, "Nothing is visible. Move around."

Bolt walked around and turned to face Casper.

"Still good. Now, lean forward."

Bolt did as the cop instructed.

"Perfect. Now, sit."

Bolt sat.

"It looks good."

"How do I activate it?"

"Are you driving to a meetup location?"

"Yes."

"Good. I recommend you activate it in the staging area, like the parking lot, before you get out of your car. At that time, you can state the day, time, location, and who you're meeting."

"I understand."

"You're leaving soon, right?"

"Yes."

Casper took his phone out. "They got an app for everything these days." He tapped his phone and said, "You're good to go. It's counting down to voice activation mode."

"Thank you. Please remember to keep this confidential."

As Casper picked up his briefcase, he said, "Of course. Good luck."

As the cop left, Bolt recited a silent prayer that it would all work out.

Chapter Fifty-One

The boat ride from the Naples City Dock to Port Royal was faster than Bolt remembered. The captain slowed as he approached the dock for Borelli's mansion.

Once the captain tied up the boat, he extended his hand to Bolt and helped him onto the dock.

"I've been told to wait here."

Bolt nodded and started up the slope to the home. He turned toward the water and said aloud that he was at Borelli's home and noted the time was 4 p.m.

The pool deck was empty, as was the oversized lanai. He climbed four stairs and a uniformed woman opened one of the giant sliding doors that made up the rear of the home.

"Ms. Borelli will meet you in the library."

Following the woman, Bolt heard two people talking. It sounded like Borelli was talking to a man.

The woman opened a pair of carved doors revealing a double-storied space lined with bookshelves. A pair of comfortable club chairs and floor lamps faced a fireplace, and a second pair of chairs and lamps backed up to a window with a view of a garden.

"May I get you something to drink?"

"No, thank you."

The woman backed out of the room, closing the doors as she did. Bolt circled the room reading the spines of the books begging to be read. He pulled a volume of Solzhenitsyn's *The Gulag Archipelago* off the shelf.

It had been years since Bolt had read the literary investigation of the Soviet forced-labor-camp system. As he paged through the second volume, the doors to the library opened.

Bolt's smile disappeared when he saw Borelli's face was dripping with disgust. The financier closed the doors and motioned to the seating area by the window.

Bolt waited until Borelli chose a chair before sitting opposite. He perched himself on the edge of the chair to get the best audio quality possible.

"I'm sorry to bother you again, but I had to talk to you."

Borelli glared at him but remained silent.

"I realize meeting is not optimal, but I'm concerned."

"Spit it out, Conrad."

Bolt said, "Cindy's boyfriend, Willie Perez, was murdered in jail."

"And wasn't he the one giving you grief?"

"Yes, he was, but I didn't want the man to end up dead."

"People are killed every minute of every day. It's not out of the ordinary."

"Did you have anything to do with what happened to Cindy's boyfriend?"

"You came crying to me."

"That didn't mean—"

"I told you I would handle things, didn't I?"

"Yes, but—"

"You want to keep our little secret? Do you want to stay on the bench?"

"Of course, but it's just that things have, uh, escalated."

Borelli sneered. "What, do you think it was luck that kept us from being discovered?"

"No, but first David and now—"

"They represented risks I couldn't allow, and just like the fence, they had to be eliminated."

Bolt's eyes widened. "You eliminated the man we sold the jewelry to?"

"For a judge, you're exceedingly naive."

"Well, I'm not cold and calculating like you."

"And you wouldn't be free if it weren't for me."

"I can't believe all this. I had no idea."

"Again, your naivety is stunning."

"What is Cindy going to do?"

"She has no idea of the lengths I've gone to protect us."

"But she threatened me with going to the police, she's unstable."

Borelli mocked. "She knew you were weak and that you'd cave in to her demands."

"So, you have it all managed."

Borelli crossed her legs but said nothing.

"And what about the investigator, Luca? He called me this morning. He's not going away."

The financier stood. "It's time for you to go back, Connie."

"But—"

She pushed the doors open and said, "The boat is waiting for you."

Bolt heard her heels clicking on the stone floor as she

disappeared into the home. The judge got out of his chair and walked to the doorway.

As he stepped in the threshold, a man appeared. He put his hand on Bolt's shoulder.

"Get back inside."

"What do you want?"

"Just a security precaution, Your Honor."

The man took a wand and waved it over the judge's body.

Bolt tried to step around the man, saying, "I'm leaving."

"We can do this the easy way . . ."

"Get out of my way. Elena!"

The man reached into his jacket and pulled out a pistol. "Shut up and do as I say."

"Take it easy, I don't want any trouble."

"Take off your shirt."

"What? That's ridiculous."

"Take it off."

"Elena! Call your dog off!"

The man put the barrel under Bolt's jaw. "Take your jacket off and unbutton your shirt."

Trembling, Bolt removed his jacket and then started to unbutton his shirt.

"Ouch," Bolt said as the man ripped the recording device off his chest.

The man examined the unit and Bolt said, "I can explain."

"Shut up. Let this be a warning to you. Next time you won't be so lucky."

"Okay, okay. I don't want any trouble."

"Get dressed and get out of here."

Bolt pulled his jacket on and buttoned his shirt as he left the house. He jogged to the dock and leapt onto the boat before the captain had a chance to help him board.

Chapter Fifty-Two

As the boat pulled away from Borelli's dock, Bebe held up the device he'd taken off Bolt.

"It's a wire, per se. It's a self-contained recording unit."

Borelli asked, "How is the technology?"

"A couple of generations behind, standard LE issuance."

"Do you think he'll be a problem going forward?"

The former Mossad officer said, "Based on the way he was sweating, I think he'll heed the warning."

"I agree, he'll toe the line."

"In any case, my advice would be to limit contact to an absolute minimum and say nothing you'd wouldn't say in public."

"I'm always careful."

"Does Bolt have anything incriminating?"

"Nothing."

"Good. If he tries to cut some kind of deal, he's going to need evidence and someone to corroborate it."

"There's only Clermont who could back him up, and I believe that would never happen."

"But it's in the realm of the possible?"

"Yes. But highly doubtful."

"We'll have to keep a close eye on this."

"Yes. And let's move up what we discussed about bringing you inside the company. I'd like you close, and the timing is right to end this cloak-and-dagger thing."

"That's your call."

"I'd feel better, and you'll get the monetary guarantees you wanted."

BOLT PULLED into his garage and shut the motor off. He hit the garage door switch and kept his eyes on the rearview mirror. When the door finished closing, the judge got out of his car and went into his house.

He disarmed the alarm system and quickly rearmed it to the stay setting. Bolt went around the house, checking that the doors were locked and closing the shades and drapery.

The judge sat in the darkened family room. His plan to catch Borelli on tape had gone terribly. Not only had he failed to get something to trade in on a plea deal, but the financier and her security detail had discovered the attempt.

Borelli had orchestrated the deaths of the man they fenced the jewelry to, Clermont's boyfriend, and David Flan, one of the team members he and Borelli had assembled to hold up the diamond store.

Was he next in line for elimination?

He and Borelli were far different than Clermont and Flan. He hadn't created a problem for Borelli. The dismissal had brought unwanted attention to him and Clermont, but

Clermont was the instigator. If anyone should be next, it was Clermont, not him.

Bolt thought killing a judge was dangerous and a possible connection to the crimes they'd committed. It could possibly be pieced together by someone tenacious like Luca.

If he was going to be murdered, he wanted to make sure Borelli would be found out. Maybe he could document everything down and give it to a lawyer, who would release the information to the public after his death.

Besides Borelli, the other threat was being found out and going to jail for it. Borelli thought Clermont would never talk, but Clermont was a drug user and unreliable. She was also bound to be angry about her boyfriend being murdered. If she found out Borelli was behind it, there was no doubt Clermont would rat them out.

Bolt got up and made himself a cup of tea. As he sipped the chamomile brew in the dark, he reviewed the murder cases where plea deals had been cut to close unsolved cases.

The judge had a decision to make: He could do nothing and maintain the life he had. It was the easier option, but he'd live in constant fear of being killed or found out. The messier choice was trying to make a deal in return for coming clean. He'd disgrace himself in the process. Was a clean conscience worth the shame and ostracization?

Bolt realized he'd also lose his job and likely have to spend every penny he had on lawyers. He might avoid prison, but what kind of life would he have?

LUCA AND MARY ANN were reading on the lanai. Luca said, "I'm going to put the grill on."

"Okay. The burgers are in the fridge."

He sprayed the grill with Pam and went inside.

Luca checked the temperature gauge and placed the turkey burgers on the grill.

Mary Ann swung her legs off the chaise. "I'm going to make a salad."

Luca read a chapter and flipped the burgers over. After reading some more, he checked the burgers and took them off the grill.

He opened the slider. "Come on, Mary Ann. The burgers are ready."

"I'll be right there."

Luca sat and looked at the setting sun.

His wife came out, carrying a bowl of salad.

Luca said, "I can't believe how cool the sky looks."

"It's beautiful. It's hard to believe it after the thunderstorm we had a couple of hours ago."

"That's Florida, it's not only the lightning capital of the world, but if you don't like the weather, wait an hour."

Mary Ann used tongs to fill her plate with salad. "That's so true."

"Have a burger too."

"I will."

Luca cut a piece. "Where'd you get these?"

"Fresh Market. They didn't have any in the display, but when I asked, a guy came out of the butcher's room and said he'd make them for me."

"Good customer service."

Mary Ann said, "Oh, the mosquito company came today to service the mister."

"Really? Was everything all right?"

"I guess so, they didn't say anything."

Luca put his utensils down. "What time is it?"

"Ten after six."

"I just realized the misters never fired."

"Are you sure?"

Luca pushed his chair back. "Definitely. I didn't hear them." He inhaled deeply. "And I don't smell anything, do you?"

"No."

"I'll bet the tech monkeyed around with the timer or forgot to fill the tank."

"Finish eating first."

"I don't want to forget to check it. The mosquitoes start coming out now."

"We have the screens, I'll be fine."

"I can't take that chance with your MS." Luca smiled. "If you get sick, who's going to cook?"

Luca walked around the perimeter of the screened lanai. He went through the screen door to the side of the house where the mechanics of the pest system were.

The system hadn't been on. He checked the reservoir and hesitated. The color of the liquid looked different. He bent down examining the liquid through the glass top of the reservoir. It wasn't the usual amber color of the cedar-oil repellent they used. This stuff was a milky green color.

Maybe the tech used a new product. Luca unlatched the door to the control unit. The circuit breaker had been tripped. The GFI outlet the system was connected to had probably gotten wet from the rain and triggered the breaker.

Luca was about to reset it when he noticed a wire

leading to a small, chip-like unit taped to the underside of the control unit. He peered at it. What was this?

He looked toward the street. Parked across the street was a white van emblazoned with the logo of the Skeeter SWAT Team. Luca headed for the street. The van's tires screeched and the vehicle took off.

Luca went back to the unit and unplugged it.

Going back onto the lanai, he said, "Get inside."

"Why?"

"Go in the house. I'll bring the food in."

"What's the matter?"

Luca picked up the platter of burgers. "Something isn't right."

Mary Ann lifted the salad bowl. "What's not right?"

"I don't know, but it looks like someone tampered with the mister."

As Mary Ann headed into the kitchen, she said, "Why would they do that?"

Luca lied. "I don't know."

After they moved everything inside, Luca called the Skeeter SWAT Team. The representative said there was no record of a service visit to the Luca residence.

Luca said, "Can you double-check that?"

"I'm looking right at it, sir. The last visit was about six weeks ago."

"Okay. We use cedar repellent, which is a brownish color. Do you have any that are green?"

"None of the natural oils we use are green, sir."

"Nothing like milky green?"

"No, sir."

Luca hung up.

Mary Ann said, "What did they say?"

"No one came today."

"But I saw their guy and their van."

"I'll call in the morning. The rep probably didn't update the system."

"Why did you want to eat inside?"

Luca felt he had to lie again, telling himself when he figured out what was going on he'd tell Mary Ann.

"The system looked weird. I think it was hit by lightning, and if it malfunctions, we could be breathing in an unhealthy dose of repellent."

"The lights didn't flicker or anything. I don't think it was lightning."

"Who knows? What time did the tech get here?"

"About one o'clock. A couple of minutes after you left."

Luca's gut pulled. Whoever it was had to be watching him. He had only been out of the house for an hour at that time of the day.

Chapter Fifty-Three

Luca left the Skeeter SWAT Team's office after confirming what he already knew: The man who came to their house wasn't an employee, and the liquid in the mister reservoir wasn't a product they used.

He looked at the milky liquid he'd ladled into a glass jar, wrapped it in a towel, and set it in the trunk of his car.

Ten minutes later, he pulled into the parking lot for the sheriff's office. He explained to Donovan what had happened, who said, "Are you sure, Frank?"

"A thousand percent."

"All right, I'll take it down to the lab and see what they say."

"Donnie, I know I've jumped the gun a few times, but whoever it is was targeting Mary Ann as well. So we need to know how dangerous the threat is."

"Don't worry. I'm going to push them."

Luca's phone pinged with a notification. When Borelli had climbed the suspect ladder, he had asked Google to monitor the appearance of Horizon Investments and Elena Borelli in any news report.

He checked the summary. There were two stories where either Borelli or her firm were mentioned. He clicked open the details.

The first was a *Wall Street Journal* article listing the top-performing hedge funds.

The second article was an announcement that Horizon Investments had opened an office in Geneva, Switzerland. Luca knew Switzerland and wealth went together, but the piece stated it was the first overseas office that Borelli's firm had opened.

Switzerland wasn't in the European Union and was famously independent. Switzerland and the United States had an extradition treaty, but Luca remembered a case in New Jersey where the Swiss had proven difficult.

Was Borelli preparing some kind of exit ramp?

Four hours later, Luca's phone vibrated. It was Donovan. He stepped into his den.

"Hey, Donnie, what do you have for me?"

"It's not good, Frank. The liquid is a neurotoxin, one that can be aerosolized."

"Are they sure?"

"Yeah, they ran it through the chromatography unit."

"So, was it deadly?"

"The lab said that it was dependent on the level of exposure. But this is serious. Somebody is gunning for you."

"I guess so."

"I already got the authorization to post a patrol unit at your house twenty-four seven."

"Thanks, you read my mind."

"Who do you think is behind it?"

Luca hesitated. "I'm not sure. The last time I was way off."

"Come on, Frank, don't try and be a hero."

"Trust me, I'm not looking to endanger my family. I'm not sure, but I want to think things through."

"Bullshit. You had to do that already."

"I promise, Donnie. When I know who it is, you'll be the first to know."

"Don't screw around, Frank. I don't like wearing my funeral suit."

Luca hung up. He sat, knowing his home was no longer a sanctuary. He had to tell Mary Ann that he was being threatened. Again.

After framing the attempted poisoning as a scare tactic, Luca retreated to his den.

He closed his eyes and reviewed what he knew: Using a toxin was a danger to whoever handled it. Using a mister to spread it spoke to a level of sophistication ordinary criminals did not possess.

Then he considered the use of a van with the pest company's logo. It was also at another level and required resources.

Luca defaulted to the fundamentals which had served him so well: Who had the means and motivation for such an attack?

The only answer was Elena Borelli. But it stretched credibility to think a prominent woman would try to kill or poison him and his innocent wife.

The doorbell interrupted his thoughts. Luca went to the front door. It was a uniformed officer with short blond hair and bulging biceps.

"Hello, sir. I just wanted to let you know I'm here."

"Thanks. If you need something to drink or want to use the bathroom, just knock on the door."

"Thank you, sir. I'll be in the car."

As the officer turned around and headed down the walkway, a Cadillac pulled into the driveway. It was Dr. Bilotti.

Luca went to greet his friend.

"Hey, Doc. What brings you around?"

"A friend of mine in the lab told me what happened."

"It's crazy, right?"

The medical examiner followed Luca into his house. "Frank, you must take the threat seriously."

"I am. Can I get you something?"

"No. I just came to find out how you are doing."

Luca lowered his voice. "Let's talk in the den. Mary Ann is upset."

"That's understandable."

Luca closed the door behind his friend and sat behind his desk. "You don't have to worry. We're going to find out who did this."

"You must have an idea."

"That's the thing, Doc. I do, but it just doesn't make sense."

"You want to share it with me?"

"Sure." Luca told Bilotti about Elena Borelli.

"That's about as high profile a lady as this town has ever seen, and we've seen a lot of wealth."

"I know. I keep thinking it's her, but she'd have to be some kind of a sociopath."

"Not a sociopath, but possibly a psychopath."

"I forget, what's the difference?"

"Sociopaths are erratic, hotheaded, and impulsive. Borelli seems to be a charmer. She couldn't achieve what she did by burning bridges and not being a long-term planner."

"That's true."

"You talked with her several times. Has she lost her cool or become emotional?"

"No. She's been as cool as a cucumber, even when I stormed into her office when they tried to kidnap Jessie."

"If she's anything, she'd be a psychopath, but that's an open question."

"They don't show remorse or empathy, right?"

"Correct."

"Let me ask you, if she was protecting a secret, that she was involved in the robbery where two people were killed, could that make her a psychopath?"

"It's believed that psychopathology is largely innate or genetic, so you shouldn't be able to turn into one. And sociopathology is environmental, things like abuse and trauma lead to it. I'm not a psychiatrist, but I think it's possible to exhibit some traits of a psychopath if, as you suggest, she is trying to keep a secret from getting out."

"How would they do that?"

"By mimicking the behavioral traits of a psychopath. It's not that someone chooses to become a psychopath. They can act like one, staying unnaturally calm and confident, for example, instead of displaying anxiety. But emotional leakage is hard to stop and exhausting to hide."

"Making it likely they'll screw up."
"Yes, but it also makes them dangerous."

Chapter Fifty-Four

All the lights were off in Bolt's house, but Luca noticed a bit of blueish tinge he figured was coming from a TV.

Luca walked to the door and rang the bell. Bolt froze. He reached for the remote and clicked off the movie he'd been watching.

Luca noticed the reduction in ambient sound and used the palm of his hand to beat on the door. When Bolt failed to answer, Luca took his phone out and called the judge.

When it went straight to voicemail, Luca left a message: "I know you're in there, Judge Bolt. I'm not leaving, so you better answer the door, or I'm going to have the sheriff send a squadron of cars to conduct a wellness check on you. If you don't want your front door broken down and neighbors out in the street, answer the door."

Luca hung up and smiled. He figured it wouldn't take more than a minute for Bolt to rationalize opening the door.

A light came on and Bolt unlocked the door.

"Uh, sorry, I was in the bathroom."

"We need to talk."

Bolt's shoulders dropped. "Okay, but I've had a very exhausting day and would appreciate it if you kept it brief."

"That's up to you."

Luca stepped inside the house. Bolt flicked two light switches, and the foyer and family room lit up. The judge motioned toward two club chairs to the right of a TV hanging on the wall.

"Let's sit over there."

Luca surveyed the room where Bolt had been watching TV. His eyes settled on a black gun sitting on the cocktail table.

Bolt eased himself into a chair, and the investigator sat next to him.

Luca said, "You said you wanted it quick, so I'll get right to it."

"I appreciate the consideration."

"It's time for you to come clean about your role in the Waterside robbery and murders."

"I had nothing to do with that. I told you that already."

"You can say whatever you like, but I think you did. Why else would you dismiss the case against Clermont?"

"It was entrapment."

"That was your excuse, but I talked to the prosecutors, and they know something fishy was going on."

Bolt mustered as much indignation as possible. "What are you implying?"

"I'm not implying, I'm stating Clermont blackmailed you into it."

"My guardianship of the legal process is not for sale."

"Everybody and everything has a price."

Before Bolt had a chance to respond, Luca followed with, "And why was David Flan murdered?"

"How would I know?"

"Blackmail again. Borelli was tired of shoveling money to Flan to buy his silence. He represented a threat, and Borelli had him eliminated."

"How do you know all this?"

"I'm right, aren't I?"

Bolt shrugged.

"You probably know you're next on her list to eliminate possible leaks."

"Me? I don't think so."

"Then why haven't you gone to work the last couple of days?"

"I didn't feel well."

"You always sit inside your house without lights?"

Bolt picked at his thumbnail.

Luca said, "You know the system; if you help close this case, you'll get leniency. Depending on your role, you could avoid a prison term. But you have to move fast."

Bolt pinched the bridge of his nose. "You don't know these people."

Luca softened his voice. "What people? Tell me, I can help you."

Bolt hissed, "Elena Borelli."

"We can work together to bring her down."

Bolt's voice cracked. "I tried. I really tried to get something to bargain with."

Luca scootched to the edge of his seat. "What did you do?"

"I wore a recording device, went to see Borelli, and got her incriminating herself."

"Where is it?"

"Before I could leave her house, her security man—I believe he's possibly ex-CIA or something similar—anyway, he threatened me, made me take my shirt off, and he took the recording."

"That's not good, Judge. That's evidence that Borelli can no longer trust you. I hate to be blunt, but you have a target on your back. Just like I seem to have."

"She's coming after you?"

"I think so." Luca pulled out a small notepad. "What did her security guy look like?"

"He was taller than me, say about six two and solid looking. He had dark, reddish hair, which was cut short, and cold, almost black eyes."

Luca jotted the description down. "Anything else you can tell me about him?"

"He had a slight accent. I couldn't place the origin, but it wasn't Hispanic."

"That's useful. I'll see if we can track him down. Now, let me bring you into the sheriff's office."

Bolt recoiled as if the Prince of Death had tried to take his hand. "The sheriff? No, no way. I can't do that."

"How else can you make a deal? I'll set it up, you come in and tell the prosecutors what you know."

"No, I don't know anything."

"You can do it, Your Honor. You've got to."

"I can't."

"It's the only way you get to stay a free man."

"I'm sorry, but I can't."

Luca pointed at Bolt. "Today, you have a choice, but if you don't cooperate, I promise I'll come after you with everything I have, and they'll be no mercy for you."

Bolt blinked several times before saying, "Can I think about it?"

"Yes. But I wouldn't take too long to decide."

Luca stood. "Take a day or two, and don't do anything stupid."

"Don't worry, I'm not going to tell Borelli you came here."

"I wasn't talking about that." He pointed at the pistol. "I meant don't try to kill yourself."

Luca was shown out of the house. Stepping outside, he instinctively scanned the area. A dark sedan was parked five houses down. It wasn't there before.

The lights went off at the judge's house. Luca pictured Bolt holding the gun in his lap, hoping the man wasn't going to commit suicide.

Luca climbed into his SUV. Before starting his car, he moved the headlight knob to the off position. He put the car in gear and slowly rolled forward to the next driveway.

Luca floored the gas and his car leaped forward. With his eyes on the other car, he turned the headlights on.

The person behind the wheel ducked down. Luca hit the brakes, and the other car took off. Luca tried to grab the plate number, but the vehicle's lights were off. Instead of giving chase, Luca went back to Bolt's house to let him know someone was watching him.

The judge agreed with Luca that the surveillance was probably being conducted under orders from Borelli.

Chapter Fifty-Five

Luca swung by his old partner's house. Lynn told him her husband was playing tennis at the community center's courts.

Derrick was hitting balls coming out of a ball machine. He hit a ball that just missed the back line.

Luca snuck along the chain-link fencing and called out, "Your backhand is terrible!"

Derrick smiled. He tapped his racket against his hand and walked over. "You should have seen it a month ago."

"All kidding aside, you look good out there."

"Thanks. I wish you would've taken the game up."

Luca pointed to his old partner's green-dusted footwear. "And get my sneakers dirty?"

As a group of ladies in tennis skirts passed by, Derrick said, "Tell me what's going on?"

Lowering his voice, Luca said, "I need to talk, privately."

"Sure. There's a bench in the shade on the other side of the court."

Derrick headed for the shade.Luca walked around the court and met Derrick.

Derrick said, "Hey, before you get started, I wanted to let you know about Loretta Gulliver."

"What about her?"

"After she left Naples, her mother got sick. Her mother pleaded for her to come back, but she was living with some guy, and she never did until she passed away. Three of her friends said she was wracked with guilt and is still dealing with it."

"That kind of fits."

"I think so. Tell me what's going on."

"Someone is coming after me again."

Luca told him about the toxin he found in the insect repellent system.

"This is out of control, man. You're going to end up dead."

"I want to find out who is actually executing Borelli's orders."

"Let's get the sheriff to bring Borelli in. If he leans on her, she might crack."

"She won't. Plus, she's overseas right now."

"Lie low and wait till she's back."

Luca pressed his forefinger and thumb together. "Judge Bolt is this close to coming clean. The more information I get, it might put him over the edge and he'll incriminate Borelli."

"Or I might be going to your funeral."

"Don't worry. Donovan arranged to station a patrol unit outside our house twenty-four seven, and I'm being careful." He flashed his hidden holster and then lifted the leg of his pants, revealing another pistol attached to his ankle.

"If this guy is a pro, that might not be enough."

"I have an idea to identify him, and I think he'll know that I know. But I need your help."

"Whatever you need."

DERRICK CHECKED the logo on his polo shirt. The property management logo was generic enough to work. He grabbed the yellow hard hat from the passenger seat and put it on. He got out with a clipboard and tablet from the rear seat and headed for the office building.

He waved to the security guard and, his eyes on his clipboard, breezed to the bank of elevators.

The receptionist for Horizon Investments was transferring a call when Derrick got off the elevator. He examined the ceilings and made a note on his clipboard.

"May I help you?"

"Hey there, I'm with Building Tech Services. The company on the floor below is getting some signal bleed from the encrypted lines in this suite. The property manager said Ms. Borelli's private team runs their own loop. I just need the name of the security director so I can sync our 'null' channels." He held up the tablet. "From what I see, the interference isn't coming from you guys. But they want me to get the information from every tenant."

"Sure. That would be Bebe Herzog, he took over recently."

"Bebe? How do you spell that?"

The receptionist spelled it out and Derrick said, "Bebe is an unusual name. I never heard of anyone with it."

"He's an Israeli."

"Oh, got it. Thanks."

Derrick took the stairs down to his car and called Luca.

"Frank, it worked. The guy's name is Bebe Herzog. He's from Israel."

"He's probably ex-Mossad."

"Those guys are as good as they get. You better watch your ass."

BORELLI WAS BACK from her European trip and had dodged Luca for the second day. He sat in the dark, waiting for the financier in the parking lot of her office building.

The sparkle from her Bentley's distinctive headlights meant she had arrived. Luca slipped out of his car as she parked in a reserved spot.

Borelli wore a dark pantsuit and hustled into the building. She waved to the guard and pushed the elevator button.

Luca came into the building's lobby. "I'm with her."

Borelli turned her head. Her frown morphed into a smile. "Good morning, Mr. Luca."

"Morning, ma'am."

They stepped into the elevator, and as it rose, Borelli said, "I'm trying to accommodate you, but must tell you I don't have much time this morning. I recently returned from an overseas trip."

"Where did you go?"

"Switzerland."

"I saw something in the paper that you opened a branch office there."

The doors slid open. "We did."

"Good luck with it."

The lights came on as she walked down the hall to her office.

They passed an office with a light on. "Good morning, Elena."

"Good morning, Marco."

"Oh, you have a visitor?"

"We'll be quick."

She unlocked the door to her expansive office and sat behind her glass-topped desk.

Luca's eyes settled on a red booklet. It was a Swiss passport.

"You've got dual citizenship?"

"Yes. I've had it since my teenage years. My mother was born in Geneva."

"So, that's why you decided to open a branch in Switzerland?"

"No. It was purely a business decision. Now, what can I do for you?"

"Bebe Herzog."

"He heads the firm's security operations."

"You need a Mossad agent to run your security?"

"I've learned to get the best available person for any position in the firm."

"Does he handle your personal security as well?"

"As I stated earlier, I have to play catch-up, so, if you have a meaningful question, I'll do my best to address it."

"From what I know, Mossad agents used toxins against Hamas and Hezbollah."

"You're better informed on that than I but—"

"Do you condone the use?"

"I haven't given the matter much thought, but Hamas

and Hezbollah are terrorist organizations, so I guess anything goes."

"The system we use to make sure my wife, who has MS, is safe, uses an essential oil to keep mosquitoes away."

"Over cocktails these subjects would be fascinating to explore, but unfortunately I don't have the time."

"Bebe Herzog was behind the attempt to poison my wife and me."

"Mr. Luca, you have a penchant for making unfounded accusations. This is the second or third time you've engaged in slander."

"It's not slander; it's the truth."

Borelli stood. "I'm going to have to ask you to leave. Please don't force me to call security."

Luca got up. "You're not getting away with this."

As he trudged down the stairs, Luca contemplated Borelli's dual citizenship. Was she planning to flee?

Chapter Fifty-Six

Luca wasn't a big ravioli fan, but Mary Ann enjoyed them, especially the Pastosa ones stuffed with broccoli rabe. He was hoping they'd have some of the fresh bread he liked. And he'd check out what pastries they had.

Luca turned off Livingston Road, making a right onto Progress Avenue, then a left, then a right to get to Domestic Avenue. As he rode down the deserted street, the sound of a motorcycle caught his attention.

He checked the rearview mirror. A high-performance sport bike was approaching fast. Luca kept his eyes on it. Two people dressed in black were on it. As the motorbike veered to pass him, Luca saw the passenger pull a gun out of his jacket.

Luca jerked the wheel to the left and into the motorbike. The biker swerved to avoid getting crushed, causing the gunshots to miss.

Luca slammed the brakes and pulled his pistol out. Riding the shoulder, the motorcycle gunned it and blew past Luca to safety.

Heart hammering, Luca knew he'd been targeted. He also knew the route he'd taken to Ambrosio and Son wasn't direct.

That could mean only one thing—there was a GPS tracking device on his car. Luca thought back to when he went to Bolt's house. The car he'd seen when he left was probably not watching the judge but tracking Luca.

Luca had the impression he was being tailed but had ignored his instincts. The fact that his gut was right instilled confidence in the dangerous scheme beginning to form in his mind.

Luca decided he wouldn't tell Mary Ann what had just happened and drove to the Italian delicacy store as if nothing had changed.

He dropped off the groceries and called Derrick, telling his ex-partner he needed to talk.

DERRICK THREW OPEN his front door. "What's going on?"

Luca motioned for him to step outside.

A landscaper was blowing grass cuttings off the driveway as Luca said, "Things are heating up."

"What happened?"

As Luca relayed the close call he'd had on the way to buy raviolis, Derrick shifted his stance. "You're going to get yourself killed!"

"Hold on, let me finish. I got a plan."

Luca told him the outline of his idea to catch Bebe Herzog in the act.

"You've lost it, man."

"What are you talking about?"

"You're going to use yourself as bait?"

"I guess so. I never touched the GPS tracker. I'll lure them to an isolated location where they'll feel confident they can—"

"What, are you trying to get your picture on the memorial wall?"

"Come on, it's a good plan."

Derrick shook his head. "You're crazy. If you don't go to the sheriff's office, I will."

"What are they going to do? There's not enough evidence to charge anybody. I catch them in the act, and it's game over."

"It's too risky, man. You don't even know how many of them will be coming."

"I will, if you come and help me."

"What do you mean?"

"You get into a position to monitor their arrival and then radio or text me. If it's an overwhelming force, we shut it down and I'll take off."

"No. It's still dangerous."

"Well, if I don't do anything, I'm still going to be a target."

"Quit the damn case."

"That's not going to stop them. I know too much. They can't take a chance."

"I don't like it."

"I'm doing it with or without you, and I'd rather have you with me."

LUCA KEPT his eyes on the rearview mirror before he turned onto Immokalee Road. The dark SUV behind him pulled into the turning lane. Approaching Collier Boulevard, he saw the SUV again. He was being followed.

Using a burner phone, he called Derrick. "It's a go. A dark-colored SUV, looks like it might be Japanese, is a quarter mile behind me. It seems like it's just the driver inside."

"Okay. Be careful."

"Are you in position?"

"Yes. Everything is ready to go. I parked in the Bird Gardens of Naples lot and got about a hundred mosquito bites walking in."

"I owe you, pal."

"Let's make sure you're around so I can collect."

Traffic thinned the further east Luca traveled. He went through the Oil Well Road intersection, and Immokalee Road narrowed to a lane in each direction.

As he passed the street leading to the county fairgrounds, the SUV fell back. Luca acknowledged the smart move. There were no cars around, and the stalker could follow his taillights.

Just before Immokalee Road began to bend to the right, Luca put his turn signal on. The SUV was about half a mile behind, and as Luca turned onto Sanctuary Road, the SUV shut off its headlights and used its running lights.

Luca sped up to get closer to the next turn. He put his left turn signal on and waited at the intersection. When the SUV turned onto the road, Luca hit the gas and drove to the lot for the Corkscrew Swamp Sanctuary boardwalk.

Night vision goggles on, Luca made sure not to look in the direction of where Derrick was positioned. Holding a heat-dispersing camouflage suit, he scampered down the boardwalk.

Luca slipped the ghillie suit on. He checked the swamp for alligators and climbed over the railing into the water. It took less than thirty seconds to wade out to a fallen cypress tree. He climbed out of the water and onto the tree.

The sounds of the thirteen-thousand-acre preserve amplified with his stillness. He took the bag with his phone out and stared at the screen.

DERRICK WATCHED as an SUV entered the parking lot of the sanctuary. Someone got out and opened the trunk. Derrick adjusted his binoculars to see through the heavily wooded area.

Luca's ex-partner held his breath as a figure, clad in black and wearing night vision goggles, approached the entrance to the two-mile-long boardwalk. The visitor was carrying a rifle.

Derrick tapped out a text to Luca. "One person, on my way."

Chapter Fifty-Seven

Bebe took two gentle steps onto the boardwalk. His rubber-soled boots were nearly silent. He raised his rifle to the shooting position and headed into the dark.

Every couple of steps, Bebe would look through the expensive thermal scope mounted on his rifle. Working for someone with a limitless budget had advantages over even the best-funded police agencies.

The ex-Mossad agent smiled. A private investigator like Luca was out of his league, just like the radicalized factions who wanted to destroy Israel were.

Splash!

Bebe froze. He turned toward the sound. Bebe trained the rifle on the ever-expanding ripple rings in the water. He homed in. Two green eyes reflected the moonlight. Bebe lowered the gun. It was an alligator.

Borelli's enforcer continued down the meandering walkway. He put an eye onto the cup on the rifle's scope and panned left to right, then farther ahead. In the distance through the trees was an area that lit up red. A shot of adrenaline coursed through his body. Bebe took a moment to slow his heart rate.

The boardwalk bent to the right, and whatever the scope had picked up was on that stretch of the walkway. Bebe advanced to the point where the wooden footpath pivoted. He stood motionless and looked through the scope. He needed to get closer.

Bebe took several steps forward and zeroed in on the spot where the scope had detected heat. He studied the colored form. He considered whether it was Luca sitting on one of the benches that dotted the boardwalk or an animal. Bebe didn't know what kind of mammals lived in the area and certainly couldn't tell which ones were nocturnal.

He assumed the heat was coming from Luca and began to gently close in for a kill shot.

NIGHT VISION GOGGLES ON, Luca kept watch on the boardwalk. A green figure was moving toward him. The grainy image made it difficult to discern details, but it was clear he was carrying a rifle.

Luca made himself as small as possible and made sure to exhale behind him to lower the heat profile he emanated. He avoided swatting the mosquitoes looking for a sliver of skin.

An owl hooted and the figure came to a halt. Luca willed the assassin to get closer. The figure raised the rifle and Luca regretted not having a backup plan.

A strong gust of wind blew through, filling the air with pine needles. The figure lowered his rifle and tiptoed his way nearer.

Derrick grabbed the high-powered rifle he'd left leaning against a tree earlier. He hoped he wouldn't have to use it.

Derrick crept through the woods to a position with a sight line of where Luca was stationed.

Bebe didn't know much about wildlife but enough to know the hooting sound was coming from an owl. And that was one animal he knew was nocturnal.

He looked through the scope. He was within range. As he braced himself for a shot, a gust of wind blew through. He took his eye off the scope and waited for it to pass.

When the air stilled, he raised the rifle. He wrapped his finger on the trigger and zeroed in. He slowed his breath, but a swarm of bugs encircled him. He swatted with his free hand and took several steps forward.

Bebe leaned against the railing and shouldered the rifle. He trained the scope's bullseye on the head of human heat signature sitting on the bench. Bebe widened his stance and squeezed the trigger.

The head of the figure exploded and Bebe rushed forward.

Bebe pulled a flashlight out of his jacket and directed the light to the bench. It wasn't Luca's head that he blew off.

"What the fuck?"

Bebe kicked the heated saltwater bag draped in Luca's old jacket.

The ex-Mossad agent reached for his shoulder. "Ow!"

Luca pocketed the Taser and slid off the tree. He splashed into the water and climbed onto the boardwalk and stood over Bebe, who lay crumpled to the ground.

Luca ripped off the man's balaclava. It was Bebe Herzog. Luca put the gun to Bebe's temple.

"You tried to poison my wife. I should blow your frigging head off."

Derrick swatted Luca's side. "Easy, Frank."

Luca scowled and used his phone to take several pictures of the assassin.

Bebe started to thrash.

Luca straddled him, pointing his pistol at him. "All that Mossad training is great for Tel Aviv and major cities, Bebe. But out in the Florida swamps? You're nothing but a snack for the alligators."

Derrick chided. "I bet the most nature this guy got was from watching a documentary."

Luca said, "Get on your back, you piece of shit."

Bebe struggled to roll over and Luca assisted him, cuffing his wrists together.

Luca put a hand under Bebe's armpit and told Derrick, "Grab the other side."

They propped the prisoner against the railing. Bebe turned his head away from the beam of light Luca shone on him.

"Who are you working for?"

Bebe remained silent.

Luca grabbed Bebe's chin and said, "I know it's Borelli, but if you tell me, I can tell the prosecutors to go easy on you, especially if you cooperate."

The assassin looked away but said nothing.

Luca turned to Derrick. "Let's get him on his feet."

They pulled Bebe up to a standing position. Luca motioned and Derrick got close to his ex-partner. Luca whispered in his ear.

Derrick smiled. "Let's do it."

They bent Bebe over the railing and, with each of them

holding one of the assassin's legs, lowered Bebe's head to the water.

Luca said, "The gators aren't going to have to hunt for their next meal."

Derrick chimed in, "I see one coming."

Bebe didn't struggle or say a word.

"Get him down further. I want his head in the water."

They shimmied Bebe's body lower. His head was inches from the surface of the black water.

Luca said, "Start talking or you're going in."

Bebe shook his head.

"Dunk him in."

They lowered him into the water. Bebe craned his neck to keep his nose above water.

"You're going down unless you start talking."

Bebe wagged his head again.

"Let's put his whole head in."

They submerged him up to his neck and pulled him out after counting to twenty.

"You going to talk or what?"

Bebe remained silent.

Derrick said, "These Mossad guys are tough."

"We'll see how he likes getting his face chomped on by a gator."

They lowered Bebe's entire head into the swamp again.

Derrick said, "Pull him up."

"No. Wait another ten seconds."

"Ten, nine eight, seven, six, five, four, three, two, one. Pull him up."

They yanked him out. Bebe started coughing.

"You going to talk now?"

Bebe shook his head no.

Derrick said, "Where the hell are the alligators when you need one? You want to try dunking him in another area?"

Luca whispered, "At this point, I don't think he'd going to talk. And we can't risk pushing this any further."

"What do you want to do?"

"Let's bring this bastard in. We turn him over to the sheriff, charge him with several counts of attempted murder, and let the prosecutors cut a deal to get him to talk."

"We can't let him get off scot-free."

"I can't worry about that now. Maybe they'll deport him, or he serves some time, but the main focus is nailing Borelli."

Chapter Fifty-Eight

Luca took his muddy clothes off in the garage before coming into the house.

Mary Ann called out, "Frank? Is that you?"

"Yeah, it's me."

She froze when she saw him half naked in the hallway. "What are you doing?"

"I got a little dirty and didn't want to track the dirt into the house."

"Where were you?"

"It's a long story, but we don't have to worry about the threat anymore."

"What do you mean?"

"The guy who was doing it is now a resident of the county jail."

"You caught him?"

"Yep."

"Who was it?"

"The guy who runs security for Borelli."

"Oh my God. So that woman is really behind all this?"

"She sure is."

"How did you get him?"

"Me and Derrick set a trap and he fell into it."

"What kind of trap?"

He didn't want to tell her he used himself as bait. "It was nothing big. I'm going to hop in the shower."

Luca was towel drying his hair when Mary Ann came into the master bathroom.

"Are you going to tell me what happened?"

"It was no big deal. I lured Borelli's security guard to a swamp, and Derrick nailed him."

"A swamp?"

"Look, the only thing that counts is he's behind bars. They'll press him to make a deal so we can get Borelli."

"Let me call Jessica and let her know."

"Okay, but tell her to remain vigilant."

"Is there something you're not telling me?"

"No. Just being careful. I told the sheriff to keep the car out here there just in case they try something."

"You think they will?"

"No. Trust me, we cut the head off of these bastards."

"But Borelli is still out there."

"She's got to be looking to protect herself. She's not going to take a chance with her main guy in prison."

"That's true."

Luca's cell phone began to buzz. "Let me get this, it's Donovan."

"Hey, Donnie, what's up?"

Collier County's lead homicide detective said, "Bebe Herzog tried to kill himself."

"What the hell happened?"

Donovan said, "They were fingerprinting him, and he

apparently took what they think was a cyanide pill he had hidden on him."

"How is he?"

"He was in rough shape when he left here for the hospital. I heard they pumped his stomach out, but cyanide works fast."

Luca finished the call and shook his head. "Unfrigging believable."

"What happened?"

He told his wife what happened.

She said, "There's nothing you can do about it now."

"If he dies, we'll never get Borelli."

"It'll be okay, Frank."

"How the hell does crap like this happen?"

"Take it easy, Frank."

"I busted my ass and—"

"Frank, you're exhausted and need sleep. You'll figure out what to do in the morning."

"If Bebe dies, I just won't believe it."

"Stop, already. Let's go to bed."

Even though he was wide awake, Luca climbed into bed.

THE ACID from Luca's morning coffee crept up the back of his throat. He hung up the phone and said, "Damn it! Can't I catch one frigging break?"

Mary Ann said, "Who was that?"

"Donovan. It looks like it might be too late to save the guy we brought in last night."

"I'm sorry."

Luca picked up his phone and made a call.

"Donnie, it's not a butt call."

"What's up?"

"I'm afraid Borelli might take off and go to Switzerland."

"Why would she do that?"

"To stay out of reach until she sees if we got anything on her."

The head of homicide said, "I think we have an extradition treaty with the Swiss."

"Yeah, but they're not in the European Union, and they love to play the independent neutral part."

"We can't stop her from traveling without charging her, Frank."

"I know, but can you ask to be alerted if she's taking off?"

"I guess we could, but I don't know what that will do."

"I don't know, I guess I'm fishing at this point."

"Hang in there, Frank. I've got to run to a meeting with the captain."

Luca hung up and sighed.

Mary Ann said, "You need to take a break from all this."

"I can't."

He punched in another number. After five rings, voicemail answered. "This is Conrad Bolt. I'm either in court or indisposed at the moment. Please leave a message and I will return your call as soon as possible."

"Judge, this is Frank Luca. Call me as soon as possible. It's urgent."

Mary Ann said, "You called the judge?"

"Yes. It just hit me that with Borelli's henchman out of the way, he may want to cop a plea and help us nail Borelli."

"That's a good idea. It'll probably work. See? I told you you'd figure it out."

"I hope so."

"It will."

"As soon as the courthouse opens, I'll leave a message there too."

—

LUCA DISCONNECTED THE CALL, leaving a third voicemail for Judge Bolt. He paced the kitchen and called the judge's chambers again.

After being told Bolt hadn't come in yet, Luca got testy with his secretary and hung up.

Mary Ann said, "Why don't you go for a walk?"

"That's a good idea."

Luca went into the garage and was putting his sneakers on when his phone buzzed. It was Donovan.

"Hey, Donnie."

"Hi, Frank, I wanted to let you know, the guy died."

"Bebe Herzog?"

"Yeah. I just got the call. They couldn't save him."

"Damn it! I was counting on him to make a deal and give up Borelli."

"Intelligence agent-type guys ain't the talking kind."

"I don't need the reminder."

Luca finished the call and said, "I'm taking a ride to Bolt's house. I know he's hiding out in there. I got to talk to him before he finds out Borelli's guy is dead. Otherwise, he might want to hang in and not talk."

Luca got into his car, convinced this was his final shot at closing the Waterside Shops murders and robbery.

Chapter Fifty-Nine

Luca parked in front of Judge Bolt's home. All the shades were down. He sidestepped a sprinkler and headed up the paver walkway. Luca hit the doorbell twice, muttering, "Let's go, Your Honor."

He strained to hear any sounds coming from inside the home. The only noise was coming from the hum of the air-conditioning units and the *psst* of the irrigation system.

Luca pounded on the door. "Judge Bolt! It's Frank Luca. We need to talk."

He put his ear to the door but couldn't detect any activity coming from inside the house. He twisted the door-knob, but it didn't budge.

Luca checked the front windows, but the shades were down and nothing was visible from the outside. He went around the back of the house and tested the sliders but couldn't gain entry.

He went back to the front door and pulled his phone out. He called Bolt's cell phone and put his ear to the door. He could hear the phone as it rang inside the home.

Luca considered breaking a window and walked across the driveway. He saw the keypad for the garage door, and on a lark punched the #1 key four times. Nothing happened. He tried 1-2-3-4 and smirked when the door groaned and lifted.

Luca crouched under the opening door. He knocked on the interior door before he went inside the home.

"Judge Bolt! It's Frank Luca."

Silence.

He kept his hand near his hip but didn't draw his pistol. The sharp smell of liquor grew as he passed through the kitchen.

Luca froze.

Bolt was slumped in a chair, tilted toward the coffee table.

His hair was neatly combed, but the side of his face was destroyed. The pistol Luca had warned Bolt about was on the floor, under his limp hand.

Luca hurried over, checking the judge's neck for a pulse, though he knew there'd be none.

"Damn it, Bolt. You frigging coward."

The judge's neck was cool. He had passed.

Luca called 911 and surveyed the scene.

A bottle of Macallan lay on its side in a puddle of booze. On the table was a nearly empty glass of Scotch and a single sheet of cream-colored stationery.

The judge's handwriting was elegant. Luca began reading the suicide note:

I have spent the last twenty years passing judgment on men far better than myself. The irony has not been lost on me.

Though I tried to compensate by ensuring justice in the criminal cases before me, every time I pounded the gavel I heard the echo of that fateful day at Waterside Shops. Elena Borelli and I planned the robbery at Van Dores, and it went horribly wrong.

The fact is, I have lived a lie, and the weight is too much to bear.

Apologetically,

Conrad Bolt

As the sound of sirens closed in, Luca took a picture of the note with his phone and several more of the depressing scene.

He tucked his phone away and went back over the position of the body and weapon. He knelt and sniffed Bolt's hand. The acrid smell of gunpowder residue was present.

Luca stood. He was confident the judge had taken his own life.

LUCA CAME into his house and plodded into the kitchen.

Mary Ann was playing mahjong on her iPad. She said, "What's the matter?"

"Judge Bolt killed himself."

"Oh my God. That's terrible."

"I know, I feel bad, like it's my fault."

"That's ridiculous. As sad as it is, any pressure he was feeling was of his own making."

"Bolt had a gun, and I warned him not to do anything stupid with it."

"That's exactly what you should have done."

"If I would've taken the weapon away from him, he'd still be around."

"That doesn't mean he wouldn't jump off a bridge or take pills or something."

"Maybe."

"Did he leave a suicide note?"

"I took a picture of it."

He handed his phone off.

Mary Ann read it and said, "Maybe you can use this to get Borelli."

"You know it can't be used as evidence. Her lawyers will have it thrown out because they can't challenge Bolt about it."

"I know, but you can still let Borelli know you know she was involved."

"I'm not sure that'll help. It could put her on edge. She could take off to Switzerland. She's got a Swiss passport."

"We have an extradition treaty."

"We do, but at this point we don't even have what we need to charge her. If she's overseas, the appetite to go through with this is going to die, and she'll never be brought to justice."

"What are you going to do?"

"I don't have the slightest clue."

"You need to take a break, step away from it, and something will come to you."

"Maybe."

"Relax for a while. Dinner is going to be ready in an hour."

"What are we having?"

"Pasta with lentils."

"Sounds good."

Luca went onto the lanai and flicked the TV on. As WINK News came on, he adjusted the angle of the screen so he could see it from a chaise lounge. He pulled his phone out and read Bolt's suicide note again. Lingering on the apologies the judge had left behind, the anchorwoman caught his attention by saying, "We have sad news to report this evening."

A picture of Bolt in his black robes filled the screen.

"Earlier today, Judge Conrad Bolt was found dead in his home, the victim of a self-inflicted gunshot wound. The sheriff has ruled the death a suicide. Judge Bolt was known to be tough on crime and had served on the bench for nearly fifteen years.

"We're going live to the Collier Courthouse, where Carol Asbury is speaking with colleagues of Judge Bolt."

A blonde reporter replaced the image of Bolt. Luca clicked the remote and the screen went dark. He closed his eyes and tallied the bodies from the Waterside crimes: the security guard, the jewelry store owner, David Flan, Willie Perez, Bebe Herzog, and now, Conrad Bolt.

Six people, that he knew of. Were there others? And he was no closer to solving it. In fact, there were fewer people living that he believed had the knowledge to close the coldest case he'd ever worked.

In the middle of that night, Luca got up to use the bathroom. He shuffled to the toilet and sat. As he coaxed a leak out, his mind drifted to the image of Bolt slumped over in his chair.

He wondered how Bolt felt as he wrote the suicide note. Luca tried recalling exactly what the judge had written when an idea popped into his head.

He rolled the scheme around as he washed his hands.

As he slid back under the covers, Luca believed the idea had a fifty-fifty chance of working.

Chapter Sixty

Luca tried to remember how long it had been since he'd been to Tin City. The section along the Gordon River, named for its corrugated metal roofing, had been a hub of fishing a hundred years ago.

He mused it was hard to believe the economics of Naples had once been clam shelling and oyster processing. He walked along the water to the Riverfront Restaurant, where Cynthia Clermont was seated at an outdoor table.

Luca approached. "Thanks for seeing me."

Clermont took a deep drag on her cigarette before asking, "What do you want?"

"The truth."

Clermont said, "There is no truth, just versions of it."

"I didn't come here to talk philosophy. What I want is justice for a dead man's daughter."

"And what do I got to do with that?"

"The man died twenty years ago, during the Waterside robbery."

She sipped her glass of draft beer. "I told you, I had nothing to do with it."

"Conrad Bolt did."

Wiping her lips with the back of her hand, she said, "No way, he's a judge."

"And he's dead."

Clermont's jaw dropped. "What? How?"

"Suicide."

"That's sad. But some people can't handle their shit."

Luca stood. He threw a twenty on the table. "Let's take a walk."

Clermont drained her beer before getting up.

They stepped away from the restaurant and Luca said, "I was the one who found Judge Bolt. I know all about what you did, blackmailing him into dismissing the drug charges against you."

She wagged her head. "You're making shit up. I didn't do anything like that."

"Look, you can say what you want, but I don't care about your drug case. What I want is to nail Elena Borelli."

"Borelli? For what?"

"She tried to kill me and my wife, who had nothing to do with anything."

"Come on, why would she do that?"

"Because I'm close to proving who was responsible for the Waterside murders and robbery twenty years ago."

"I wouldn't know anything about that."

"I get why you keep denying your involvement, but I—"

"I'm denying it because it didn't happen. I didn't do—"

Luca put up a hand. "Hear me out, okay?"

She shrugged. "Whatever."

"I spoke to the prosecutors, and we can make a deal with

you. You tell me what you know about Borelli's role in the Waterside crimes and you'll get immunity. You'll have to testify, but you'll walk away from it."

"You're crazy. I don't want anything to do with all this."

"It's a once-in-a-lifetime deal. You'd get off scot-free in return for helping."

She shook her head. "It's not going to happen. I didn't do anything."

"What if I told you Borelli is the one who got your boyfriend murdered in prison?"

"What?"

"That's right. She had Willie Perez killed as he waited to go on trial."

"That's bullshit. You'll say anything, won't you?"

"I can prove it."

She popped another cigarette into her mouth. "Yeah, right."

"Take a look at this."

As she lit her smoke, Luca took his phone out, opened an image and handed it to Clermont.

"What is this?"

"The suicide note Judge Bolt left."

"How did you get it?"

"I was the one who found him, remember? It was lying right there. Now, read it."

She held the phone out. "This could be just a fake, something you made with AI."

Luca took the phone from her. He swiped the screen and stuck the phone in front of Clermont's face.

"Oh my God."

She looked away from a picture of Bolt slumped in his chair.

Luca switched to another picture.

"This is the scene in Bolt's house where he killed himself. He must have been drinking to get the courage. It's upsetting to see, but the guilt got to him."

"Fucking Connie. Why'd you do something like that?"

"I wanted him to make a deal and thought he was going to, but he put a bullet in his head. So it's your turn. Take the deal, or you'll find yourself going to prison for the rest of your life."

"I'm not making any deals."

Luca held up his phone. "Read what Bolt wrote."

Clermont blinked. "That's creepy, man. He's dead, for God's sake."

Luca handed her the phone. "Read it! Aloud."

Clermont cleared her throat and began reading:

"I have spent the last twenty years passing judgment on men far better than myself. The irony of sending people who committed lesser crimes than I has not been lost on me.

Though I tried to compensate by ensuring justice in the criminal cases before me, every time I banged the gavel I heard the echo of that fateful day at Waterside Shops.

The fact is, I have lived a lie, and the weight is too much to bear.

The truth is, four of us, Elena Borelli, Cynthia Clermont, David Flan and I planned the robbery of the Van Dores Diamond Showroom at Waterside Shops."

Clermont paused, and Luca said, "Keep reading."

Clermont continued:

"I am not offering an excuse; however, I want it known we did not plan to harm anyone. The fact that two people lost their lives is something I am no longer able to live with.

Shamefully, I also stood silent as Elena Borelli, attempting to keep this dark secret from being exposed, killed David Flan, Willie Perez, and was attempting to murder the investigator, Frank Luca.

I can no longer live with my cowardly behavior.

Apologetically,

Conrad Bolt

Clermont stared at the phone. "I can't believe that bitch killed Willie."

Luca took the phone from her. "Believe it. It was her."

"What a lying piece of shit. She told me she'd always protect me."

"Well, now you've got an opportunity to turn the tables on Borelli."

Clermont sucked on her cigarette and the tip turned red. She exhaled and said, "How can I be sure I'm not gonna be arrested?"

"You have my word."

"Your word ain't worth shit. I need guarantees or I'm not saying anything."

"We can call Prosecutor O'Leary. He's the one I'm dealing with. He'll assure you this is real."

She nodded. "Go ahead."

Chapter Sixty-One

The sound of the garage door had Mary Ann heading down the hallway to meet her husband.

Luca pulled into the garage, saw his wife, and frowned. He got out and shook his head.

Mary Ann said, "What happened? You've been gone forever."

"I don't know. Everything went to crap."

"What do you mean?"

Luca smiled. "Just kidding. I brought Clermont in and handed her off to Donovan and O'Leary. She's going to come clean, and we'll use her to nail Borelli."

"That's wonderful."

"It sure is."

"How did you get her to confess?"

"I tricked her. I got to thinking about Bolt's suicide note, the one I told you about."

"Yes. What about it?"

"It didn't give me anything to work with, so I figured I'd make one that would have what I thought would work."

"What? You made a fake suicide note?"

"Yep."

"But is that going to be okay?"

"Criminals lie all the time. Clermont was lying each time I talked to her, denying her involvement in the Waterside case. So I got creative, saying Bolt's note revealed that Borelli murdered her boyfriend. I figured she'd want revenge. Besides, we believe Borelli was responsible for killing the guy anyway."

"That was a good idea, but what if the real note Bolt left gets out?"

"It won't be released, but even if it became public, it'll be too late; she made a deal."

"I can't believe it worked."

"Better than I thought."

"Thank God this is over."

"We're almost there. I'll feel better once Borelli is in custody."

"Did you tell the security guard's daughter?"

"No. It's too late, I'll call her in the morning."

Luca rinsed their coffee mugs and put them in the dishwasher. Mary Ann breezed into the kitchen in a bathing suit.

Luca said, "A bikini? Is that new?"

"No, I've had it forever."

"You always say that."

Mary Ann smiled. "I'm going to do my laps."

Luca ran his hand down his wife's back. "You sure? You don't want to, you know?"

Mary Ann spun away and opened the slider.

Luca said, "I guess I'll have to take a walk for my exercise."

He went into the garage and put his sneakers on.

A text came in from Donovan: *We have an arrest warrant. We're going to grab Borelli.*

Luca typed back: *Great. Let me know when you have her.*

He scrolled to Tanya's number and called the security guard's daughter.

"Hi, Tanya, It's Frank Luca."

"Hello, Mr. Luca. It's nice to hear from you."

"Do you have a minute to talk?"

"Sure."

"Well, I'm happy to tell you we got the people responsible for your father's death."

"You did? Oh, thank God. Momma would be so happy."

"One of the perpetrators confessed, and, just so you know, we had to cut a deal, but the police are bringing the ringleader in as we speak."

Tanya's voice cracked. "I don't know how to thank you."

"It's not necessary. I'm just happy I was able to get a bit of justice for you."

"So, who killed my father?"

"Well, there were four of them who pulled the robbery. They went to high school together, but now two of them are dead, one of them murdered by one of their own, and another one committed suicide. I don't want to release the names at this point, but it'll be all over the news."

"I wish I could look them each in the eye and tell them how much suffering they caused my family."

"Well, if there's a bail hearing, you'll have an opportunity to address the court. If not, and they're convicted, you can make a victim's statement before sentencing."

"I will definitely do that."

"That's up to you. It can be emotional, but many find it helpful in dealing with their loss."

Luca finished the call and went for a stroll.

An hour later, he turned onto his street. A white Ford Focus was parked in front of his house. Luca picked up the pace.

As he got a view of his front door, he saw Mary Ann speaking to a woman. It was Tanya, the security guard's daughter.

Luca jogged up. "Hi. We just spoke, is everything all right?"

Tanya said, "Yes. I just wanted to drop this off."

She handed him a check. "I hope it's enough."

"I appreciate the offer, but I can't accept this."

"Why not? I hired you to find the killers, and you did."

"That's okay. I'm just happy I was able to help."

"You worked so hard on this, it's not fair."

Luca shook his head. "I'm not taking it."

Mary Ann said, "Trust me, Tanya, he doesn't do what he does for the money."

"But I feel bad."

Luca said, "Spend it on yourself and your kids."

<hr>

LUCA CARRIED a plate of shrimp marinating in a spicy sauce onto the lanai. He flicked on the remote, and the TV came to life. He checked the temperature of the grill, and using tongs, put the shrimp on to cook.

As the news anchor summarized the day's Wall Street activity, Luca stepped past the pool. He took a deep breath. The air was tinged with the cedar scent of the mosquito repellent.

Luca went back to grill. The shrimp had turned pink. He turned them over as the Fox news weatherman gave a forecast for the coming week.

Mary Ann came onto the lanai with a bowl of salad. "Is it on the news?"

Luca put the shrimp onto a platter. "Any minute now."

The camera zeroed in on the anchorman, who said, "And now to today's top story. It's hard to describe the amazing turn of events for Elena Borelli, a leading Wall Street financier and prominent member of Naples society.

"Earlier today, Ms. Borelli was taken into custody at Naples Airport.

"The sheriff's office apprehended Ms. Borelli as she was attempting to flee the United States for Switzerland by private jet. Ms. Borelli, who holds dual US and Swiss citizenships, was arrested in connection with the murders of Michael Martinez and Valerie Van Dore.

"The pair were killed during a robbery of the Van Dores jewelry store at Waterside Shops. The twenty-year-old crime had been unsolved until Frank Luca, the former head of the sheriff's homicide division, took it upon himself to investigate the cold case."

Mary Ann said, "Don't be getting a big head over this."

Luca smiled. "Can't I get any credit?"

Mary Ann wrapped her arms around him. "I'm just kidding. You're my hero, Frank."

He pressed his hips into his wife's as she grinded back. "That's more like it."

"If you play your cards right . . ."
"Now we're talking."

The End

Thank you for reading, ***The Waterside Secret: A Luca Thriller.*** We hope you enjoyed this book in the Luca Series. You can find a complete list of the authors work on the following pages, and on his website where you can subscribe for his newsletter of future books, story insights, and on very rare occasions special deals and recommendations.

www.danpetrosini.com

THE LUCA MYSTERY SERIES

THE BARROW CASE

AM I THE KILLER

VANISHED

THE SERENITY MURDER

THIRD CHANCES

A COLD, HARD CASE

COP OR KILLER?

SILENCING SALTER

A KILLER MISSTEPS

UNCERTAIN STAKES

THE GRANDPA KILLER

DANGEROUS REVENGE

WHERE ARE THEY

BURIED AT THE LAKE

THE PRESERVE KILLER

NO ONE IS SAFE

MURDER, MONEY AND MAYHEM

THE GOLDEN SELLOUT

THE WATERSIDE SECRET

SUSPENSEFUL SECRETS

CORY'S DILEMMA

CORY'S FLIGHT

CORY'S SHIFT

ART OF PAYBACK

RACE TO REVENGE

BEYOND REVENGE

THIS ISN'T OVER

OTHER WORKS BY DAN PETROSINI

THE FINAL ENEMY

COMPLICIT WITNESS

PUSH BACK

AMBITION CLIFF

Dan is a USA Today and Amazon best-selling author who wrote his first story at the age of ten and enjoys telling a story or joke.

Dan gets his story ideas by exploring the question; What if?

In almost every situation he finds himself in, Dan explores what if this or that happened? What if this person died or did something unusual or illegal?

Dan's non-stop mind spin provides him with plenty of material to weave into interesting stories.

A fan of books and films that have twists and are difficult to predict, Dan crafts his stories to prevent readers from guessing correctly. He writes every day, forcing the words out when necessary and has written over twenty-five novels to date.

It's not a matter of wanting to write, Dan simply has to.

Dan passionately believes people can realize their dreams if they focus and act, and he encourages just that.

His favorite saying is – "The price of discipline is always less than the cost of regret"

Dan reminds people to get the negativity out of their lives. He believes it is contagious and advises people to steer clear of negative people. He knows having a true, positive mind set makes it feel like life is rigged in your favor. When he gets off base, he tells himself, 'You can't have a good day with a bad attitude.'

Married with two daughters and a needy Maltese, Dan lives in Southwest Florida. A New York native, Dan has taught at local colleges, writes novels, and plays tenor saxophone in several jazz bands. He also drinks way too much wine and never, ever takes himself too seriously.

He puts out a twice-a-month newsletter featuring articles, his writing and special deals and steals.

Sign up at www.danpetrosini.com

www.ingramcontent.com/pod-product-compliance
Lightning Source LLC
Chambersburg PA
CBHW051541030726

47592CB00001B/77